In Too Deep

Books by Mary Connealy

From Bethany House Publishers

THE KINCAID BRIDES

Out of Control
In Too Deep
Over the Edge

Also by Mary Connealy

SOPHIE'S DAUGHTERS

Doctor in Petticoats
Wrangler in Petticoats
Sharpshooter in Petticoats

LASSOED IN TEXAS

Petticoat Ranch
Calico Canyon
Gingham Mountain

MONTANA MARRIAGES

Montana Rose
The Husband Tree
Wildflower Bride

WILD WEST WEDDINGS

Cowboy Christmas
Deep Trouble

Nosy in Nebraska (a cozy mystery collection)
Black Hills Blessing (a contemporary romance collection)

IN TOO DEEP

MARY CONNEALY

BETHANY HOUSE PUBLISHERS
a division of Baker Publishing Group
Minneapolis, Minnesota

Published by Bethany House Publishers
11400 Hampshire Avenue South
Bloomington, Minnesota 55438
www.bethanyhouse.com

Bethany House Publishers is a division of
Baker Publishing Group, Grand Rapids, Michigan

Printed in the United States of America

Library of Congress Cataloging-in-Publication Data
Connealy, Mary.
    In too deep / Mary Connealy.
        p.   cm. — (The Kincaid brides ; bk. 2)
    ISBN 978-0-7642-0912-3 (pbk.)
    I. Title.
PS3603.O544I5 2012
813'.6—dc23   2011040755

Scripture quotations are from the King James Version of the Bible.

This is a work of fiction. Names, characters, incidents, and dialogues are products of
the author's imagination and are not to be construed as real. Any resemblance to actual
events or persons, living or dead, is entirely coincidental.

Cover design by Dan Pitts

Cover photography by Mike Habermann Photography, LLC

Author is represented by Natasha Kern Literary Agency

12   13   14   15   16   17   18   7   6   5   4   3   2   1

In Too Deep is dedicated to the newest member of our family, my grandson Isaac. The first boy born into this branch of the Connealy family in over fifty years and well worth the wait.

Fear thou not; for I am with thee: be not dismayed; for I am thy God: I will strengthen thee; yea, I will help thee; yea, I will uphold thee with the right hand of my righteousness.

Isaiah 41:10

CHAPTER
1

AUGUST 15, 1866

"Ethan! Where's Maggie?"

Ethan's head snapped up at Audra's sharp tone. "What?"

Audra, rounding a boulder, just coming into view, dropped an armload of kindling. With baby Lily clutched to her chest, she charged forward, calling, "Maggie! Maggie!"

"I thought she was with you." Ethan rose from where he was crouching by the morning fire and turned in a circle, searching for the toddler.

No sign of her.

"I thought you took her." Audra's voice rose in agitation. She'd been gathering sticks while holding her baby. The confounded woman refused to just sit and rest and watch the children while Ethan got a meal.

"Maggie! Honey, where are you?" She raised her voice, did her best to sound playful, when under it Ethan heard panic. Audra turned, looking frantically, her eyes wide with fear.

"Maggie . . ." He tried to copy Audra's easygoing tone. Scaring the toddler wouldn't get her to come in.

"You're sure Rafe and Julia didn't let her ride along with them to Rawhide?" He charged toward a clump of aspens and shoved his way in to see if she'd crawled behind them.

"No. I was holding her when they rode off. Maggie was running after them. I told you I was going for firewood."

"You said you were taking the babies."

"I said baby, not babies. Maggie was sitting under those aspens, playing with your hat when I—" Audra's voice sharpened. "Ethan, where's Seth?"

Audra strode around to the back of the boulder she'd just circled. "Maggie? Maggie, come to Mama."

Mentioning Seth made Ethan's gaze swing to the cave opening. Ethan's hat lay on the ground by the entrance. A knife of fear slashed Ethan's chest as he looked at that black opening that led downward forever.

"My hat! Over there!" Ethan started running. "Maybe she went in the cave. Maybe Seth went after her. Seth!"

"Maggie, honey, come to Mama." Audra's falsely chirpy voice faded as Ethan left her at the camp. He dashed into the cold tunnel and stumbled to a stop. The dark was like a choking hand. His throat closed. He forced himself to drag in a breath.

"Seth! Where are you?" He forced each word out, forced his feet to move forward. Each step a battle of wills. His eyes went to a torch stuck in a crack. He pulled out a tin of matches.

"Maggie! Maggie, come back." Audra caught up and passed him.

"Wait outside for me." He was talking to her back. Fumbling with the tin box, he struck a match and it snapped in half. With shaking hands he tried again and finally got the torch lit.

Audra rushed deeper in, Lily cradled in her arm. The baby was just a month old. Where was Rafe when Ethan needed him?

"Don't bring the baby in here. It's cold." And dangerous, but he didn't say that out loud. Audra vanished around a curve. Ethan's torch cast flickering shadows that grabbed at him.

"Maggie!" Audra's voice echoed from ahead. Ethan hurried to catch up.

"Audra, wait!" Ethan got to the split in the tunnel. One trail descended a long, long way, and he saw Audra moving down it. No lantern. Was the woman crazy? The other way led to a larger cave. A hole in the ceiling let sunlight in. "Let's check ahead first."

Audra paused at the downward trail and looked back. "She wouldn't have come in here. Not this far."

"She moves fast." Ethan's breathing sped up. He imagined Maggie going down that slope. She'd fall. She might slide a long way. If she wasn't too badly hurt, she'd get up and be so lost. So lost in the dark.

"Seth had to bring her." Something flashed across Audra's expression. Pure mama grizzly bear.

"Go look around outside." He wanted her out of here for her own good, but also so she wouldn't see him if he shamed himself with his fear. "I'll hunt in here. Lily shouldn't be in this cold place."

Audra gave him a look of utter contempt. "I'm not going to stop looking for Maggie."

She wrapped the blankets tighter around Lily. "Let's look ahead, before we go down."

Heaving a sigh of relief at not being left, even as he wished she'd get out, Ethan forced himself to lead the way to the place they'd found Seth's bedroll. "If she's alone, she can't have gone far. If she's with Seth, she's all right."

I hope so—considering Seth is half loco.

They reached the small cave room with the light trickling in from overhead. It was empty.

Ethan's panic subsided just a bit with the light shining in from the punctured ceiling. Then he thought of where he had to go next, and his heart pounded until he could feel it in his ears.

Ethan turned to that downward tunnel. "Audra, this floor is steep and it's cold and wet. You shouldn't have Lily in here."

"Are you going to lead the way or should I?"

Gritting his teeth, he set out. "At least let me go first. Then if you fall, I can stop you from sliding." He caught her and pushed past.

"Maggie!" Audra's voice bounced and echoed and boomed. All those repeating voices felt like evil spirits to Ethan. How he hated this cavern.

Hated.

Hated!

Hated!

"Maggie, honey, are you here?" Audra's words echoed back to him like drumbeats. Restless, like natives on the warpath. This place was restless. Alive. Waiting.

He stepped down the slope, each step slower. He hadn't been this deep in ten years. But he cared about that little girl, so he took another step. One at a time. "Maggie! Seth!"

He knew what lay ahead from listening to Rafe and Julia and Seth. A place that dripped overhead. Rafe said the tunnel passed under the stream that ran near Audra and Julia's old shack. They weren't near it yet, but Ethan felt that stream break through the roof, drowning him, washing him into a deep grave. A ride that went all the way to the devil.

Each step, each breath was forced. But he did it. He moved. Then he couldn't.

His feet stopped.

Audra caught up and poked him in the shoulders. "Hurry up."

"I . . . I . . ." He could not take another step. He would have to admit he'd let a child die because he was so useless. A coward. He hated caring what Audra would think. Hated caring about a little lost girl.

He'd sworn to never feel this much again.

"Ethan, come on. Is something wrong?"

He was smothering. His heart pounded so loud he could hear it, and then the walls seemed to have a heartbeat, as if he were inside a living creature. He had to get out. He had to admit it.

It shamed him but he couldn't move. Not forward.

Before he could confess his fear, he saw a light.

"Look! In that gap, someone's in there." Audra grabbed Ethan's shoulder and shoved him forward. She would have passed him, but the tunnel was too narrow.

"Seth! Are you in there?" Audra's voice echoed off the walls.

"Hey, Audra, Ethan. What are you doing in here?" Seth's voice came from a narrow side tunnel. A light appeared. Seth, torch in hand, poked his head out of a crack Ethan thought was nothing but a shadow.

It was the worst thing about this cavern—danger hidden in the shadows.

Seth was empty-handed.

"Where's Maggie?" Audra's voice was so tight it squeaked.

Ethan's heart, already trying to hammer its way out of his chest, doubled in speed.

"She's with me." Seth looked down at his feet and frowned. "She was right here." He turned around and vanished back in that crack. "Maggie, come on out."

Audra wedged past Ethan and rushed into the little fissure. With stumbling steps, Ethan approached the opening. It was tall and narrow, as if someone had slashed the stone with a knife.

"Where is she, Seth?" Audra was fighting to stay calm. "You shouldn't have let her go. We might never find her down here."

Ethan could tell she was about one second away from screaming.

"I just put her down for a second. Don't worry. She can't get into any trouble in here."

Ethan knew for an absolute fact this wasn't true. He needed to help. He needed to search.

Uphill, movement caught his eye. Maggie toddled into view as if she had stepped straight out of the rock. Ethan dashed for her and almost had her when she ran into another crack across from where she'd appeared. He dove at her and felt the fabric of her little skirt, but his fingers closed on air. She squealed happily as if they were playing a game.

"She's out here." Rushing after Maggie, he'd realized how tight the tunnel was. He crouched and scrambled faster.

"Come back, Maggie." He heard the anxious tone and fought to control it, to keep from scaring her.

She giggled and her little doeskin shoes scuffed on stone.

Banging his head on the ceiling of the tunnel, he stooped lower. The tunnel twisted one way, then another. His torch cast light on a flicker of white. It had to be Maggie.

"Magpie, wait for me." The ceiling dropped more until Ethan had to crawl. The walls began scrubbing his shoulders. His torch gave him only one hand to spare. If this got too tight for him—but not for Maggie—how would he get to her?

"Maggie, let's go see Mama." Ethan hated the phony sound of his voice, his fear not concealed at all.

"Where are you, Ethan?" Audra was hollering, echoing, panicking.

"Call for her, Audra."

A flash of white showed in the tunnel ahead.

"Maggie, come to Mama."

The white quit moving. Ethan lunged forward and grabbed Maggie's skirt with his left hand just as she toppled forward with a scream of fear. Her weight hung from the dress. Her little arms lifted as the dress slipped up and threatened to pull off.

Ethan, flat on his belly, pulled her back. The loose dress hitched up and almost dragged over her head. To free his other hand, he tossed the torch forward to keep it from burning Maggie. At the same time he made a desperate grab and caught her flailing arm.

The bright arc of the torch curved up, then plummeted out of sight. Dropped into nothingness. Ethan knocked rubble forward and he heard rocks echo and bounce. Falling after the torch. He didn't hear anything hit bottom.

Maggie's screams changed to sobs of pain.

He pulled Maggie back, his grip too tight on her little arm.

Tucking her against his chest, he let go of her arm the instant she was safe. She fought him.

"Hey, Ethan, you shouldn't've taken Maggie down that tunnel. It's not safe." Seth sounded concerned. The idiot.

"We're fine." Ethan was about as far from fine as a man could be. The tunnel ceiling was only inches over his head. He couldn't turn around.

Maggie's crying announced that she was alive and had the energy for tears.

"It's not safe?" Audra asked. "That tunnel's not safe?"

Ethan was having the devil's own time backing up. With the ceiling too low to let him get to his hands and knees, and Maggie wiggling in his arms, he could barely move. He inched backward. Maggie cried and kicked. He kept her hugged awkwardly against his chest with his left hand and used his right to shove himself backward.

"Maggie, don't cry." Ethan felt the whole mountain pressing on all sides. How many dead drops were there in here? How many ways to die that a man could never know about—until the moment he was dying?

"Ethan, what's going on?" Audra sounded close to hysterics.

Ethan couldn't say as he blamed her. "I've got her. I'm coming back. It's slow because it's a tight squeeze. But we're fine."

The chill of the tunnel told Ethan his shirt was drenched with sweat. His heart pounded. He could barely draw a breath in the tight space.

Finally he got back far enough that he could hold his head up. It was pitch-dark because he'd thrown his torch away. He could imagine little side tunnels tricking him into following them away from where Audra and Seth waited. The tunnel got bigger. On his hands and knees now, he sped up.

Maggie's cries faded to whimpers. Ethan whispered nonsense

to her, trying to push back both their fears. The ceiling rose. Ethan got to his feet, ashamed of his wobbly knees. He crouched, but he at last managed to turn around and move much faster. Almost running. Hoping he hadn't gone off down some side tunnel.

The thought struck him and he stopped, terrified to take another step. Just then Audra appeared, torch in one hand, Lily in the other. His breath whooshed out in relief.

In the flickering firelight, his eyes met hers. He saw such fear he wondered that she could stand upright. He looked past her and saw Seth with his own torch.

"Go on back." His voice broke, so he couldn't say more.

Audra wheeled around, pushed at Seth to get him moving, and in a few steps they were in the larger tunnel.

Finally Ethan was out of the tunnel—the small side one—and into a bigger tunnel. Always another stupid tunnel that led God only knew where.

He hated this place.

Seth hoisted Maggie out of Ethan's arms so casually that Ethan didn't have time to stop him.

"Here, hold my torch, Eth." Seth shoved it at Ethan. "Maggie, you shouldn't have run off." Seth tickled her under her chin and Maggie quit crying and smiled.

Ethan heard Audra breathing—it had a sort of low growling quality that reminded Ethan of a grizzly bear getting ready to pounce. She caught Ethan's arm and almost strangled his elbow.

"Let's go on out now." No anger sounded in her voice—just a phony tinkling cheerfulness.

"But I wanted to show Maggie the big room with all the towers." Seth looked at Ethan and Audra, who were blocking the way down. He glanced at the side tunnel he'd been in . . . the safe one.

"No, it's time to go up." Audra dragged Ethan forward to cut Seth off from the "safe" little side tunnel in case Seth made a break for it.

Fingernails sank into Ethan's arm—and his shirt was good, thick material, so judging by the way her nails cut into his arm, she was furious.

Maggie had tears running down her cheeks, but like the good-natured baby she was, she'd cheered up and was now smiling and waving at Ethan.

"What are you doing down here, Seth?" Audra's voice lost the phony calm. In fact, she almost blistered Ethan's ears.

Seth's smile shrank like long woolen underwear in boiling lye water. "I . . . I was just going for a walk. Maggie was tagging after me, so I brought her along."

"Into this cave?" Audra's voice rose. Lily jerked in her sleep. "Without telling me?"

Maggie whimpered. Ethan knew how the little tyke felt.

"Seth, you shouldn't have brought Maggie in here," Audra yelled.

"Sorry." Seth didn't sound one speck sorry. "I thought she'd like to see it. It's real pretty."

"But I was worried." Ethan heard Audra's fury, banked like a nighttime fire but still smoldering, ready to erupt. "Didn't you think I'd be worried when I couldn't find her?"

"Uh . . . I didn't think of that, no. Our ma never cared much where we went."

"Your ma never—" Audra cut off whatever words she intended to say next. There was an extended silence. Her breathing slowed

until Ethan couldn't hear it anymore. Finally, sounding less furious, Audra said, "Let's go." She removed her claws from Ethan's
arm and made a shooing motion.

With a shrug, Seth took his torch back from Ethan, turned,
and headed up the tunnel with Maggie. Audra went next with
Lily. Ethan brought up the rear.

Seth carried Maggie, but when they reached the turn in the
tunnel to go out, Audra snatched Maggie out of Seth's hands so
that now she carried both children.

As Seth strolled toward the exit, he extinguished the torch
by jamming it against the stone wall, then tossing the smoking
wood onto the floor by the cave entrance. Handy for the next
time he came in here.

Ethan's heart slowed once he saw daylight. He was almost
completely calm by the time they got outside, not counting his
shirt being soaked with nervous sweat.

Audra stepped out into full daylight and stopped so suddenly
that Ethan almost ran her down. Audra turned, both children in
her arms. Ethan took Maggie to lessen the burdens this fragile
woman carried.

The second Maggie was out of her arms, Audra leaned close
and whispered hoarsely, "What happened in that tunnel?"

Seth went on ahead. From Audra's quiet question, Ethan
knew she didn't want Seth to overhear.

His shoulders square, his feelings tucked away, Ethan slipped
past Audra, into the sunlight as if he went cave walking every
day.

"Nothing happened. Much." Ethan wasn't sure he could talk
about it anyway, so why try?

Audra examined Maggie, running her hands over the little

girl, checking for injuries. Her eyes narrowed on Maggie's waving arm. Grabbing the child's hand, Audra asked, "What's this?"

Maggie's upper arm was bright red and swollen. Ethan knew exactly what it was. It was where he'd grabbed her. Seeing that bruise was like taking a blow to the stomach.

"I hurt her." He swallowed hard and forced the words out. "I caught her there. I . . . I didn't mean . . ."

Audra looked away from Maggie's arm. "What happened in that tunnel, Ethan?"

Shaking his head slowly, Ethan wished himself far away from the guilt and fear. But he couldn't look away from Audra. "It's hard to say. It was pitch-dark, so I threw my torch away to get both hands free."

"Tell me." Audra, for a fragile little woman, had a surprisingly determined tone.

"There was a ledge. She ran away from me. I grabbed her dress just as she . . . she fell."

"Fell off a ledge? How high a ledge?"

"I couldn't see but . . ." Ethan heard those stones falling without hitting bottom. He saw his torch arc up, then fall and vanish from sight.

Audra brought her hand up to cover her mouth, to stop the words. "Go on. How did her arm get hurt?"

"I almost pulled her dress off. For a second I was afraid she'd slip out of it and fall, so I caught hold of her arm, but I was too rough."

Audra's eyes fell shut as if she couldn't bear to see what Ethan described. Dragging in a long, slow breath, she whispered, "You saved her."

"I hurt her." Maggie's injury wouldn't leave a scar, but she had a reminder of that cave now, just like Seth and Rafe. Only Ethan had come away from that pit unscathed, and he was the one who couldn't stand to go in anymore.

"She'd have gone over a ledge. Fallen heaven knows how far. She'd have died. My baby would have died." Audra's shoulders heaved as if she was ready to cry, but though her lips wobbled, she kept it contained.

They faced each other. Lily in Audra's arms. Maggie in Ethan's. Time stretched as all that had happened—the danger, the fact that they'd all survived it—filled the silence. Finally, Audra lifted Maggie's arm and gave the red mark a whisper-soft kiss.

Maggie giggled and tugged against Audra's gentle hold and got her arm free. She was going to be fine. There would be a bruise, but Maggie's arm was working fine.

"What are we going to do, Ethan? My children aren't safe."

Movement drew Ethan's attention. Rafe and Julia rode up. Rafe looked overly relaxed. Rafe and Julia had taken way too long riding into Rawhide to mail off Julia's first paper about the cavern. She'd written an article about a fish fossil she'd found that she thought was an ocean fish high up in the mountains. She was hoping to get it published in some scientific journal back East.

Rafe's eyes shifted from Ethan to the tunnel entrance and all his relaxation vanished. "You went in the cave?"

Julia glared straight at Seth as she dismounted. "What is going on here?"

Audra didn't answer.

"Seth, what happened?" Julia focused on Seth. It was the honest truth that Julia wasn't overly fond of Seth. Though she did like talking to him about the cavern. Seth probably knew the cavern better than any man alive.

"I just wanted to show Maggie the cave. I didn't mean to upset you none, Audra." Seth came up and gave Maggie a worried look. The little one smiled and reached for him. After a quick glance at Audra—who hesitated, moved slightly to further block the cave entrance, then nodded—Ethan handed Maggie over. The five adults, two of them holding babies, formed a circle right in front of the cavern.

"Well, you did upset me. I didn't know where Maggie had gone. And that cave is dangerous." Audra softened her words by moving closer to Seth.

"No, it's not."

With Lily in one arm, Audra hugged Seth with the other.

Ethan saw her hands trembling, but she sounded so calm. Audra was always sweet. She liked peace.

For some reason, seeing Audra's arm wrapped around Seth irritated Ethan. When Seth's hand crept up and wrapped around Audra's slim waist, Ethan considered putting a stop to all the hugging.

Audra pulled back before Ethan could step in. "If there is anyone in the world who Maggie would be safe with down there, it's you."

Ethan remembered the grizzly tone from earlier and knew Audra was shoving her anger and fear down deep and not saying what she really meant.

Instead, she said what she thought was kindest. "But it's still dangerous. Too dangerous for a little one. Now promise me you won't take her in there again."

"Okay." Seth sounded like a child, being lovingly chastised by his mother. Except he didn't look one speck like a child. He was a full-grown man and he still had his arm around Audra.

The four of them—Seth, Audra, Maggie, and Lily—were a picture.

Seth holding Maggie. Even with his hair trimmed and his beard shaved, Seth had a loco gleam in his wild blue eyes. Pretty, fragile Audra. Fair-haired, finely made. Both of them had a baby, and when they hugged they made a family.

"Good." She patted Seth gently on the shoulder. "And I need to know where Maggie is all the time. If I don't know, then I'm going to be hunting for her and worrying about her. And I won't quit hunting or worrying until I find her. It's a terrible feeling to worry like that. You mustn't make me feel that way."

"Is that what a ma does?" Seth sounded genuinely confused. "I don't remember our ma doing much worrying." Seth looked at Ethan, his brow furrowed. "You reckon it was worry about us that made her spend all her time sittin' in her chair with her head down?"

Ethan suspected Ma had forgotten she had children for the most part. She was busy full-time worrying about herself.

"It was different for you, Seth." Audra tilted her head up as if to prove she'd never hold it down. "You had your brothers to look after you when you were little."

And a great job we did of it.

"Your mother knew you were with them. That's why she didn't check up on you." Audra's voice was so kind while she stood there lying about Ma. Where was the cranky woman who'd almost knocked Ethan aside when he'd told her to take Lily out of that cavern?

"Ma mostly just cried." Seth looked at Ethan. "She cried a lot, didn't she?"

"All the time. I think we were too much for her." Ethan

decided to break up the family and took Maggie. She grinned at him and squeaked.

He smiled, not that there was much to smile about, but it came real natural to him to laugh everything off. Then his eyes fell to her bruised arm. His gut twisted as he remembered that moment when he thought he was going to lose her over the ledge. Something had to be done to make sure Maggie never went in there again.

"Rafe, do something." Julia's voice cracked like a bullwhip.

Rafe had married himself a nagging woman. And Ethan noticed Rafe didn't seem to mind one bit. In fact, Rafe seemed to find reasons all the time to ride off with his bossy little spitfire of a wife and not come back one bit too soon.

"You want me to do something?" Rafe looked at his brand-spankin'-new wife. His voice got deeper and he seemed to speak only to her. "Like what exactly, darlin'?"

Something very personal flashed in Rafe's eyes, and Julia seemed to forget Seth. In fact, the two of them seemed to forget the whole world.

Rafe grinned.

Julia blushed.

Ethan didn't exactly know why, but the look they shared made him restless and discontented. And it reminded him of how pretty Audra was. And how she shouldn't have been hugging Seth.

And Audra's looks had nothing to do with Rafe and his wife, so it all added up to Ethan being stupid.

"I think we're going to have to make some changes," Audra said quietly.

Ethan turned to her and saw something he hadn't noticed

before. Under the kindness she was showing to Seth. Under the calm once the crisis was over.

She had worry lines drawn in her face.

"I'll take Seth back to the ranch." Ethan knew that had to happen. He had to go home sometime. Rafe had bought this mountain valley—Julia called it a caldera. It looked like a big scoop taken out of the top of a mountain. Julia said it was caused by a volcano in the far-distant past. Ethan had serious doubts that Julia knew what she was talking about, but he had no better theories, not to mention he wasn't exactly sure what a volcano was.

Rafe had given the old Kincaid homestead to Ethan, then with Seth's and Ethan's help had built a new cabin here in his caldera. But the work was mostly done now. Nothing Rafe couldn't finish alone. Ethan had no excuse to stay. But truth to tell, he hated to leave. He'd left home as soon as he was old enough, and now that he was back, he liked being around his big brother. Losing him to marriage and this new ranch didn't suit Ethan. And he didn't like Seth's strange behavior, mainly because Ethan blamed himself for Seth being so crazy. So he was losing his steady-as-a-rock big brother and taking on his runaway avalanche of a little brother.

"No, it's not Seth. Seth meant no harm." Audra patted Seth again. He smiled back like a cheerful puppy. The kind that didn't mean a lick of harm when he bit you in the backside.

"It's that tunnel." Her hand clenched on Seth's shoulder. "It's all the caves in this place. This is a wonderful place for a cabin, but . . ."

Seth flinched and gave his shoulder a nervous glance. Audra was a lot more upset than she was letting on.

"It's not safe." Ethan looked around the mountain valley

Rafe had chosen for his home. It was beautiful. Sheltered from the harsh winds by the mountain walls surrounding it. A flowing stream teeming with trout. Fertile soil and already a good-sized herd of cattle grazing in the belly-deep grass. Rafe had found a hidden valley no one had known existed. Well, honestly, Seth found it. But Rafe had tracked Seth in here and seen the value of the place and wanted it.

"We can put up gates to block the tunnels." Julia's brow furrowed. "Maggie's getting older now and we do need to be careful with her."

"I was being careful," Audra snapped. She clamped her mouth shut and breathed in and out slowly. Then she spoke more calmly. "But the mountain walls are honeycombed with tunnels and caves. We haven't begun to find them all, let alone explore them and know which ones are dangerous. No, it's not a safe place to raise a child."

Audra turned to Julia. "Not yet. You and Rafe have time to explore and make it safe. But it will take time. Months, maybe years. You have years. I don't." Her slender shoulders squared. Her spine straightened. She didn't mention Seth. Julia and Rafe had years to make sure he was all right, too. They intended to have children, and they intended to raise them right here.

"I need to leave, Julia."

"No. Absolutely not." Julia crossed her arms, stubborn and bossy as ever.

"And you need to stay. I need help to get to town and the price of a ticket to take a stagecoach back East. I'll find my f-father. The children and I will move in with him."

Her father, who had as good as sold her to Wendell Gilliland to settle a gambling debt.

"You're not going back to him." Julia came over and relieved Audra of the baby. She probably didn't mean it that way, but it looked for all the world like Julia was planning to hold the month-old baby captive so Audra couldn't leave.

"Yes, I am. This is no place for me. I've been a burden to you long enough."

"You're not a burden, Audra. I love you. You're my family. Maggie and Lily are my little sisters. No, you're not going."

Ethan itched to join Julia in refusing to let Audra go. But Julia was doing fine by herself.

"If you won't help me, I'll go alone. I don't have a penny to my name. If you don't want to help me with the ticket, I'll get a job in town. Take in laundry and mending. See if there's a diner in town that needs a cook. Or, come to think of it, didn't Wendell own some small business in town, Rafe?"

"He did, but it wouldn't be worth much."

"I don't need much. I'll sell that and use the money to go back East. Or I'll live in it while I work. I told Wendell I was leaving the night he collapsed."

"But the main thing you needed to get away from was my father." Julia's voice rose. "He's gone. You're staying."

"This isn't a decision you can make for me." Audra reached over to fold down the corner of Lily's blanket. The baby was still sleeping, having slept through the whole trauma of losing Maggie.

Ethan sort of wished he could have slept through it, too.

"It will be easiest to travel right now. The weather is good. Lily still sleeps a lot. That will leave me free to watch over Maggie."

"Who never sits still for two minutes," Julia reminded her.

"Let alone days and maybe weeks in a cramped, uncomfortable stagecoach and in a rough train car filled with strangers."

"Maggie running off is what started this whole thing." Ethan wished he hadn't spoken when Audra's eyes shot flaming arrows at him before looking back at Julia.

"You've got a new life now, Julia. And I'm happy for you. But we're part of your old life. I'm tired of being a burden."

"You're not a burden." Julia stepped away from Audra, swinging her body a bit to block her from Lily. "Rafe, say something."

"There's some sense in what she says, Julia."

"Rafe!" Julia clenched her fists.

Ethan hoped she didn't clench her whole body and squash the baby. Then he noticed he had a pretty tight hold on Maggie, too. He didn't want the little one to grow up back East. Still, that was no reason to strangle her. He forced his arms to relax.

Rafe slid one arm around Julia's shoulders. "We'll have lived here a while by the time our children get old enough to wander around. We'll know the caves well by then and can block off the dangerous ones. But right now, with Maggie so young and speedy, and Seth so drawn to the caves . . . Audra's right. It's dangerous."

"So I'll get packed up then, and you'll take me to town, Rafe?" Audra sounded determined.

"He will not!" Julia took another step back.

Ethan wanted to help Julia escape with the baby. Thinking of Audra leaving didn't sit right. She had no place to go. They could put her on a train back to her father, but who was to say the man would take her in? Or maybe he'd take her in and marry her off to the next varmint who had some kind of hold on him.

"No, I won't take you to town, but I think you should move

to the Kincaid Ranch." After Rafe spoke, the only sound was the buffeting of the mountain breeze.

Julia thawed first. "What? She can't do that."

"I have no place at the Kincaid Ranch, for heaven's sake." Audra's mouth started working next.

"What would she do there?" Ethan went from worrying about Audra to being scared to death of her.

"That'd be great." Seth reached for Maggie.

"I'll keep her for now." Ethan dodged Seth's hands.

"Audra can be the housekeeper." Rafe nodded as if everything was settled.

"Audra can't live in a house with two men," Julia snapped.

"I most certainly can't." Audra moved to Julia's side. "It wouldn't be right at all."

"She can if she's married to one of 'em." Rafe had eyes like a gray mountain fog when he was determined, and Ethan saw that color right now. Not a hint of blue anywhere.

"I'll marry you, Audra." Seth grinned like a pig in slop.

"Not you." Rafe turned to Ethan as if picking a wife was just another order Rafe could give. "Ethan."

CHAPTER
2

Julia had married a lunatic.

"That sounds great, as long as she's at our house." Seth was even crazier than Rafe.

Audra waited for Ethan to say something equally crazy so she could peg the whole family as madmen.

"I'm not marrying Audra." Well, at least one of them had some sense. And for once he didn't have a smile on his face.

"What's wrong with Audra?" Rafe asked.

Audra kind of wanted to know the answer to that, too.

"I'm not marrying Ethan. I'm not marrying anybody. Rafe Kincaid, you can't just pick a husband out for someone because it makes life tidier."

"Sure I can." Rafe gave her a look that seemed to be . . . pity. Like he pitied her for being alone? Or did he just pity anyone who didn't immediately see that he was the one who should organize the whole world?

"Now, Rafe," Julia said, patting him on the arm, "Audra doesn't want to marry either one of your idiot brothers."

"Hey!" Ethan said.

"My brothers aren't idiots." Rafe crossed his arms and glared at his fiery redheaded wife.

Seth said, "Can Maggie and I go hunt around in the cave again for a while before you marry one of us and we go home?"

Julia arched a brow at Rafe.

With a sheepish jerk of one shoulder, Rafe said, "Well, Ethan's okay. He's the one Audra needs to marry."

"I'd be proud to marry you, Audra." Seth sat down on the ground and started pulling off one of his boots. "It's more fun in the caves barefoot. The rocks are nice and cold. Ethan, get Maggie's shoes off."

Ethan swallowed so hard, Audra thought he must feel a noose tightening around his neck. "Maybe she could be our housekeeper," he ventured.

Audra scowled at him. "I can't live in a house with two unmarried men."

"Why not?" Ethan looked offended.

The idiot.

"We're decent men. We wouldn't treat you wrong."

"As long as the food was good." Seth was tugging on his sock. If he got his feet stripped down and headed for the cave, Audra decided she'd just let him go and live in there forever. But without Maggie. She didn't have a baby in her arms, which left her free to punch someone. Her only problem was deciding who.

"No, you need to marry her." Rafe pulled his hat off his head. Audra sincerely hoped his hatband was too tight and that would explain his idiocy. "It don't make no sense to put it off. You're bound to marry her eventually."

"Why would I do a thing like that?" Ethan shifted Maggie on his hip. She grinned at him and pulled his hat off his head and swatted him in the face.

"Because she's young and beautiful, and she's taking care of your house." Rafe's voice rose as if he was sick and tired of everyone not falling in with his plan. "She'll be cooking and sewing for you, and you'll be supporting her. Maggie already treats you like you're her pa. And you're bound to figure out she's your wife in every way except you can't sleep in her bed at night."

Utter silence cut through the group. Ethan's eyes swung to Audra.

Audra was pretty sure either her cheeks had caught fire or she was turning a ridiculous shade of red. Julia bit her lip, so maybe she had something to say but thought better of it. Seth's toes were wiggling and distracting him.

Maggie swatted Ethan again and said, "Papa."

"I'll take the housekeeper job." Audra said it quick to forestall Rafe's charming proposal. And to get Ethan to quit looking at her.

Then after she'd said it, it sounded a little like she was angling to get herself into Ethan's house.

"Nope, you can't live in a house with two unmarried men." Rafe crossed his arms. "Ride on into town now and get it over and done. The parson is still around. We saw him."

"Rafe Kincaid!" A voice Audra had never heard before came from her lips. "You need to quit talking. Now! I'm not letting you order me to get married to anyone and especially not to your grinning fool of a brother."

"Now listen here." Ethan shifted Maggie to his other side. "There's no call for you to keep calling me a—"

"Whose side are you on?" Audra snapped.

Ethan fell silent.

"And if I'm the housekeeper, I cannot live in a house with two unmarried men. You and Seth have to move out."

"Move out?" Ethan's brows shot up. "What's the point of having a housekeeper if we don't have a house?"

"He's got a point, Audra." Seth looked up from the ground and smiled. "I'm looking forward to getting home. I don't want to move out."

"Well, you're doomed to be disappointed then." Audra preferred to be kinder to Seth. She had a lot of compassion for him. But right now kindness was beyond her. And her main compassion was for herself. Somehow she'd dug deep, despite her near panic over Maggie, while she'd talked to Seth. But now that it was Ethan she was thinking about, she seemed to have no control of her mouth at all. Where had all that good sense gone?

"You two can bunk with the hands and come in for meals. I'll do your laundry and mending and tend a kitchen garden and keep house."

"Keep house for yourself." Ethan scowled and she wanted to smack him.

"But you'll have your hands so full, Audra." Julia shook her head. "Two babies, alone."

"We'll have to think of something else." Ethan looked like six full feet of stubborn and another few inches of dumb. He hadn't grinned in a while, though.

34

"So now you *want* to get married?" Her fist clenched and she was shocked at her violent impulses. This wasn't like her at all.

While Ethan was busy sputtering, Audra looked at Julia and Rafe, a matched set, and she could see their determination. Julia to keep her here. Rafe to get her married.

Add in Ethan to keep his house and avoid her presence, and Seth to go on his merry, cave-exploring, furiously mad way—probably with Maggie in tow.

She was by far the weakest-willed person in this group. She'd planned to grow herself a backbone, but obviously she was outclassed at every turn, even by the barefoot lunatic.

"So what'll it be?" Rafe asked.

"I'm going back East." Audra hated the idea of going back East.

"No, you're not. I'm not going to let that happen," Rafe said with a tone of such absolute assurance that Audra gave that option up, with a lot of relief.

Which left her with some mighty poor choices.

Marry Ethan?

Eject Ethan and Seth from their house?

Stay in this pockmarked deathtrap of a caldera?

The wind gusting through the caldera carried the scream of an eagle. The aspens quaked with a quiet rattle. Everyone stared at her, waiting.

Except Seth, of course—the little maniac.

Audra had given birth twice. She'd traveled out West, great with child, a nursing babe in arms, on a brutally uncomfortable train that felt like heaven once she'd had a nice long ride in a wagon to compare it to.

She'd lived in a shack with five people. One of them her obnoxious, ill-smelling, bad-tempered crank of a husband.

All that. And none of it had been pleasant. But right now, this was the longest moment of her life.

"I can't decide."

Ethan half raised his hand. "I'll decide for you. Stay here. Watch your baby closer. You'll be fine."

"I can't stay here. I can watch Maggie, but I can't keep an eye on"—she took a very deliberate glance at Seth—"everyone."

"So I'll take him and we'll leave?"

"Forever?" Audra knew they'd be back.

Ethan shrugged. She was sure he knew they'd be back, too.

Sounding glum and unwanted, he said, "Sure. Let's go, Seth."

Ethan pulled his hat out of Maggie's hands and she screamed loud enough to make a man's ears bleed while she grabbed at it, trying to get it back.

"What's she so riled up about?" Ethan looked with horror at Maggie while he put his hat on.

"She seems partial to you, Ethan," Rafe said.

The screaming went on and Seth got up. "I'll take her."

Audra felt all eyes turn to her. Except Maggie, who was trying to scale Ethan's body, screaming all the while.

The pressure built, the silence—not counting the screaming—stretched.

Julia's dislike of Seth.

The need to get Maggie somewhere safer.

The sick knowledge that her father would not welcome her home and might in fact sell her off again.

The screaming.

The wrongness of kicking two men out of their home.

Ethan's handsome face.

Audra caught herself. She hadn't meant to include that in her list of reasons why she felt forced to make a choice.

No money. No home. No rest. No real choice.

At least Ethan wouldn't yell at her. That mindless grin on his face had the redeeming quality of being a quiet shortcoming.

The screaming.

Her wobbly backbone bent under the pressure. "If you'll have me, Ethan, I'll marry you."

Ethan got a look in his eyes like a scared calf at branding time. She wondered if he'd start kicking and bawling. She had a sudden image of herself twirling a loop of rope over her head and lassoing herself a husband.

Then his fear faded. He smiled and shrugged as if she'd asked him if he wanted a cup of coffee, and said, "Okay, why not? I don't want to sleep in the bunkhouse."

It was so far from the romantic proposal of a girl's dreams that Audra was glad she wasn't carrying a loaded shotgun.

She might've started blasting.

CHAPTER 3

"You certainly smell better than Wendell."

"I can barely stand all the sweet-talk." He was sorely afraid that was the closest he was ever going to get to a compliment out of the contrary woman.

Audra gave Ethan a strained smile as they walked out of the abandoned shack that Rawhide called a church.

They each had a baby in their arms.

Good grief, I'm the father of two children. I didn't see that coming when I woke up this morning.

Then he realized he'd forgotten to take off his hat for his wedding. He remembered well that he'd said "I do," though. Ethan had the sudden image of a bear trap snapping shut on his leg.

The rest of their wedding guests—Rafe, Seth, and Julia—followed them out of the miserable excuse for a church.

"Hold up, Ethan, Audra. I want to talk to you while Parson Stamper's still here." Rafe's voice acted like a lasso thrown over Ethan. He'd never had much luck standing up to his big brother. It was easier to let Rafe run things and for Ethan to keep his mouth shut and curved up into a smile.

Turning around, he and Audra stepped back into the church and formed a small circle with the wedding guests and the parson.

A very small circle.

Rawhide wasn't a real welcoming place for a man of the cloth. This ten-by-ten-foot derelict building was the church, the parson's home, and when the parson was out of town—which was most of the time—it served as the closest thing Rawhide, Colorado, had to a hotel. Bring your own blanket.

They'd been surprised to find that Parson Stamper hadn't moved on yet. Rafe had called that luck.

Ethan had another word for it.

The parson stayed this long because his horse had come up lame, so the parson didn't see it as good luck, either.

Rafe said, "I want to talk to the sheriff while we're in town."

"I'll go along." Ethan waited to see what other orders Rafe would give.

"And I intend to search Father's building. He had to hide that money somewhere. Let's split up so we can get home." Julia could give orders well enough, too.

"No." Rafe wasn't real good at talking things over. "You stay with me. This is a wide open town and I'm not going to let you out of my sight."

Ethan was standing right in the doorway. He looked over his shoulder at Rawhide. Eight buildings stood almost swallowed up by the forest. The unpainted wooden shacks faced each other, four on each side of a rutted street. The forest pressing in from all directions until the town looked ready to be reclaimed by the wilderness.

Which might not be such a bad thing.

Rawhide was a mountain settlement mostly abandoned since the Pike's Peak Gold Rush had played out.

There were another two dozen cabins scattered around, mainly up the slope to the west. Ramshackle log buildings peeked out of the woods here and there. Not a single person was visible besides themselves. But one building had a horse and wagon parked in front of it, marking it as the general store, and another had the word Sheriff painted over the door.

"It doesn't look all that dangerous, Rafe," Julia said dryly.

"Parson," Rafe said, "can you keep this wedding a secret? Just don't mention it to anyone."

Parson Stamper shrugged. "Don't see why not. I'm a man who can keep a secret. But why?"

"It occurs to me that no one in these parts has the name Gilliland anymore. There's trouble following my wife's pa. He's dead. If someone comes hunting for Wendell, they'll find that out, and no one knew he had a wife and family." Rafe's arm slid to Julia's back. "Maybe they'll just believe it's a dead end and leave us be. Of course Tracker knows Julia's married, but I'll make sure the sheriff doesn't let Tracker send any messages. And even if they do find out about Julia and Audra, they won't know they've both moved and changed their names."

Ethan swallowed hard to think that, yes, Audra had changed her name. To Kincaid. The whole thing seemed like a dream, so he smiled and ignored it. A dream or a nightmare. He smiled bigger.

"Fine with me." Parson Stamper nodded at a building on the south end of town. "My horse is better and I'm leaving town today. I won't mention the wedding to anyone, here or on my circuit. And I'll be praying for the trouble that's dogged you all."

"Obliged, Parson." Rafe stepped aside to let the parson head for the livery, then turned to the rest of the group. "Julia, you come with me to talk to Tracker. Ethan and Audra, why don't you go hunt around in Wendell's building?"

Rafe pointed to a tumbledown shack up the hill from town. No windows, a door hanging from one leather hinge.

"That's an even worse building than the one Father bought for a house." Julia looked at the building, then turned to Audra. "He couldn't have spent much of the money he stole. I wonder what he did with it?"

"I wish we could find it and send it back to the man he took it from." Audra hugged her sleeping baby closer. "Then he'd leave us alone."

"The man he stole it from probably came by it in a dishonest way." Ethan was sorely afraid this was a problem without an easy solution.

"There's no reason to believe that." Audra frowned.

"No honest man sends vermin like Tracker Breach to regain his money." Ethan shifted a sleeping Maggie in his arms so her head was resting in his right elbow. "Sending Breach was the choice of a bad man. If we find the money, we should turn it over to the sheriff and let him get to the bottom of who it really belongs to."

Audra nodded. "Agreed. Let the law handle it."

"Julia and I will come up to Wendell's building when we're done. Seth, you go with Ethan and Audra. I don't want you talking to Breach."

"Why not, Rafe?"

"Because you tell a mixed-up version of what happened because of the laudanum he was feeding you, and I want everything clear. You go hunt. We'll come shortly to help you." He took Julia's arm. It might have been a romantic gesture, but to Ethan it looked more like he was taking her prisoner.

"I'm looking forward to seeing Tracker again." Julia sounded dangerous. Grim. Possibly violent. Ethan hadn't much wanted to get married to anyone, but the Gilliland brood had the only women available, and he'd gotten the pick of the litter.

Ethan watched Rafe and Julia head down the street. He took Audra's arm. "Well, Mrs. Kincaid, shall we go find your money?"

He smiled. Nothing much to smile about, but he tended to smile over anything and everything, so why not this?

Audra seemed to study his smile for too long. Then she frowned. "Yes, let's go. Maybe we can find it and get all of this behind us."

"Then can we go home?" Seth asked, heading toward the building, leaving them behind.

"We'll sleep at home tonight, Seth. But first we'll tear Wendell's building apart, board by board if we have to." Ethan eyed the decrepit building. "That won't take long. And where else could that old fool of a husband of yours have hidden it?"

"Oh, there are plenty of places. Including he could have dug a hole somewhere."

With a sigh, Ethan said, "You're right. That building is the only place he could have hidden the money where we have a prayer of finding it."

Audra nodded, frowning. "And if we don't find it and return it, then the man Wendell stole it from may send someone else."

"You look tired. You only had a baby a few weeks ago. We should have waited to do this until you were rested."

Her pretty white eyebrows snapped low. "Ethan!"

He touched her lips gently with one finger. When she stopped talking, he said, "I don't mean you're weak or fragile." She was, but he knew she hated to hear that. "You know a woman who's just had a baby needs a while before she starts riding long hours and tearing apart buildings."

"You're right." Audra smiled behind his finger. "I'm holding up, but we've got a long ride h-h-h—"

Ethan felt her smile burn into his finger and he jerked it back.

He couldn't quite manage a smile when he said, "Home. The word you're trying to say is home. You're going home with me. Mrs. Ethan Kincaid. Hard to get that idea in my head."

Their eyes caught and held. Ethan saw a world of understanding there.

Then she nodded. "We've got lots of time to get used to it. Our whole lives."

Ethan slid his hand to her waist and turned her to face Wendell's shack. "Let's get this hunting over and done, then head for . . ." He inhaled slowly.

Audra said, "Home."

Julia felt dangerous. She would have liked about five times her normal strength and a few minutes of privacy to pound on Tracker Breach for almost killing Rafe.

"Now be mindful to not mention Audra marrying Ethan." Rafe paused at the jailhouse door.

"I will." Julia frowned and crossed her arms. "But I want to let him know that all his evil didn't hurt us in the end. I'd like to stand there on the outside of those bars and tell him he needs to repent of his sins before it's too late. And then I'd like to tell him he's the ugliest man I've ever seen."

A crack of laughter from Rafe surprised Julia. Then he caught hold of her arm, a gentle vise, and dragged her into the gap between two buildings.

"Hey, I want to go yell at that awful man."

Rafe kept going until they were swallowed up in shadows, then turned her to face him and kissed her senseless.

Seconds passed, then minutes. Maybe longer. Julia sort of lost track of time. When Rafe eased her away from him, she chased after his lips with her own.

He let her catch him.

"Have I told you yet today I'm glad I married you?" He smiled.

She traced the smile with one finger. "I like seeing a smile on your face, Rafe."

"I find myself smiling all the time since I managed to corral you, wife." He kissed her again.

"This isn't the time or place—" Her scolding, which was halfhearted anyway, was silenced by his lips.

"I know we've got to go and see the sheriff, and I'll let you scold that man as long as you like, but it just came to mind that my brothers are finally going home."

That lifted Julia's spirits to a shameful degree. "I like your brothers."

"Your favorite term of affection is 'your idiot brothers.'"

"They do try my patience, Rafe." Then a frown turned her swollen lips downward. "But they're taking Audra and the babies."

"Yeah, even better. Now I can get you alone." Rafe laughed again.

Julia slugged him in the arm, but she didn't put one lick of force behind it. "Audra needs me."

Although now that Rafe mentioned it, it would be nice to be alone with him. They'd camped out a good distance from everybody else since their wedding. Rafe had insisted. And being close to him, intimate with him, was so beguiling that Julia had gone right along with the idea. Audra had slept in the tumble-down cabin she and Julia had lived in with Father until the new cabin was weather-tight, then she'd moved in there. The rest of them slept under the stars. Rafe's brothers had camped near the house while Rafe and Julia had gone elsewhere nightly, and to Julia's shock, occasionally Rafe had managed to lure her to a private place during the day.

Since she was finding her new husband downright irresist-ible anyway, she decided it was right for newlyweds to get away.

During the day, the men had built the new cabin in the caldera, and Julia had chiseled a few fossils out of the very easi-est and safest tunnels and done some writing. She wasn't even close to satisfied with her explorations yet. But she was satisfied as all get-out with married life.

"We needed to let Audra rest up for a while after she had the baby, and we needed Ethan and Seth to help us get the cabin up and a corral and stable built. But Audra's rested. The building is done. The cattle are loose in our valley. There aren't any crazy people living in the caverns."

A chill of fear raced up Julia's back and goose bumps rose on her skin. Rafe must have noticed, because he ran his hands up and down her back as if to warm her. And if his hands pressed her close to him, well, that warmed her all the more. "We're safe enough for now. It's probably even okay for you to go exploring deeper in the caverns."

Julia forgot her fear and smiled. "You're going to let me go in?"

"As long as I'm with you, right?" Rafe jabbed one finger right at her nose. "You promised."

"I won't go in alone." She wanted company. She'd spent too much of her life alone.

"Good, then I think it's time to send everyone away and have you to myself for a while."

"That does sound nice." Julia rested her hands on his upper arms, marveling at his hard muscles and endless strength. "Your brothers really are idiots."

"No, they're not." Rafe laughed and hugged her until she squeaked. "But they are more company than I want right now. I'll tell Ethan to send over a few men, but not right now. We'll need cowhands. But we can wait a few weeks on that. And when they do come, we'll build a bunkhouse, so they won't be in the cabin with us. It's been a nuisance having to find excuses to go for long rides with you, just for a chance to get you to myself." Rafe's strong arms encircled her waist, and he hugged her tight enough that her toes lifted off the ground. "And it gets mighty cold at night camping out."

Julia looked into Rafe's gray-blue eyes. In the shadows of the alley, they shined blue. Her hands slid from his muscular arms to wind around his neck. "Do you think it was the right thing to push Audra and Ethan into getting married?"

"Sure it was right."

"But what about love, Rafe? Audra wasn't happy with Father. I wish she could've married for love."

"Now, honey. I'm sure they'll get around to loving each other when they've got a little spare time. But they needed to tie the knot now. Audra needs to get away from those caves before Maggie ends up hurt, and your little stepma needs to change her name in case someone comes hunting your pa. And besides, a single woman needs a man. Those young'uns need a pa. Ethan'll take good care of them. Maggie is so attached to him, we couldn't have let them be separated."

"Those aren't the best reasons in the world for two people to get married."

Rafe leaned down and whispered a really good reason for two people to get married. His breath on her ear tickled and she giggled. Embarrassing. She wasn't a giggling kind of woman.

"Now you quit distracting me with all this nonsense and let's go see to our prisoner." He smiled so she'd know he was teasing and not start smacking him. Then he led her back to the street. Opening the door to the jailhouse, he let Julia go ahead of him. Sheriff Amos Meese sat at his desk with one boot off, spinning the rowel of a spur.

"Howdy, Rafe." The man apparently had the crime in Rawhide completely under control.

"Howdy, Amos."

"Howdy, Mrs. Kincaid." The sheriff tipped his hat to Julia. "It's a mighty rare and precious sight to have a beautiful woman in town."

Julia hated the dismal little jail. She felt as sorry for the sheriff as she did for the prisoner, or very nearly. Bars caged off about a fourth of the one-room building, and Tracker Breach lay on a cot in a cell, only inches longer than the bed. He tugged absently on the scraggly beard that covered his scarred face.

He turned and sat up, swinging his feet to the floor. He had an eye patch and a scowl that did an already unsightly man no favors.

"Afternoon, Amos. Have you heard from Judge Steinhauser yet?" Rafe moved so he was between Tracker and Julia, as if the bars weren't quite enough protection.

"No one got hurt in that cave," Breach snarled. "We had us a tussle, but there ain't no law against that."

"No one got hurt?" Julia clenched her fists. "Why, you—"

Rafe grabbed her around the waist to keep her from charging the cell. "You're lucky you've got bars to protect you, you low-down polecat."

"Quiet, Breach." The sheriff slipped his boot on. "Don't pay him no mind, ma'am. We've got him for more than what he did to you. Tracker Breach is a wanted man in Texas and he broke jail in New Mexico Territory. He knows he can't talk himself out of a long stretch behind bars."

Julia calmed down enough that Rafe let her go. But she noticed he stayed close. It might've been to protect her, but she suspected he wanted to be able to grab her again if the need arose.

The sheriff stood from his squeaky wooden chair and stomped his foot to seat it in the boot. The lawman looked so happy to see them that Julia felt sorry for her grouchy behavior. Sitting all day in the jailhouse of a mostly law-abiding—and nearly deserted—town with one cantankerous prisoner couldn't be a fun job.

Tracker subsided onto his cot and went back to yanking on his scraggly whiskers.

"Judge Steinhauser was in Colorado City a couple of days ago," Sheriff Meese said. "A rider came through and seen him. So we're hoping we can have the trial real soon."

"When the judge shows up, send a rider and we'll come in and attend the trial."

"I will if need be, but chances are the judge'll just send him back to Texas with the next U.S. marshall that comes through." The sheriff settled back into his chair. There was no other furniture in the room besides that chair, the desk, and the cot in the jail cell. "Heard you weren't staying at your ranch anymore, Rafe."

"I claimed a piece of property nearer town. And while we're in here, Seth is going to get another chunk."

"He is?" This was the first Julia had heard of it.

"Yeah, I just now remembered I'd planned on him doing it sometime. I scouted the water holes and know right where he oughta stake his claim. He might as well do it now. We can make the whole Kincaid property into a solid stretch."

"Have you mentioned this to Seth?" Julia didn't think Seth was a real solid choice to own a ranch at this point.

"Nope. Forgot. Remember to send a rider for us, Sheriff."

"Will do, Rafe." The sheriff got up again. Maybe he was a gentleman, rising when a lady entered and left a room. Or maybe he just wanted them to stay and talk awhile longer. A lonely job being sheriff of Rawhide, Colorado. "I had no idea Gill had family in the area, ma'am."

Her father had run a small-time gambling operation here in Rawhide and he'd kept his wife and daughters a secret, using them to hide his tracks when he'd run from trouble. No one was looking for a family man named Wendell Gilliland. Julia had been dragged across the country, then left to live in remote locations most of her life as her father set up shop, then ran from the unsavory people he gambled with. He had married Audra when he'd realized Julia was getting ready to leave him and take his disguise with her. Then Julia had found she couldn't leave her delicate new stepmother to her lonely fate.

"That was Father's way," Julia said. "He always kept us away from his business. I suspect he didn't like us to know what he was up to."

The sheriff nodded.

"If you think my boss is gonna forget about your pa stealin' a fortune from him, yer loco," Breach said. "He'll keep coming."

"A fortune? No, my father didn't have any fortune with him."

"The man who hired me was mad as a rattlesnake. But what really made me know it was a fortune was that he was scared, too. He's a wealthy man, and I'd say your pa took almost everything he owned."

Shaking her head, Julia said, "I helped pack the house. I helped carry things. There was no money."

Breach shrugged. "Maybe your pa took gold."

"No, I helped tote everything we brought at some point or other. Gold is heavy. Father had no fortune that I could see." It was the first Julia had heard about any fortune. "Whatever amount he stole, I don't know where it is."

"Has Breach here contacted anyone, Sheriff?" Rafe asked.

"Not since you brought him in, but I can't say about before. No telegraph in town."

"It doesn't matter if I contacted the boss," Breach said. "When I don't come back, he'll send others. And Wendell Gilliland might've slipped away quiet, but I didn't bother coverin' my trail. When he don't hear from me, the boss'll just figure I found you and took the money for myself. He'll follow my trail and it'll lead him right here. And he'll come with more trouble this time. He hired me 'cause I'm a tracker. The next ones he'll send will be gunmen. When he gets here and finds what's what, he'll be after you same as me, figuring a daughter would know her father's favorite hiding places."

"But I don't." Julia's breathing picked up. "I can't tell him where the money is."

Tracker cackled like an old hen. "Reckon you'll get a chance to tell the boss that, Mrs. Kincaid. Face-to-face."

"I don't want him in contact with anyone," Rafe said.

The sheriff nodded. "If the judge don't come this week, I'll send out a rider and find him. We'll either get him over here or take the prisoner to him. Then we'll get him locked up tight. His boss won't be able to ask any questions. And I'll put the word out to keep quiet about Gill's family. Anyone comes looking will find a dead end."

Julia didn't like it. No sheriff could promise the silence of everyone in town. Not even a small town like this. But it was the best they could do for now.

She turned to Breach. "More than a tussle went on in that cavern. You kidnapped me. You shot Seth and your gunfire caused a cave-in that nearly killed Rafe. That's no tussle, Mr. Breach. It's a whole cavern full of serious crimes. If they go easy on you, they'll lock you up for the next twenty years. You'd do well to contemplate the state of your soul."

"I spent my childhood blind," he said, "then later, when I could see, I saw people avoid me, turn their eyes away. Step back in disgust. The world ain't been too nice to old Tracker Breach, so I don't see any reason to be nice to it." He turned his terribly scarred face to her and glared with his one good eye.

"I suspect it's hot in a Texas prison, isn't it, Sheriff?" Julia felt a moment of compassion for the man. What had he gone through that had turned him into such a villain? But it didn't matter what excuse he had. Seth had terrible scars. Rafe had a nasty one on his temple. They hadn't let those scars etch evil into their souls.

"Hot as Hades at high noon in July, ma'am." The sheriff crossed his arms and looked at Breach.

"So you'll be living in blazing heat and surrounded by evil people. That pretty much describes the life you'll have in the next world if you die in your sins."

Breach scowled. Julia had to control a shudder at the sight of his scarred face. "I think you ought to use that time in prison to decide if that's how you want to spend eternity."

Breach suddenly lunged at the bars. "Get her out of here, Sheriff. I don't need no woman preaching in my ears. I can do for some peace and quiet."

"You're wasting your time, Julia." Rafe rested a hand on Julia's lower back. "His soul is mighty rocky ground."

"I said get out." Breach jerked on the door of the cell, rattling the bars until Julia couldn't hear herself think.

"Fine," she said. "I've had my say. I'm going. Maybe sometime during the twenty years you spend in prison, what I've said will take root."

CHAPTER
4

"He said he ran a general store." Audra stepped into the wreck of a building her dead husband had owned. Which meant she owned it now. Two shacks to her name, she was still a long way from becoming a land baron.

Four walls. Three windows—one in each wall except the one with the door. Three battered tables made of split logs. Two jugs on the floor, tipped on their sides, no corks.

"I suppose those were whiskey." She pointed to the heavy crockery jugs.

"Most likely," Ethan said. "And a few decks of cards. Not much else here."

Audra saw cards scattered on the floor. Stumps of logs turned on end served as chairs. There were shelves wedged into cracks in the log cabin.

"How do we search for money inside a mostly empty building?" Audra looked sideways at Ethan and saw him studying the derelict shack.

Seth went all five paces across the room, and as he walked, Audra noticed how the building creaked.

"Under the floorboards?" She crouched down, Lily in her arms, to tug at a knothole in the floor.

"Good idea." Ethan pointed at the nearest log. "Here, sit down. You can't tear up a floor while you're holding a baby."

"Ethan Kincaid, I have told you I don't want to be treated like an invalid. I am fully capable—"

Ethan caught her arm and pulled her to her feet and kissed her. She jerked back in surprise. "What was that?"

"It's my new plan for keeping you quiet when you start in yammering at me. I've noticed Rafe doing that to Julia and I think the idea has merit."

"I did not—"

"I'd say," Ethan said, cutting her off again, "you're asking for another kiss—is that right, little wife?"

Audra's eyes slid to Seth, who was watching with unseemly curiosity. "Ethan, this is not the time nor the place for kissing. In fact, because we have married under unusual circumstances, I doubt there will ever be a correct time and place for it."

"Whatdaya mean by that?" Ethan arched one dark brow.

"Yeah, what?" Seth stepped closer.

Audra growled.

Both of them stepped back. Which she rather liked.

"Well, if this isn't the time for it, then stop your fussing about letting us search, and sit down. If it'll make you feel more useful, you can hold both babies."

Maggie chose that moment to stir in Ethan's arms. Him talking in such a loud and bossy voice no doubt helped nudge her from sleep. Fine, now she had herself a job.

"I'll sit then." She did, and wondered if a hard, overly narrow log for a chair wasn't worse than standing.

Ethan sat Maggie in her lap. Maggie woke up enough to squall and reach for Ethan. He took her back, completely relieving Audra of her only real job since Lily was fast asleep. Then he began to tear the cabin apart one-handed. Seth threw in with him, yanking at the floorboards.

Audra wondered if, given time, they'd take it down to toothpick size.

Rafe and Julia arrived, and Rafe joined the search while Julia took Maggie from Ethan. They pitched the rotting split logs used for the floor into one corner with a continuous roll of crashing wood. Audra had to move from her log seat so they could tear the floor up under her. About the time the floor was gone, Lily started fussing.

Audra leaned close to Julia and whispered, "I need to find a private spot to nurse Lily."

All three men froze. Clearly she had not whispered quietly enough. The three men turned to stare at her. She'd made the Kincaid men blush. Even her own husband.

"Get back to your search." She waved a hand at them to shoo their attention away.

With a sigh, Ethan said, "We'll step out. We need to search the outside anyway and see if there's any soil that looks freshly turned."

The three men trooped out the door.

"I'll keep looking in here. There can't be many more places to hunt," Julia called after them.

"I've never felt so useless in my life." Audra adjusted her clothing so Lily could eat.

"Nonsense, you're taking care of a baby. You're the only one here that can do that, you know." Julia began running her hands along the top of the wall. There was a level spot all around where the roof touched the building. Audra didn't bother to tell Julia that the men had already looked there, twice each.

"True." Lily looked up from where she lay in her mother's arms. Audra loved her children so fiercely. Two daughters. Would the day come when they'd get married with only a few moments' discussion? Audra prayed it would not be like that for her girls. She smiled down at her precious baby, then whispered, "Can you believe I got married today?"

"No, I can't. I can barely believe I'm married." Julia finished her hunt in the tiny room and turned to Audra. "Is it okay? I don't like it that you married a man who . . . who . . ."

"Who doesn't love me?" Audra said it firmly, glad it had been spoken aloud. "Just like my first husband."

"It's a terrible thing, the way women are just handed out to whatever man is available. I should have stopped it. I should have—"

"Now it's my turn to say 'nonsense,' Julia." Audra sat up straighter. "Ethan is a decent man. I know you weren't overly fond of your father."

"That's putting it mildly."

Clearing her throat, Audra went on. "Yes, well, then you won't be hurt to hear me say Ethan is a big improvement."

"There's no denying that. I just wish he wouldn't stand around grinning all the time."

"Smiling is also a big improvement. Ethan is a fine man."

She hoped. "I'm sure he's got his own quirks, just like I do. But we'll learn to deal well with each other in time. And I needed to get away from that caldera, you know that. Maggie wasn't safe."

"But Seth was a big part of the problem and you're taking him with you."

"But the tunnels were such a lure to him. If we can't keep him from going down in those tunnels, I hope we can at least keep him from taking Maggie with him when he goes."

"He's a lunatic, you know that, right?" Julia dropped to her hands and knees and felt along the ground where the floorboards had been torn away.

"I feel a lot of compassion for Seth."

Julia lifted her head up so suddenly the bun in her hair, always unruly, tore the pins loose. "Really?"

"Of course, really." Audra rolled her eyes. "He isn't really a madman."

"Ummm . . . yes he is." Julia's hairpins scattered around her. She quit her search for money and started chasing pins.

"Where's your compassion, Julia? He was terribly hurt as a child. He was a prisoner who suffered only God knows what during the war."

"Which has made him a lunatic." Julia found her last pin. Audra noticed Julia was a lot more interested in gathering every last pin than she was in the money.

"I think a woman's kind touch, children in his life, a strong brother at his side will help him find his way back to good sense."

Julia looked doubtful as she twisted her hair into a knot and refastened it. Once she was finished, she said, "I hope you're right. I hope you'll be safe with him."

"I'll be fine."

Julia looked around the room, now torn to bits, though it hadn't had far to go anyway. "Can you remember Father carrying anything that would've held a lot of money? Breach told us there was a fortune missing."

On a gasp, Audra said, "A fortune?"

"That's what he said. But in what? Dollars? Paper money? That would fill a large satchel at least, if not a chest. I don't even know how much space that kind of money would take up."

"Gold maybe?"

Julia shrugged. "A fortune in gold would be heavy. I carried every bag and box at one time or another on our trip. Besides, I helped pack. I filled every square inch."

"Where could he have hidden it?"

"Picture Father when we were packing." Julia's bright green eyes closed. "Did he have something bulky or heavy that he kept with him at all times? Did he say or do anything that drew your attention to a satchel or a certain box?"

Audra shook her head, yet did some thinking before she answered. "When he was dying, he said something about the money."

"Like where he'd hidden it?" Julia jumped to her feet.

Audra lifted Lily to her shoulder and patted her back. "Yes. He said deep."

"Deep?"

"He said he hid it 'deep, deep, deep.' I think he said the word three times. Maybe more. He did a lot of muttering. He said we'd never find it."

Julia looked around the room. "I suppose that means he buried it?"

"Which means Wendell was right." Audra heard a little

burp out of her baby and got more satisfaction from that than she had from her recent marriage. A sad commentary. "We will never find it."

"Was there anything more?"

Frowning, Audra tried to remember what exactly he'd said. " 'The rest of the money I've hidden in a deep, deep hole.' He said that just before I hit him."

"Stop saying you hit him."

"No, I'm glad I hit him. The fact that it knocked him down when he was so sick doesn't take away from me doing a good thing." Audra realized how that sounded. "Not that I'm glad I hit him."

"You just said you were."

"Well, I am, but I'm not. I mean—"

"Don't worry about it. He had it coming and there's no doubt in my mind you didn't hit him one tiny fraction as hard as he deserved."

"He said more, right before he died, but it was the same—I think. He said, 'I've hidden it in a deep, deep hole where no one will ever find it.' "

"I'll go tell the men to stop hunting. Unless we want to dig up all the land around this cabin and the one where we lived, and with no assurance that we will find a thing, we might as well forget it."

Audra nodded. "It's been a long day. I'm ready to go home." And face her fate. She needed to have a longer talk with Ethan about just exactly what her fate was. Certainly nothing could pass between them as a husband and wife anytime soon. She'd just had a baby. Although she remembered Wendell had expected to claim his rights the night of their wedding and far too soon after Maggie was born. And she'd known him less than she did Ethan.

Julia went outside, and Audra faced with dread the fact that she was a married woman again.

Then she made a mental comparison between Wendell and Ethan.

Things had to get better.

Considering the last couple of years of her life, they couldn't get worse.

"I don't care who you have to kill!" Jasper Henry slammed both fists on his desk. "I want that money found!"

He hit the desk so hard the massive oak slid forward. He split the skin on his knuckles and saw blood on his ink blotter.

Bleeding him dry. That's what this mess with Wendell was doing.

He looked up and did his very best to scare his men to death.

"We haven't heard from Tracker lately, but we know where he's gone."

A chill of rage settled in Jasper's gut. A lot better than fear. Wendell had taken too much. And he'd taken it at just the wrong time, so Jasper couldn't pay a man even more powerful than himself. Even the two thugs before him didn't know the full truth of it, or they wouldn't keep working for him. Their loyalty stretched just as far as Jasper's money, and no further. Now Jasper was spending his last bit of money trying to restore his fortune. But his instincts were telling him to run. Take what little he had left and get out of town. He'd been planning his escape before Wendell's theft, which was why nearly all of his accumulated wealth was in one spot and easy to grab.

"He found him, didn't he?" Jasper didn't have anyone among

his men who knew the western lands, so he'd hired Tracker Breach. Jasper could track a man on brick streets right here in Houston, but he'd needed the best tracker he could find who knew the wild places. That is, the best tracker who wouldn't ask too many questions.

"Yeah, Tracker found Wendell. He probably killed him, grabbed the money, and ran," Mitch said.

Jasper nodded at his man Mitchell Wilks. Trouble was, by hiring Breach, he'd hired someone who didn't have the sense to be afraid of him.

"Wendell was an expert at leaving a hard trail to follow, sir," Mitch added. The cowboy stood in his sharp black suit with his hands folded in front of him, a nasty piece of humanity. He'd made his living slipping guns and whiskey and runaway slaves past blockades during the War Between the States. He hadn't cared what he was smuggling. He'd taken slaves north and taken them back south. He'd been with Jasper since the war ended, and so far there was nothing that was too low for the man.

No one he wouldn't kill. No vice he wouldn't enjoy. But all in his tidy way. His suit never got wrinkled while he carried on with the worst kind of depravity.

Jasper considered him the next thing to a brother.

"Tracker didn't hide his trail." Grove Cassidy was cadaver-thin with a face drawn into grim lines that Jasper had never seen bend into a smile. He scared grown men into turning over everything they had to escape his wrath. Jasper's gut clenched when he thought of some of the methods Grove used. He was the reason Jasper had such a choke hold on his territory. Between Grove and Mitch, no one ever crossed Jasper Henry. And now, Wendell had.

"Tracker could hide in the wilderness." Jasper had lived off the land after Pa had thrown him out. He knew how to survive, but it was a life with no comforts. And the people who lived there were tough men. His easiest prey was in a more civilized world. But he had to have that money. Wendell was small-time, but he'd put his hands on the wrong bag at the exact right moment, and he'd taken enough to ruin Jasper's empire.

"He might." Grove rarely said a sentence when a word or two would do.

Mitch was all charm, though. "We've found a clear trail the man left heading west. We've gotten a steady stream of telegrams from Tracker and lists of the towns he searched. And we've checked with some men in those towns and they confirm Tracker was there when he said he was. He may have gone into hiding once he found the money, but we should be able to find the exact time and place he went missing. And from there, we can start searching."

"I made it clear the price he'd pay for betrayal. Real clear. You know the system we set up to leave letters, care of general delivery, in each town. Check for those letters. They'll have a lot more details than a wire."

"We've gotta get moving." Grove's cold eyes spoke of eagerness to hurt anyone who'd betray Jasper.

"We leave on the train west in two hours." Mitch pulled his pocket watch out and flicked it open with a sharp metallic click. "We'll find Tracker, and if he has the money, we'll get it. If he doesn't have it, we'll find it."

"Don't make me come after the two of you." Jasper knew exactly the kind of men he hired. Neither could touch him for ruthlessness.

"If you had any doubts about our loyalty, we'd've been dead long ago," Mitch said, snapping his watch shut.

Grove's steady gaze was all the agreement Jasper was going to get.

Both of them left the room as silently as avenging demons.

Jasper's throat almost swelled shut when he thought of some of the men he owed money.

Fear.

He'd dispensed his share, but he hadn't felt any since he was young and had learned to deny everything weak. And nothing was weaker than fear.

And right now . . . he was terrified.

CHAPTER
5

Ethan was on his way home. He was taking along his wife and two children.

He paused to see if he might wake up—but nope.

And he had Seth, who had just claimed a homestead. Ethan wasn't sure Seth even fully realized that, but Seth was the owner of all the good water holes for a thousand acres. It was mostly forests and yet there was some decent grassland included, too. Seth's land connected Rafe's caldera to where Ethan lived on the old homeplace. It gave the Kincaids control of over ten thousand acres of rugged mountain range, lush with grass and thick with timber. A lot of people would've seen wasteland, but the Kincaids had lived here long enough to know the wealth to be found in these mountains.

Ethan and Rafe would explain the land he owned to Seth

more clearly, later, after he settled down. And the first step to settling him down was taking him home.

Home.

Home without Rafe.

That wasn't how Ethan had pictured things when he'd decided to quit his wandering ways. At least now Audra and her daughters were miles and miles away from that ugly hole in the ground.

"What are we having for supper, Audra?" Seth, leading the way, eager to get home, pulled his horse back so he could ride alongside them.

"I have no idea." She looked from Seth to Ethan. "Is there any food in the cabin?"

Ethan tried to remember. "I haven't hardly been home since I've been home."

"You haven't been home since you've been home?" Audra smiled at him. A cold, mean-hearted kind of smile. A shiver of fear raced up Ethan's back.

"Being married is kind of strange, isn't it?" Ethan looked down at Maggie, sitting on the saddle in front of him, flopped over his left arm, dozing. Lily was asleep in Audra's arms. He had two children.

Strange for sure.

"I'll say it is." Audra shook her head. "I had hoped that man who hurt Rafe and Julia and Seth would be shipped away by now."

"Tracker was my friend." Seth bent toward Audra to look at Lily.

Audra shuddered. Ethan sure hoped she was shuddering because of Tracker and not because of Seth. Life could be a trial if Seth made her shudder.

"He was a bad friend, Seth." Ethan wondered if Seth would ever start thinking clearly enough to remember Tracker had shot him.

It wasn't just being married that was strange.

"The sheriff said the judge would be in Rawhide soon." Audra's worry lines seemed deeper all the time. "I had hoped he'd be locked up in a penitentiary by now."

"Can you cook, Audra?" Seth asked.

She smiled.

Ethan was curious about that, too, and happy to hear a question that wasn't quite so life-and-death.

"Yes, I think I'm a decent cook. I did a lot of cooking before I married Wendell. Julia handled most of it while I lived with her, but I know how."

Ethan met her eyes and smiled. "I reckon having a woman around the house will be pleasant." Then his smile faded. "Unless you're planning to cry day and night like our ma did."

"I hardly ever cry."

"Well, good. If you do feel such an inclination, I'd appreciate it if you didn't act on it." Ethan saw the cabin come into view as they rounded a curve in the trail. "We're home."

He pulled his horse to a stop and looked at the pretty cabin nestled in the valley, tucked up against a mountain, with a barn and corral. There was meadowland to the west and north. Horses grazed on lush grass. The mountain shaded them from the worst of the August sun and kept the grass green all summer. Rafe had turned his skilled hand to improving the cabin after Ethan had left.

"The barn is painted red," Audra said as she stopped her horse beside him. "A log barn painted red. I've never seen that before. The whole place is really beautiful."

"That's Rafe." Ethan loved his big brother, but right now he was just a touch jealous. "He's a hand at carpentry. You saw how hard he worked on his own cabin."

Audra nodded. "And he said he isn't close to done with it."

"Our place didn't look like this when Pa was alive." Seth reined his horse to a stop, and they sat, three in a row, staring at home.

"Nope, Pa never had much use for prettifying things. He wouldn't do it himself, and he wouldn't put up with Rafe doing it. Reckon once Rafe was here alone, he figured he'd run things his way. I got the feeling Rafe was mighty glad to see me. It'd be a lonely place to live with only a bunch of cowhands."

Ethan looked at Seth and saw his little brother watching him. Ethan said, "We should've never left him."

"And now we're home and Rafe isn't here," Seth said.

"Let's ride in. Audra, the inside is as pretty as outside."

His wife smiled, and something tugged on Ethan's gut that wasn't jealousy but somehow reminded him of it. It also reminded him that he was a married man.

Ethan had done a lot of traveling around, but he'd stayed to manly places, spent time in the mountains trapping or mining, spent time on ships at sea. He'd never been around women much, except for his ma. And that hadn't been any fun.

The sun was low in the sky, but there was plenty of daylight left as they rode up. "Seth, will you hold the horses while I get Audra inside with the babies?"

"No," Audra said. "Let me go with you to see the barn. Then we can go inside the house for the first time together. Is that all right?"

Ethan smiled. "Sure." He steered his horse toward the barn. Steele Coulter, Rafe's foreman, came out of the bunkhouse. No, not Rafe's foreman. He was Ethan's foreman now. Ethan had to try and remember that.

Steele walked into the barn just behind them. "Howdy, Ethan, Seth, Mrs. Gilliland."

Steele had been over helping build Rafe's house and he'd run for supplies and done other work for them. Ethan had come home and brought Seth a few times, too.

"She's Mrs. Kincaid now, Steele. Audra and I got hitched today."

Steele's bushy gray brows arched, but he was a man of few words and one to mind his own business. He said nothing, just took the reins of Audra's horse. Ethan helped her down, with the baby asleep in her arms, as Maggie was asleep in his.

"Can you get my horse, too, Steele? Unless you want to hold the baby." Ethan smiled at the grizzled old-timer, who took both sets of reins and grumbled but did a top job of stripping leather and brushing down the horses.

"Have you had any luck hiring more men? Rafe looked in town today, but there wasn't anyone hunting for work."

"I've taken on a couple of new men and put the word out for more. We're set pretty well for now. Rafe said in about two weeks he'd be ready to take on hands, so we can see how they shape up here before we send 'em over."

"Sounds good. And Seth filed on a claim today. He doesn't need to live over there for a while, so we might put off building him a house on his new property, but it should be up before the snow flies. You'll stay with us for a while, right, Seth?"

"Well, sure." Seth looked confused, and Ethan wondered if he remembered filing a claim at all. "I want to live here at home, Eth. What are you going to build? Another house for Rafe? He don't need two."

Ethan slid his eyes to Steele, who had some idea of how strangely Seth had been acting.

A barely perceptible nod from Steele assured Ethan the

foreman would see that Seth got inside and didn't end up hanging from the rafters like a bat, or whatever crazy notion took him.

Ethan wanted just a few minutes in the house with his wife and children. Strange business having a wife and children with barely any notice.

They walked in and Ethan found things in good order. "Let's lay the little ones down. The room Rafe slept in is in good shape. I can pull the mattress off the bed and they can both sleep on that. Then if they roll out of bed, they won't get hurt."

Audra nodded and followed Ethan upstairs. He noticed Rafe had changed the railing. The old one had been made of a slender young pine. Now it was carved wood. Rafe had taken his tools to his own place, so Ethan knew he had a lathe and a fine set of razor-sharp wood chisels.

They reached the top of the steps. "There are three bedrooms. I put Seth toward the back of the house the few times he's slept over here. I was afraid he'd run off and figured I had a better chance of catching him if he had to walk past my door."

They were in a hallway with three doors opening off it. Ethan's room was closest to the top of the stairs on the right. It was the room his folks had slept in and stretched the length of the cabin. The bedroom straight across from his would be for the children. That room was about half the length of the cabin. Down the hall a second door opened to the left into Seth's room.

Ethan swung the door open, and holding Maggie in one hand, he dragged the mattress off Rafe's bed with the other.

"I think I'll put Lily in one of those drawers." Audra pointed at a chest. "Can you pull the largest drawer out and put a blanket in it? I'd like her to be somewhere with sides. She can't roll yet, but I'd just feel better about it."

"She didn't sleep anywhere with sides at your other house."

"No." Audra gave him a sad smile. "She certainly didn't. I'd like to do better for the children now."

Ethan pulled the drawer out with a whisper of polished wood. "Rafe made all this furniture since I left. There are nice things all over the house." Ethan set the drawer down, found a small quilt he remembered his mother using, and lined the drawer with it. He took Lily from Audra and laid her in the crib. Neither of the children so much as stirred.

"I'll show you our room." Ethan led the way out and entered his own room. The nicest bedroom in the house by far. When he got inside it, he noticed Audra hadn't followed him. Just as he was beginning to wonder where she'd gotten to, she came in hesitantly.

"It's a pretty room. It's got a nice view of the yard and we get shade most of the day. The house stays cool in the summer, and we've got shelter from the wind in the . . ." He noticed Audra's silence. "Don't you like it?"

"No. I mean yes, I like it. It's not that. It's just that . . ." She looked at him and her cheeks were flushed pink. Her hands twisted together until her fingers had to hurt.

"What's the matter?" Ethan smiled. He solved all his problems by smiling.

"Ethan, you know I just had a baby."

"Uh, yeah. I just laid her down. I'm not likely to forget her."

"I . . . I can't be with . . ." The flush turned redder. Her eyes seemed to plead with him to understand.

"Can't be with what?"

Audra gestured toward the bed. "You. I can't be with you. Not as a wife. Not so soon after—"

"Oh, wait. Stop. Sure, I understand." Ethan didn't exactly

understand. "Look, Audra, that's fine." It wasn't fine, except he didn't really know what she meant by not being with him. The ways of married life were a mystery to him. Did she want to sleep with the children?

His ma sat around and cried a lot. His pa worked the cattle or took off to check his traplines. That's all he knew about marriage. Oh, he knew about man-woman things in a general sense. He lived on a ranch after all. He'd helped deliver his share of foals and calves, and he'd certainly known how the babies had come to be in there. But beyond that, he was ignorant.

"Look, Audra. You'll have all the time you want. We need to get used to each other for a while before . . . before . . ."

The downstairs door opened and slammed shut. "Ethan?"

Seth.

With a sigh of relief, Ethan veered his mind away from before. Or more honestly, he veered it away from after, or really the truth was he had to veer it away from during.

"Anyway, you'll have all the time you want." For whatever she was thinking about. Before whatever was supposed to happen happened. "So stop worrying. Let's go down and see about getting some supper."

Audra smiled and looked so relieved it irritated Ethan for no reason he could understand. And that made about the tenth thing he didn't understand about being married.

She turned and fled from the room.

Ethan decided to just chalk it up to the woman being hungry.

He was a little hungry himself, though food didn't seem to be the exact right solution to his hunger.

CHAPTER

6

"Ethan, you have yeast!" Audra turned from the cupboards and threw herself into his arms.

It was at that moment Ethan decided being married was going to work out fine.

"I can get you all the yeast you want, little darlin'." And he meant every word. Her arms were strong and warm and the rest of her was real nice, too. He hugged her back hard just to make sure.

Audra laughed, then whirled away to go through the rest of the cupboards.

It wasn't long before he sat chewing on a thick, savory venison steak, eating the smoothest mashed potatoes he'd ever tasted. She ladled on steaming hot gravy and set biscuits on the table straight from the oven.

"We'll have bread for breakfast, but I had to make do with biscuits tonight."

Ethan smiled at her and their eyes caught. "It's all real good, Audra. Thank you for this fine meal."

Her smile changed to something warmer and kinder. Her eyes widened. And for a second Ethan thought she might be able to smile and cry at the same time.

"I'm never gonna say a kind word to you again, woman, if you start crying."

That made her laugh for no reason he could understand, but if threatening her made her happy, he'd go ahead and do it real regular. Women were a mystery.

"My last husband never complimented a thing I did. You just took me by surprise is all. I won't cry a single tear, not even tears of happiness."

"See that you don't."

She laughed again and whirled back to the stove in such a pretty way it was almost dancing.

"I think she's a good trade for Rafe, don't you, Eth?" Seth was smiling while he scooped food into his mouth.

"We've done well for ourselves for a fact, little brother."

Audra looked over her shoulder and grinned, then went back to work. She straightened from her pots with a plate of food for herself and then sat down with them.

"Ethan, something's been worrying me and I'd like to ask you what you think."

Her smile was gone, and Ethan braced himself for some new strange female request. "Go ahead."

Audra rested her fingers on her lips while she gave Ethan a worried look. He decided then and there he'd do anything to

76

keep her smiling. "I've told you about my little sister and brother, haven't I?"

"I know you've worried that your pa might not treat your little sister right."

"Her name is Carolyn. She's eight now, so I don't think Father would force her to marry anyone for a few years." Little worry lines appeared on Audra's brow.

Ethan wanted to reach over and smooth them away. "What can we do to get her away from him?"

That did it. The lines disappeared. Ethan was surprised by the feeling that he'd performed some heroic deed.

Audra's smile returned. Not so full and carefree as before, but a beautiful smile all the same. "Thank you, Ethan."

"I haven't done anything yet."

"Yes, but knowing you want to and you're willing to help makes all the difference." Audra drew in a slow breath, as if she was working up the nerve to say something. Ethan waited, hoping he could rescue her again.

"Do you think we could . . . get her and bring her to . . . to live with us?"

Ethan was quiet, thinking of how to get to the girl, get her away from a pa who might not want to give her up, get her all the way out West. How long would it take? Who should go?

"We don't have to, Ethan. I'm sorry." Audra cut into his thoughts.

"What?" Ethan had been lost in his planning. "What are you sorry for?"

"I can tell you don't want to do it." Her brow was wrinkly again.

"I was just planning whether I should head for Texas myself

and snatch her away and bring her home, or take you with me. Reckon she'd be scared if I showed up. If she didn't want to go, I'd be kidnapping her." Ethan looked at Seth. "The law might take a dim view. But if I take you, Audra, then I have to take the babies—"

Audra cut off his planning by laughing. "So we can do it? We can bring her here?"

Ethan nodded. "Sure. She's my sister now, too. Your pa sounds like a polecat, so we'd best get her away from him. And we probably oughta fetch your little brother along. Your pa's gotta be a mighty bad example of a man for him to grow up learning from."

Audra leaped out of her chair to throw her arms around his neck. He scooted back in time to make room for her to end up on his lap. And a whole lapful of Audra Kincaid was one of the sweetest things Ethan had ever known. Ethan decided he was taking to this husband business right quick.

"There's no rush." Audra kissed him on the cheek, then stood up way too soon to suit Ethan. She sat back down in her chair. Her eyes were shining with unshed tears, but Ethan decided they weren't all that scary, so he didn't scold her for them.

"You want to bring your ma out, too?"

Audra laughed.

"Because if it'll get a kiss and a hug out of you, I'd probably let you move your whole family into the house."

"Probably not Mother." Audra giggled as if she couldn't quite get herself under control. "I suspect she'd kick up a fuss if we stole her away. But thank you for offering. Now let's eat. The food's getting cold."

They were about halfway finished with the meal when the first baby cried.

"Lily's awake." Ethan pushed his chair back. "I'll fetch her."

He left the kitchen quickly, thinking to prevent Maggie from waking up, but it wasn't to be. By the time he swung the door open, Maggie was crying, too. She was sitting on the edge of her mattress on the floor, her little bare feet hanging down. She looked forlorn in her little white dress, all crumpled from sleep, rubbing tear-stained eyes, her bottom lip trembling, her fine white hair sticking up in all directions like thistledown.

Lily lay on her back in the drawer, her arms and legs kicking, working her way up to a temper tantrum. Ethan needed to get a crib built for the baby. Maybe a big one for Maggie, too.

He smiled at Maggie and she instantly smiled back. Ethan picked them both up without coming even close to dropping one of them on her head. He was real proud of his handiness.

When he got downstairs, Audra already had potatoes dished up for Maggie.

"I heard her." Audra smiled at him as if they were a real team at being parents, and Ethan liked being married even more. "Hang on to them for just a second, Ethan, while I pour some milk. Then I'll take Maggie."

"I'll take one of them." Seth reached out his arms.

Maggie smiled at him and stuffed about eight of her fingers into her mouth. Ethan looked at Audra, who gave him a very hesitant nod of approval.

With Maggie on Seth's lap, Ethan could finish his meal and bounce Lily at the same time. Audra scooped potatoes into Maggie's wide-open mouth.

Except for Seth ending up splattered with potatoes, the meal went well.

Ethan figured they'd feed them and tuck them back into

bed. But he still had a few things to learn about children. They were rested.

The evening grew late as Maggie played on the floor in front of the fireplace. Seth applied himself to keeping her out of the blazing fire while Ethan bounced a fussy Lily. They had one rocking chair, which Ethan sat in until Audra came in from cleaning up the supper dishes. Then Ethan scooped up Maggie and took her along as he grabbed a chair from the kitchen for himself.

Ethan came back in with his chair just as Audra sat down in the rocker. She gave a worried look, and Ethan wondered what was sitting uneasy on her pretty little head this time.

She nodded at Seth.

Without Maggie to distract him, Seth had turned to sit, staring at the fire as if it held the meaning of life.

Ethan put his chair beside Audra's, wondering what his little brother was so interested in. "Seth?"

There was no response. No sign Seth had heard Ethan say his name from a couple of feet away.

"Seth!"

No reaction.

Ethan gave Audra a worried look. He reached forward and grabbed Seth's shoulder. "Seth, what's wrong?"

With a shout, Seth whirled and leaped to his feet, stumbling backward almost into the flames. He clawed for a gun that wasn't there.

Ethan was mighty glad it wasn't.

Seth froze, looked between Ethan and Audra as his eyes focused. "Uh . . . I-I'm sorry, you startled me."

Ethan wondered just how dangerous Seth could be. "What were you thinking about?"

Seth shoved both hands deep into his hair, then turned to face the fire. "I . . . I guess it was the war." Staring hard at the crackling flames, he said, "When fire talks to you, Eth, what do the voices say?"

Ethan's throat went dry. "Uh . . . fire can't talk, Seth."

He exchanged a glance with Audra, who gave a tiny shrug.

"Sure it can. If you listen real close, it calls to you. In the war we were always burning something. A house, sometimes a whole town. The people would run, the ones we didn't kill. But the houses would howl like the flames caused them pain. And the fire would laugh, like it was having fun. And sometimes it would call to me, tell me to join the fun."

With a short, hard shake of his head, Seth turned from the fire, almost as if he had to wrench his eyes away. "You can't hear it?"

Ethan thought maybe there was a right and wrong way to talk to Seth right now, but he'd be switched if he knew what it was. He decided to just tell the truth. "Nope. I think maybe this is a notion you've got in your head from being burned so bad when you were a kid. Then the war made it worse. The idea that fire is alive and wants you is coming from inside your head. Fire's just fire. It doesn't have a voice."

"I wonder if you're right." The tension left Seth and he sank back to the floor, turning away from the fire this time, resting his back along the warm stones of the hearth. "Reckon I oughta give up trying to make sense of what it says to me, huh?"

"Might as well." Ethan leaned back in his chair, trying to act calm.

Maggie squirmed to get off Ethan's lap, and he left her to toddle around. Seth kept a watchful eye until the little girl started to yawn and finally tugged on Ethan's leg to be picked up. She fell asleep in his arms. Seth fell asleep leaning against the fireplace. Ethan nudged him with the toe of his boot and told him to go up to bed.

When Seth's bedroom door clicked shut, Ethan said, "He might be dangerous, Audra. We need to take care."

"How do we do that?"

"I think I'll start by putting the guns somewhere kinda hard to get at, so he won't ever grab one in a bad moment."

"Good idea." Audra swallowed hard. "Take Maggie up to bed. You might as well get to sleep, too. I'll nurse Lily and hopefully she'll settle for a few hours."

Ethan went upstairs, but he had no plans to sleep while his wife was up working. That was his last thought before the long day caught up with him.

Ethan jerked awake when Audra came slipping into the room. "How late is it?" he asked.

Audra squeaked and pressed both hands to her chest. "I didn't mean to wake you, I'm sorry. I'll get my nightgown and go change in the girls' room."

It was a strange business having a woman walk into his bedroom.

"I'll just turn my back. No need to leave." Ethan slid to the far side of the bed and rolled to face away from her. He listened for the door to open when she left, but that noise never came. Instead, she said, "O-okay."

It was a strange business having a woman stirring around, dealing with her clothes—right in the same room with him. They'd brought Audra's meager clothing, as well as that for the girls. It had been mostly diapers and not too many of them. He needed to buy Audra more clothes. Fabric probably. He couldn't remember much female fabric in the store in Rawhide. He probably ought to make the long trip to Colorado City before long.

He was wide awake and could swear he heard every button slip through its hole.

A scratching sound surprised him into glancing over his shoulder, and he saw Audra sitting on a stool near the little dresser Rafe had made. She moved rhythmically in the dim light, and it took Ethan a few seconds to figure out she was brushing her hair.

Her nightgown was white, or at least it appeared so in the starlit room. He realized he'd never seen her hair loose before. It was long, nearly to her waist, and very fine. Very beautiful.

She finished with her brushing and stood hesitantly. Ethan looked away quickly before she could catch him staring.

Sweat broke out on his forehead as he heard her take one slow step at a time toward the bed.

He was glad he'd dozed off, because that might be the only sleep he got tonight. He didn't think it was going to be possible to sleep with her right next to him.

It was a strange business having a woman in the same bed as him. Wildly strange. A good kind of strange.

Quiet as a ghost, she lay down beside him. The bed gave; the covers shifted on his body as she adjusted them.

Ethan was glad he was lying down—because he was suddenly a little dizzy.

"Ethan?" Audra whispered.

"Yeah." He was lucky to get that much to come out of his suddenly dry throat.

"I . . . I feel like this needs to be said." He heard her shift—felt her shift, too. That's when he realized his eyes were clamped shut and he faced away from her.

He'd frozen like that.

But her tone, so sweet and worried, gave him no choice but to turn. He could smell her.

A strange business noticing what someone else smelled like, but she smelled fresh and innocent and sweet. None of those things was a smell, but Ethan swore it was what it made him think of. He breathed a little deeper.

"Okay." Another word. Ethan was amazed he managed it as he rolled onto his right side and looked at his very own sworn-an-oath-before-God-and-man wife.

Wife.

Strange business being married.

Strange for sure.

"What passes between a man and wife . . ." She fell silent. There was a window behind Ethan and the night was bright. Her white hair glowed and her skin was as pale and fine as her hair. The starlight cast all the shadows in deep blue. She was stunningly beautiful.

Ethan knew it for a fact because he was fully stunned.

"Go on." He swallowed hard to make his throat work and he might've gotten up to get a drink of water if he'd been able to make himself leave the bed.

"Well, I know about a wife's . . . duty. I expect to . . . to honor you as a wife must. In that way."

Ethan wasn't sure if she was talking about making meals or what. "That's good then. I'm glad to have you for that."

"I'm not surprised." She sounded disgruntled. Maybe she hated cooking. He wondered if she hated good-night kissing.

Ethan rose up on one elbow so he could look down on her. His body blocked the moonlight, but he could still see her enough. Then, driven by an urge he couldn't control, he bent slowly down and kissed her. She lay still for seconds while Ethan marveled at the touch of her lips on his. He marveled at a few more things that came to mind. Some of them shocked him.

Then she sighed and her lips softened and suddenly she was kissing him back. He'd never kissed a woman besides her, so he didn't know there was more than a touching of the lips.

There was a whole lot more.

She lifted one hand to touch his chest and that delicate female touch stirred him, made him restless and hungry for more. Her hand moved and for a terrible moment he thought she meant to stop touching him, to push him away. Then instead of pushing, she slowly, an inch at a time, let her hand creep up his chest until it slid around his neck.

She pulled him closer . . . so close.

He felt something that tugged on his heart. It was terrifying. More terrifying than if she'd shoved him away. He refused to feel this deeply. He'd learned that lesson when he'd taunted his little brother to get him to climb out of a pit. He'd learned it when, right in front of Ethan's eyes, Seth had lost his mind.

Seth had never really found it again and it was all Ethan's fault.

The guilt drove him to move away from Audra, and he was planning to, in just another minute.

Her other hand crept around his neck and he forgot exactly why feeling this good was a terrible idea. His arms moved without his giving much thought to it. They circled her waist, pulled her closer still. He reveled in the miracle of a woman and ignored the danger of what woke up inside of him.

The draw was so powerful that he had to risk feeling, even knowing it led only to pain.

How could a man have a woman in his arms and in his bed and not care, not love? What if he allowed himself to care and he lost her?

He ended the kiss and was surprised to find just how close he'd gotten to her.

"Ummm . . ." Audra's eyes flickered open. He could see them shining in the darkness because he no longer cast a shadow on her, not with her tucked beneath him.

"We can't . . . that is . . . the baby is too young."

"Too young for what?"

"A woman can't . . . well, she can't."

Can't what? Ethan was afraid to ask, since he really didn't know exactly what she was talking about. He only knew that he wanted to kiss her a lot more than he wanted to talk.

"I suppose—I mean I know because of, well, after Maggie it was probably too soon. Yes, much too soon." Audra's delicate hands caressed the back of his neck as she talked. "And now there's Lily."

It was so distracting, Ethan had his hands full listening to her. He kissed her again, hoping she'd stop talking.

She did.

For a long time.

Then she turned her head aside. "But she . . . I mean, we shouldn't, Ethan."

Lily shouldn't do something? Babies didn't do much but sleep and cry and eat. He wondered which of those Audra wanted to put a stop to.

"Shouldn't what?" Ethan liked his wife better when she wasn't talking. He suspected that was the way it was for all men and their wives. He leaned down to kiss her again and get her to quiet down.

He was too slow. She started talking again.

"Anyway, we mustn't. Not yet. You agree, right?" She sounded really uncertain. Like she maybe didn't know what she was talking about.

Ethan figured that made them about even, because he didn't know what she was talking about, either. He only knew he didn't want to care about anyone as much as he was afraid he could care about his wife.

Ethan felt Audra's arms leave his neck. She whispered, "Let's get some sleep."

Common sense said they should. "Lily will be waking you up before long, won't she?"

He ached as she slipped an inch farther away, until they weren't touching at all. The ache made him all the more determined to not let her sneak her way into his heart.

He finally moved away too and lay flat on his back and stared at the ceiling, fighting the need to look at her again. Then her hand touched his. Slowly, gently, her delicate hand slid into his and he held on, their fingers entwined.

Ethan felt a peace descend on him that he hadn't felt since before Seth's accident. No. It had been longer than that. Before the first time he'd come upon his mother crying for no reason.

That peace scared him to death because it went so deep, to a tender place in his heart that couldn't bear to be hurt. It must have been fear that made him hold her hand tighter, and knowing there was no chance he could sleep tonight, not with her here, he just hung on and tried to deny that she'd touched him all the way to his heart.

The scream tore Ethan out of a deep sleep.

He was on his feet before he remembered he was a shallow man.

A shallow man with a brother who tended to scream in his sleep. Nothing to get upset about there.

Of course he had to shut Seth up. He'd wake the children.

Another scream, more awful. He might stampede the horses.

Audra hit the floor running, and only then did Ethan remember he'd gotten married.

"I'm burning!"

Ethan took a second to prove he didn't care about anything. He ran his hands through his hair and felt them shaking. Stupid to let it upset him.

Seth screamed again.

Ethan followed. He knew how to handle this. Seth had been having nightmares ever since he'd come home.

Ethan got to his bedroom doorway in time to see Audra freeze, her hand on the door. "Charging into Seth's bedroom a little forward for you, darlin'?"

"I'm on fire!" Seth's scream would have shriveled Ethan's soul if he'd let himself care.

Audra paused in the darkened hallway. She wore her nightclothes, which covered her from neck to toe, but still . . . "You go first."

"Get back to bed. I'll wake him up." Ethan reached her side in time to see a mighty cranky look. "What?"

"Your brother needs help."

Ethan couldn't deny that. Help and maybe a straitjacket.

"The fire! Ethan! Rafe! Help!" A bloodcurdling scream

88

almost honestly curdled Ethan's blood. His heart was pumping hard and erratically as if there were lumps slowing it down.

Audra shoved open the door, rushed to Seth, and grabbed his arms. "Seth, wake up!"

He heaved himself forward, twisted in her grasp. "Let go. No, don't. I'm burning. Don't. Don't shoot!"

Seth swung, and Ethan threw himself forward to block the fist just in time to catch it with his mouth. Seth had sent it straight for Audra.

Ethan staggered backward, then rushed back into the space between Seth and Audra. Seth threw himself sideways unexpectedly and knocked Audra on her backside.

"Get back before he hurts you." Ethan felt his temper ignite, and since Seth wasn't awake, he yelled at the person most handy. "If you'd've stayed out of here, I'd have him awake by now."

Audra scrambled backward. Good thing. Seth swung again. This time Ethan didn't have Audra to protect, so he could duck in plenty of time.

Then, just when Ethan thought she was going to be sensible and get back, she launched herself at Seth and wrapped her arms around him.

"Wake up, Seth. You're okay. You're fine."

Audra was too close to really get hit. Seth rolled away from her and dragged her onto the bed.

It was a fur ball for a while.

Seth thrashing.

Ethan trying to grab a handful of someone, to break this up.

Seth screaming like he was in agony, on fire.

Audra crooning at Seth like he was a frightened child.

Ethan doing his best to get his brother off Audra without hurting either of them.

A wild heave of Seth's body sent Audra away from him and she tumbled straight for Ethan, who went down under her like a pine tree in an avalanche.

Audra ended up sprawled on top of Ethan, nose to nose with him.

Seth quit screaming.

Ethan's head went in a whole wild direction that honestly surprised him.

"Are you all right?" he asked.

Her pure white brows slammed together. "Quit treating me like I'm a fragile piece of China." She shoved against his body to get up.

There was the Audra he knew. Irritated, he grabbed her and jerked her back against him. "I don't treat you like that. But Seth outweighs you by about a hundred pounds and he just bucked you off like you were riding a wild mustang. I'd've asked anyone if they were all right after that."

Audra quit shoving and settled against him, flowed really, like melted candle wax. "Really?"

"Well, sure." Ethan slid his hand up her back. A trim back. He might've been going to give her a reassuring pat on the shoulder, but his hands sort of wandered.

"Well, okay."

He felt her breathe. He was distracted for a second by how wonderful a breathing woman could feel. He only distantly remembered what they'd been talking about. Audra's face was shadowed, what with her being on top of him and everything. But he could see the shine of her eyes, even though they seemed colorless and mysterious.

Something shifted inside Ethan. Something deep, painful, frightening. He'd caught a glimpse of that deep pain and longing earlier and he'd ignored it with a lifetime of skill.

But with Audra's weight on him and whatever that was that stirred deep inside, and the parson's vows still ringing in his ears, telling him she was right where God wanted her, Ethan was captivated. His hands tightened on her.

"Ethan?" Audra sounded confused. Her hand slid up his chest and around his neck. Soft hands. Pretty hands. Pretty lady.

"Should you be lying on top of my brother like that?" Seth's head appeared over Audra's shoulder.

She rolled off one way while Ethan scooted the other.

"Fell down is all, Seth." Ethan was on his feet so fast that Audra was still sitting on the floor and Seth was crouching beside her, staring at where they'd both just been.

Seth looked up and smiled, his blue eyes wild looking yet mostly normal. "Had a bad dream."

Ethan nodded. He reached down for Audra. She took his hand. Considering she'd had a baby recently, she was mighty agile.

Ethan shook his head, dropped her hand a bit too slowly, and turned away from both of these two pests to drag in a chest full of air.

"Are you all right?" Audra's voice turned Ethan around, at least somewhat against his will.

He saw her rest her hand on Seth. She really hadn't oughta touch Seth when she'd just had her hands on him. A woman shouldn't be puttin' her hands on a whole lotta different men.

Audra said to Seth, "The sun will be up in a few minutes. Why don't you go get a fire started in the kitchen stove?"

Nodding, Seth said, "No sense trying to get back to sleep. We can get a jump on the day."

"Sounds good. I'll get started on breakfast quick. I can have biscuits in the oven before the baby wakes up. And get the bread on to bake." Audra smiled at Seth. Sweet. Gentle. Worried.

Ethan wanted to punch his brother.

Seth disappeared out the bedroom door, and Audra turned to follow. Ethan caught her arm and whispered, "You need to be careful around Seth when he's having a nightmare. He could hurt you."

Audra turned. Ethan realized the sun must be near the horizon, though it rose late here in the shadow of Pike's Peak. "Seth would never hurt me."

Dropping his voice lower, he snapped, "He'd have punched you in the face if I hadn't gotten in the way."

"He needs kindness, Ethan. He needs a safe place, good food, kind words, gentle touches. I think we can really help him if we just pour kindness out on him."

"I agree that he needs all those things, but you need to be careful, too. I've helped wake Seth up from a few nightmares, and I've learned to stay back until he's awake."

Audra reached up and touched Ethan's temple. "Not this morning you didn't."

The touch helped Ethan get control of his anger. "I saw his fist coming right at you. I had to do something."

Her hand trailed down his cheek as gently as a breath of air. It still hurt. He'd probably end up with a black eye.

She lifted her hand away. "I need to get on with breakfast."

Kindness, gentle touches. Good food.

As she left, Ethan wondered if Audra was treating him the

same way she treated Seth. And if so, did that mean she thought he was a crazy man, too?

I'm crazy to let that man kiss me.

Audra pulled her clothes on quickly and rushed downstairs. She got coffee started and had just measured out the flour for biscuits when Maggie yowled. She turned back and nearly ran into Ethan. She'd been so lost in thought that she hadn't heard him coming down. And besides, those stairs were so well built they didn't squeak a bit.

"I'll get her. Better hurry before she wakes the baby." Ethan wheeled around and rushed back up to the bedroom.

Audra was glad for the moment alone. And it would only be a moment, she knew. Seth had a fire crackling in the stove and was probably fetching kindling, for the woodbox was empty. Ethan would be down right away with Maggie.

Savoring the quiet moment, she finished making the biscuits. She didn't bother lighting a lantern in the gray light of dawn. No sense wasting kerosene.

She took stock of her supplies. Plenty of venison left from last night. Eggs. A basketful of them sitting on a long, highly polished oak counter. There was milk in a pail. A rasher of bacon hung from a meat hook over a sink that had cold running water coming right into the house. And the sink had a drain that went right back out, no water to haul. Such luxury! Ethan said the drain emptied onto the kitchen garden to water the vegetables.

There was a nice square cast-iron oven with a baking chamber and water wells. A quick check told her the wells were full. She quickly sliced bacon into a big skillet. As the meat sizzled, she heard Ethan's low voice. Maggie giggled. Maybe he was changing her diaper and getting her ready for the day.

Audra sincerely doubted it. But she did thank God quietly that, though she hadn't married for love this time, she'd at least married a kind man. She thought of how he'd kissed her last night, and her cheeks heated as she turned the bacon. But she didn't for one second blame the heat of the stove for the blush.

Holding Ethan was more pleasant than anything that had ever passed between her and Wendell, and she'd had two babies with the old goat.

A hiss sounded from inside the tall black coffeepot. The bacon sizzled. She began cracking eggs into a bowl to pour in after the bacon was done, surprised by just how delighted she was with her new life.

CHAPTER
7

Ethan only stabbed himself in the finger twice while he changed Maggie's diaper.

He'd taken her out of the bedroom she shared with her baby sister, dragging along the diapers, and laid her on the floor in his own bedroom.

There was a lot of wiggling involved, and Ethan had his hands full until the diaper was in place and he was done stabbing himself. With some pride he realized he hadn't stabbed the baby. He was proving to be a mighty good pa.

He took Maggie downstairs and found his very own personal, God-blessed wife, cooking at the stove. It was a wonderful sight.

She turned from flipping bacon.

"I got her diaper changed." Ethan smiled.

"You did, really?" Audra smiled back. A real smile. Big and

so happy that Ethan decided he'd change as many diapers as he could.

"I really did."

"The bacon is done." Audra turned back to the stove. "Coffee, too." She poured a bowl full of whipped-up eggs into the skillet that had held the bacon, and the hiss of them frying filled the kitchen.

Ethan sat Maggie on the floor, thinking to keep her away from the hot stove, and kept an eye on her. It wasn't necessary, as she noticed her wiggling toes and was fully occupied trying to put them in her mouth. "It smells terrific in here. I like having a wife more every second."

He grabbed a cup and poured coffee.

Seth came in with an armload of wood. He looked at Maggie. "I think she might be hungry. Not much food in her toes."

Ethan smiled at his chawing baby. Besides Maggie, he had a helpful little brother and his cooking wife, who hadn't cried once in nearly a whole day of marriage.

He could live like this forever.

Ethan almost got on his horse and rode away from his foreman five times before the noon meal.

"Rafe always kept the cattle in the south corral." Steele twirled a lasso over his head and dabbed a loop on a pinto mustang.

Ethan fought down the need to bark at Steele. He ignored how he really felt and found his smile. He didn't want to care so much what anyone thought of him, but Steele couldn't have made his disrespect plainer.

Wanting to say something, Ethan couldn't figure out how to without admitting he cared. And he didn't. Much.

When Steele got the pony under control, Ethan walked over to him. "We need to talk about how this ranch is going to be run—Rafe's way or mine. If I want some changes, I'll make 'em. I lived on this ranch most of the first twenty years of my life, and I've got some ideas."

Silence stretched between them. Finally, Steele said, "Rafe is a mighty knowing man. He had his reasons for doing things his way." Steele's tone said he didn't think Ethan was man enough to run the ranch.

"I don't mind hearing how things worked before, but you've got a way about doing it that doesn't leave much room for me being the boss." Ethan jerked his gloves off his hands and tucked them behind his belt buckle. "And that's what I am, the boss."

"I heard Rafe is hiring hands over at his ranch." Steele's voice dropped lower to keep the fact that he was making veiled threats quiet. "I might go see if he'll take me on if I'm not needed here."

The silence continued to stretch as they measured each other. Ethan didn't want to lose the grizzled old-timer. He was a dependable cowhand and a leader the men respected. After a morning's work, Ethan could see they needed to keep Steele at the Kincaid place. None of the cowhands was very impressed with Ethan.

"Plan on coming to the house and having the noon meal with me." Ethan did his best to make it sound like a friendly invitation rather than an order. But he ruined it by adding, "We can talk about Rafe's way and why you think I need to take orders from you."

Steele's jaw worked for a few seconds as if he was afraid to speak what was in his head. Ethan countered by smiling.

Slowly, with narrow eyes, Steele nodded. "Now, where'd you want those cattle, boss?"

"Let's put 'em in the south corral . . . for now."

"I'll get right to it." Steele was too savvy a man to smirk at his boss.

Mitch came charging out of the general store in Colorado City, a letter clutched in his hand.

"Tracker left a letter for us." Mitch had found it in the mail, addressed to Mr. J. Henry, General Delivery, Colorado City, Colorado. Jasper and Tracker had developed that system so Jasper, or the men Jasper sent, could get the latest news without the letter bearing Jasper's address in Houston. Mitch tore open the letter and read fast.

" 'Tracker got wind of Wendell. Calls himself Gill now. Tracker doesn't know exactly where Wendell is, but he's in this area. Tracker is setting off to start hunting through mining towns.' "

"There's gotta be ten towns around these parts, all full of men who mind their own business," Grove said. He looked like he wanted to grab the letter and make it say something else.

"I got a list of all of 'em." Mitch frowned at the letter. "Says here Gill's not traveling alone. That's why it took Tracker so long to get a trace on him. He's got himself a family. A wife and children."

"A wife?" An evil gleam flashed in Grove's eyes. Grove had a taste for hurting women.

"Women are mighty rare out here," Mitch said, glancing at the letter again. "Children even more. If there's a woman to be found, it'll be easy. Even men who mind their own business will mention seeing a woman. Let's sniff around Colorado City awhile, then start going town to town."

Grove grunted his agreement.

"That'll take a long time." Mitch scowled. "I'll leave a letter here for Jasper to find. He doesn't want any letters or telegraphs coming to Houston that might get into the wrong hands. If we run into trouble like Tracker did, Jasper will find the start of the trail right here."

Grove pulled his reins loose from the hitching post and mounted up.

"I wonder what happened to Tracker." What Mitch really wondered was how much money they were talking about. Jasper Henry was reported to be a very rich man. Was the money still in Gill's possession? Or had Tracker really taken it and run, as Mitch had suggested to Jasper back in Texas? "We could be at this for a year," Grove muttered.

"We don't have a year." Mitch forced himself to think of the fortune Wendell Gilliland had stolen. "If we don't find that money soon, the boss is going to chase us all the way to the ends of the earth, and then he'll send us to Hades."

"Let's ride" was all Grove said.

Rafe came into the cabin and Julia pounced. "You're done with morning chores, right?"

Rafe didn't swing the door shut behind him, and for a minute Julia wondered if he'd run. She carefully set aside the fossil she'd been cleaning and stood with her very most charming smile. She was learning well that Rafe had a hard time denying her anything if she asked in a friendly way.

Though he'd sure enough been denying her the cavern.

"Now, Julia, honey, I've got—"

"Rafe, if you've got a good reason why we can't go, I'll understand." She squared her shoulders, drew herself to her full height and looked her husband straight in the eye. "But I don't think you do. There will always be work to be done around this ranch, but we agreed we would explore in that cavern and I've been very patient."

Rafe rubbed the scar on his temple and remained silent. Julia knew he was thinking. He was a very organized, sensible man. If he couldn't think of a real reason not to go down, he'd admit it. "I'll give you two hours. How does that—?"

Julia threw herself into his arms and kissed him. "Thank you, Rafe."

"You'll be careful and you'll stay right with me and—"

"I'll be the most obedient wife you've ever seen or heard of." She kissed him again as long as he was close.

Rolling his eyes, Rafe said, "That I will have to see to believe. Now, let me get the lantern and rope and—"

Julia had it all in her hands before he could finish the sentence. "I'm all packed. I've got my hammer and chisel as well as my bag for carrying out fossils if we find any we can get loose."

They headed for the cavern within seconds of Julia getting his cooperation.

Julia looked back often, half expecting Rafe to have abandoned her.

Except he wouldn't.

Julia headed into the tunnel and moved fast, leading Rafe deeper and deeper, hoping he didn't recognize their trail. They entered a disaster. A cave so jumbled with rocks it was nearly impassable.

But nearly was the key. She hoped to get past all right.

"This is where Seth got shot and Tracker grabbed you. We shouldn't have come this way. Who knows if this cave will collapse some more." Rafe came up beside her. Their torches flickered and light jumped against the walls.

"It's been weeks." Julia turned to him, scowling. "We got married."

"We sure did." Rafe leaned down and kissed her.

She ignored the thrill of pleasure. "We built a cabin."

"If we'd stayed home this morning, I had plans to build more chairs and I'd like to put shelves above the—"

"We got Audra and Ethan married and moved."

Rafe laid his torch on its side on a waist-high boulder, took Julia's lantern away, set it down, and pulled her into his arms. "I especially like the part where they moved and took Seth with them. I like being alone with you."

He kissed her until all that starch just flowed right out of her and she was wrapped around him.

"Rafe, stop." But if she really meant that, she'd let loose of him instead of hanging on tighter.

"I had no idea," Rafe whispered against her lips, "being married would be so great."

"My point was—"

His kiss stopped her from talking again for a while, until she almost forgot her point. "Rafe, I've waited and waited."

Sighing so long and hard that she expected him to deflate, he said, "I know. We're here, aren't we?"

"Yes, and I thank you for that. But I'd appreciate it if you quit distracting me. And stop all the complaining, too."

Rafe stared at her for a long moment, frowning, his brow

furrowed, then shook his head. "Nope, can't do it. I can let you explore, but I can't ever be happy about it."

Knowing it was the best offer she was going to get, she said, "Well, then fine. Complain all you want. But let's try and pick our way around the wreckage and go into that small tunnel Seth was so excited about." Julia picked up her torch, turned and sidled between two boulders, then climbed another one.

"I thought you found your fossils somewhere else." Rafe stuck with her. "Why don't we go there instead of exploring new caves?"

"I want to see what Seth was talking about." Julia clambered over shattered stone to her left, to see if there was a way through. "He said that last tunnel led to a cavern that was so beautiful, and he knew I was looking for fish fossils. There were some in there."

"We already walked right past plenty of fine-looking rocks."

Since he was mumbling, Julia decided not to respond. Complaining seemed to help him stick with the job. It must be a man thing.

She found a way over the pile of stones, slipping through a gap in the rocks, and after that her way was clear to a small opening.

"This place . . . it's hard to breathe."

Julia stopped to look back when he muttered. He had a tighter squeeze than she did. For the first time, as Rafe scooted through the gap between the cave ceiling and the avalanche of rocks, Julia really looked at the collapsed cave. Oh, she'd looked at it before, thinking of how to get through it. But she hadn't really seen how ruined it was. The ceiling on one side had come down and with it piles of rock that almost filled what had been a good-sized space. She saw deep cracks in the ceiling on the side Rafe was squeezing through. Her throat tightened. Had all the stones finished falling? Would another cave-in close off the only way to the surface? They could get stuck in here.

The small cave entrance Seth had wanted to lead them through on the day Tracker Breach had attacked them wasn't blocked, mercifully. She was used to exploring and it didn't bother her to drop to her knees and crawl, but the idea of the roof collapsing behind her, blocking her way out . . . she whirled to face Rafe as he finished descending from the pile of rubble.

She didn't want to admit it, but she didn't think she could climb in that small tunnel. How wide were Rafe's shoulders? Seth had been prepared to rush right in, so he must have known he wouldn't get stuck. But Seth was crazy, or close to it. Rafe's shoulders were broad. While Rafe was lean, he was heavily muscled. He'd fit into this cave, at the entrance, crawling, but might the tunnel get narrower as they went deeper? Might they get stuck?

The room seemed to press down in a way that threatened to wring a whimper out of her.

Julia's chest was getting tight and it made her mad. She'd never been afraid in a cavern before. This was Rafe's fault.

Honesty forced her to admit that surviving a cave-in might be at least partly responsible. But it didn't force her to admit it out loud.

Julia had the impression of that tiny cave breathing on her. Hot breath. Like she'd be crawling into the mouth of a monster that wanted to swallow her whole. The only good thing about that was she was real certain Rafe would let her quit for the day.

There could be no doubt about that.

"Rafe, I'm thinking maybe we should wait until Seth can show us that cave. I'd like to bring Seth back down here." She smiled. A fake smile if ever there was one.

"No." Rafe got that stubborn look she was already learning how to work around. "We're not bringing Seth down yet. He needs time to . . ."

She thought she heard the monster's stomach rumbling and she snapped. She couldn't stand here by that maw another second. She'd convince Rafe they needed Seth once she was outside.

She dodged around Rafe and climbed up the pile of stones she'd just crossed. Going exactly the wrong way.

"Let's go to see Seth." She spoke over her shoulder. If he couldn't hear, he could just follow along. She doubted he'd lag behind.

"No. I think it'd be a mistake."

"Seth loves this cavern." She had to lie on her belly and scoot between the rocks and the cracked ceiling, and she made short work of it. "I'm sure most of his troubles have to do with the war and that awful prisoner-of-war camp, and those drugs Tracker was feeding him."

Julia got across the collapsed cave and rushed into the tunnel. Rafe didn't catch her and force her to look at him and talk this problem through. She took that to mean he supported leaving.

It was a long, quiet, quick march, but at last they were outside, stepping into their mountain valley. Cold sweat trickled down Julia's spine. It made her furious that she was developing a fear of the cavern. She refused to feel this way. She had to explore.

I just need a different exit, Lord. I can't stand to think of being trapped in there. That's not irrational fear. That's just caution. Wisdom. Good, common sense.

Calmer now, looking sideways at Rafe as she let him catch up and walk beside her, she said, "Do you really think it will hurt Seth?" She knew, if Rafe said yes, she couldn't ask.

Rafe rested a hand on her upper arm to stop her. He looked back and she saw him staring at the cave. "The reason Ethan married Audra was mostly to get her—and even more, her children—away from here."

"Seth too, though." Julia ran both hands into her hair. Her hair had sprung loose and she juggled a few pins around to better collect the always-scattered curls.

Nodding, Rafe said, "I was afraid at first he might run into that cave and stay there. We might never find him. But I don't think he'd do that. Not anymore." He gave her a worried glance as if asking her what she thought.

It was the sweetest thing he'd ever done. Because of it, she took a few seconds to think before she answered. "I don't want to harm him. I know he's fragile and confused. I just, well . . ." She couldn't admit she was scared. Rafe would pounce on that like a hungry cougar. "I want to be careful, Rafe." Nothing wrong with admitting that, for heaven's sake. "I don't like that collapsed room." There, a little more truth.

Rafe turned back to stare at the cave entrance.

She tugged on his arm and it drew his attention to her. "What are you thinking?" A faint shudder shook him, and she wouldn't have known it if she hadn't been holding on tight. "You really hate it, don't you?"

Rafe's eyes fell closed for a long moment. Then he looked at her with a grim smile. "I hate it as much as I'd hate anything that did its best to kill my brother."

"A cave doesn't have a mind. You're giving it a personality, like it's living and dangerous."

Rafe slid his arm across her shoulders and turned her to look at him. "You know something?"

"What?"

"You're right. I am. That's how the cavern seems to me. Like it's alive and dangerous. Like it has evil intentions."

"And to me," Julia said, sliding her hands up his strong arms, "it feels like it could be a place that reveals the greatness of God."

As she said it, she remembered her dream. She remembered the fossils she'd seen of fish and plant life that she thought could be from an ocean. "It's dangerous, but it's a place full of the majesty of creation, too. It's a shining testimony to God."

Rafe breathed deeply, then said, "Okay, we'll ask Seth if he wants to go in. If he says yes, we'll bring him back with us. With the children away from here, he can't do much worse than just go in himself—and if he does, we'll just wait for him to come back. He isn't going to go in and just stay. My brother's not that crazy."

CHAPTER
8

The screams jerked Ethan out of a deep sleep. He was on his feet and in the hall before he was fully awake. He heard his wife rushing on her little bare feet right behind him.

He'd have pondered the wonder of having a barefoot woman in his bed if Seth's screams hadn't been at risk of waking the children.

"I'm burning! Rafe! Ethan! Help me!" Seth's arms blocked his eyes, then flew wide. Staring at nothing, Seth flailed and slapped at his neck and back and arms.

Trying to put out the fire.

It made Ethan heartsick.

Audra rushed around Ethan to get to the far side of the bed. Ethan beat her to Seth. Ducked the swinging fists. Grabbed Seth by his nightshirt.

"No, Ethan, don't." Audra grabbed at Seth, but Ethan was quicker.

Dragging Seth off the bed with one hand, Ethan picked up a pitcher with his other and dumped water on Seth's face just as Seth hit the floor with a dull thud.

The screaming stopped.

Sputtering, and swiping at his dripping face, Seth shook his head. Touching his neck and shoulder, probably to make sure the fire was out, he blinked his eyes and looked up at Ethan.

"That was pure mean, Ethan Kincaid." Audra came back to Ethan's side.

"No, it wasn't. Right, Seth?"

Seth's eyes, still puffy from sleep, blinked owlishly. Ethan grabbed a towel that he'd brought earlier, along with the water, for just this reason and tossed it at Seth.

Seth grabbed hold of the towel and started mopping his face. "Yep, put an end to the dream right quick. I appreciate it, Eth."

"You didn't have to drag him off the bed." Audra jammed her fists on her slender hips, and Ethan had the devil's own time looking away from her . . . her fists.

"There was no sense soaking the bed."

"That's right, Audra. He did that last night. Pure nuisance changing sheets in the night."

Audra crossed her arms across her chest and glared at Ethan.

He had the devil's own time looking away from her . . . her arms.

"He needs to be awakened gently." Her little bare foot started tapping.

Ethan tore his eyes away from his very own wife and her adorable fists, arms, and feet. A wife he'd sworn to love and honor in a ceremony duly witnessed and blessed by God and man. A ceremony that gave him responsibilities . . . and rights.

Ethan forced himself to look down at Seth. "Reckon you were in a hurry to be awake, weren't you, little brother?"

Seth stood up and went to the chest in his room. "Yep. No sense tiptoeing around with a thing like that. Best to just get on with it." Pulling out a dry nightshirt, Seth turned around and seemed to freeze at the sight of Audra, like maybe just now he was really fully waking up. "You shouldn't come in here in your nightgown."

Ethan thought about throwing more water on Seth.

Audra gasped, looked down at herself, glared at Ethan, then rushed out of the room.

"Strange having a woman around the place," Seth said, wiping at his head a few more times as he moved back to the bed.

"Stranger still having babies around," Ethan said. He listened but there was no crying. Lily had been sleeping longer every night, and he held out hope she might make it till morning one of these times. Now, if only Seth would.

Seth smiled so wide that his teeth gleamed in the moonlight. "I think you made Audra mad. Best to go apologize."

"I won't wake you up that way again if you say the word. I decided it was best." Ethan didn't think his black eye showed in the dim light, but Seth had seen it sure enough in the daytime. Quieting Seth once or twice a night had gotten to be a pure nuisance.

"Sorry about the nightmares," Seth said. "Wonder if they'll ever stop. I can move out of here if'n you want, Eth. I know I'm hard to have around."

"Nope. Not yet. We've got a few more months before we

have to get a house up on your homestead. I think you oughta be around people awhile longer. Maybe the nightmares'll stop and you'll be able to get on with building a home then." Ethan brightened. "Hey, you oughta get a wife, too. It's a fine thing having a woman around."

Seth's eyes narrowed thoughtfully, and the wildness that always gleamed in them when he woke up from a nightmare tamed a bit. "A wife? That seems like a bad idea."

"Why? You need someone to cook for you, right?"

"I don't know exactly, but the thought of taking a wife just seems all wrong."

"Well, since there aren't any women around for a hundred miles, it probably don't matter none anyway."

Shrugging, Seth jerked his head toward the door. "Get on out now. And tell Audra you're sorry. Tomorrow I'll tell her I wanna be woke up like that every night."

Ethan turned to leave. He began to look forward to apologizing before he was out the door.

His room was only about ten steps down the hallway, but he was almost running by the time he got there.

He swung open the door in time to see Audra climbing into bed. He closed the door behind him and hurried to get in on his own side.

"I'm sorry I upset you by waking Seth up that way." True enough. He wasn't sorry he'd done it—just sorry she didn't like it.

She turned on her side, lifted herself up on one elbow to face him, and whispered, "We need to be gentle with him, Ethan."

Ethan leaned closer, not one bit opposed to getting close enough to whisper. "But don't you think getting him out of the nightmare fast is better than being gentle?" Ethan forgot about

110

maybe coaxing a good-night kiss or two out of his wife and asked, "Do you think he'll ever get over the dreams?"

Audra was still for a moment, then gave a tiny shrug. "Poor Seth," she said with a frown.

Watching her lips turn down reminded Ethan that Seth was fine. Completely fine.

For a lunatic.

"Well, we can talk about a more . . . um, gentle way to, uh . . ." He kissed his wife.

Who kissed him back.

"I mean, we don't want him . . . um . . ." He snuck in another kiss.

He'd forgotten all about what had awakened him when he felt Audra push on his shoulders. It almost wrenched his muscles apart to ease back from her. He looked into her eyes. Such pretty blue eyes. Even in the darkened bedroom he knew that.

"We can't, Ethan." Audra looked almost as if she regretted saying it.

"Sure we can." He could be more careful with Seth, to make his wife happy. Even if Seth gave him a black eye every day for the rest of his life.

"No. I'm sorry."

"We can't be nice to Seth?" It seemed to him that Audra had changed her opinion kind of sudden-like. "Okay, well, good then. We agree. I'll wake him up quick. And no sense soaking the bed, so dragging him onto the floor makes sense. Maybe tomorrow I'll drop a pillow on the floor first so he don't crack his head. Plus, he keeps trying to punch me, so I don't see any reason to stand there and take a beating while my brother is locked in a nightmare. So we'll keep doing it my way then."

"Oh, I was talking about something else."

Ethan raised up on his elbow. "Really? What?"

She didn't answer for too long. "We can be nice."

"But you just said we can't."

"I meant we can't . . . can't . . ." She fell silent.

A wife was a confusing critter. "Don't you think waking him up quick is a mercy?" Ethan rolled to his back and pulled his pretty little wife close enough so her head was cradled on his shoulder.

Audra's hand settled on his chest, right over his heart. It made him think of how much it hurt to care about someone. How much it had hurt to see Seth burned. How much better it was to float along through life without getting upset over every little thing, like taking a wife or taunting your badly burned little brother. That attitude had served him well. But Audra's hand was nice. Holding her was nice. He was tempted to care about her. And the temptation was about more than feelings. It was about holding her close. Being her husband in all ways.

Ethan was a master at not thinking about how he felt. Right now it took a lot of effort to crush the image of a few ways he could be her husband. Before he got his unruly thoughts under control, he had a few ideas that threatened to make him care for his wife something fierce.

"Go to sleep, darlin'." Ethan gave her a kiss on the forehead and hugged her a little closer. "In the morning we'll ask Seth how he wants to wake up from his nightmares."

After a few weeks of owning his own ranch, Ethan had his life down to a routine.

Seth screaming in the night—which had him tired to the bone.

A warm woman to share his bed, even if she didn't exactly share it fully—which was driving him out of his mind.

A crew of cowhands who mentioned Rafe way too often and had a better idea every time Ethan gave an order—which made him mad enough to want to punch every one of them.

It was a routine all right.

A routine that made him want to hit his head against something really hard.

A snort of what could be distress sounded from the stall right below him. It was the mare Ethan had ridden home. She was a game little thing, a thoroughbred. He'd bred her to a beauty of a stallion he'd found in California.

He pitched more straw down to make sure she had a soft bed for herself and the baby she was due to have soon.

From the restless look of her, soon was right now.

"Steele!" Ethan stabbed the pitchfork hard into the straw, swung down the ladder, and moved quietly to study the mare.

Steele came rushing in. "What's goin' on?"

Ethan heard the tone. Steele figured there was trouble Ethan couldn't handle. He clamped his jaw shut to hold back the irritation. As soon as he could trust himself, he smiled.

"Looks like there's a foal coming." Ethan turned to his mare. He'd had her for a few years now and the sire was another thoroughbred. "It oughta be quite a baby."

"I'll check her." Steele reached for the gate to the stall just as hoofbeats sounded outside. They both turned to look through the big double doors of the barn to see Rafe riding into the ranch yard with Julia at his side.

"Good, glad to have him here. Rafe's a hand with horses." Steele headed for the door.

Ethan clenched a fist. Then he gave the pretty black mare one more look. Satisfied he couldn't do anything right now except bother her, he went to greet his brother. Steele had already told Rafe what was going on.

"Have you got time to stay until the baby's born?" Steele asked as Ethan walked up.

Rafe looked at Julia. "It could take a while, honey."

Rafe was asking permission.

Stunned, Ethan finally managed a real smile, instead of his handy fake one.

"I'm looking forward to a long visit with Audra," Julia said, then looked eagerly at the house. "Taking a while suits me just fine."

"You can stay the night if you have to." Steele's invitation smacked of true worry for the horse—with only Ethan to help her deliver.

"It's almost time for the noon meal," Ethan said. "Go on inside, Julia."

As if he could have stopped her.

"Rafe, come and take a look at her. I've been keeping her locked up so she'd foal in the barn, but she's just getting started. I think there'll be time to eat."

Ethan stood back and watched Rafe take over.

"How big was the stallion you bred her to?" Rafe went in the stall. The mare was lying down, looking calm enough to take a long nap. She turned her head and whickered at Rafe, but stayed down. He dropped to his knees by her belly and ran experienced hands over her.

"He was a big brute. And this is her first foal." Ethan leaned on the top board of the stall, and Steele settled in beside him. No sense all of them trooping in to scare the mother.

Seth came into the barn to join them. "Hi, Rafe."

Rafe looked up at Seth with a smile that didn't hide worried eyes. "You're looking good, Seth. Putting some meat on those bones."

Ethan knew his big brother well. The worry was for Seth, not the mare. Rafe looked between Ethan and Seth with contentment on his face. Worried contentment, but contentment just the same.

They were together.

Three brothers against the world.

It was nice, even if Seth was a little bit crazy and Ethan couldn't get any respect.

Seth went in the stall. "Is she getting ready to birth her foal?"

Ethan opened his mouth to stop him, then let him go. Seth had always been good with horses and Rafe could handle it if Seth started acting up.

"Yep," Rafe said, going back to petting the young mother. Seth went to the mare's head and began scratching her between the ears. She seemed to relax under his touch.

Ethan, with nothing to do, looked around the barn Rafe had as good as rebuilt. Nothing was the way Ethan remembered it. "Did you do all this work on the barn and the house after Pa died, Rafe?"

Rafe gave Ethan's black mare a couple of caressing pats on her shoulder, then looked up at Ethan. "I started it shortly after you two took off. Pa got so he was gone a lot."

"Running traplines?" Ethan asked.

"Yep, but instead of being gone a week at a time, he started being gone more than he was home. So I ran the ranch to suit myself. Pa always complained when he saw me fussing with things he thought of as nonsense, but finally he quit jabbing at me about it. If he didn't see how much time I wasted, he let it go."

"Your pa died while he was back here one spring," Steele said. "He came out of the mountains, gone all winter."

"We figured he'd gotten snowed in way up in the hills some- where those last few years of his life," Rafe said. "He came in with a winter's worth of furs packed on three old mules. He got here, burning up with fever. He died fast."

Ethan didn't want to think about their father. Pa had as good as quit on the family long before Ma had died, and he'd been a grouchy old cuss when he was around.

"So I sold the furs and the mules and ended up with a nice pile of money. I saved it and I reckon a third should go to each of you. A third of the ranch, too." Rafe looked at Seth. "To make that good, I'll help you build a cabin on the land you homesteaded and buy up a few more water holes in your name and we'll split the cattle. That sound fair to you?"

"I'm gonna get my own cabin?" Seth asked. He looked doubt- ful. "I like Audra's cooking real fine. I want to live here. Or maybe with you, Rafe. I like having a woman around the place." Then he froze, his hands motionless on the mare's neck. He got a strange expression on his face, as if he was looking at something that wasn't there.

"What's the matter, Seth?" Ethan hoped whatever it was didn't include any waking nightmares. His horse wouldn't appre- ciate it.

Seth shook his head. "Strange."

116

"What?" Rafe asked. "What's strange?"

"I just had a strange notion about a woman."

"About Audra or Julia?" Ethan exchanged a glance with Rafe.

"No. Some other woman. I think . . ." Seth shook his head again. "Nope, she's gone."

"Gone from your head or gone from your life?"

"I think . . . I don't know. I just pictured her in my head for a minute. I must've seen her, or maybe I spent some time in the hospital after I got out of Andersonville. She must've nursed me. I think that's it." Seth turned away from whatever had distracted him and went back to petting the laboring thoroughbred.

Ethan turned back to Rafe. "What about the fixing you did to the house? Pa didn't complain about all the work you did on the porch, all those spindles?"

"Nope. Not much anyway. And what he did say didn't interest me much. I put new cupboards in the kitchen and I did the stairway railings and put the carved molding along the ceiling and mopboards along the floors. He didn't even seem to notice. I think he thought of the place as my home then. I reckoned he had a cabin up in the mountains that suited him better than the ranch. Now I'm doing all that in my own house, and I can do it for yours too, Seth, if you want."

Ethan remembered Rafe as always whittling or fussing with wood. He had a knack for building and carving, for making things pretty. Pa had said it was a waste of time. Ethan recalled Pa's mocking words when Rafe had carved scrollwork into the back of one of their kitchen chairs. After that, Rafe had left things around the homeplace to suit Pa and started carving miniature animals and people. He'd made a tiny ranch yard with corrals and buildings.

Ethan remembered the whittled toys well. A barn and a house with a porch. Corrals and cows and horses. Three brothers living in the house. Ethan couldn't remember Rafe ever making a ma and pa, though. Ethan hadn't thought of that until right now.

That little ranch Rafe had carved looked a lot like the Kincaid Ranch did now. Rafe had been making toys back then, but he'd been planning too, whether he knew it or not.

When Maggie got older, Ethan would hunt those toys up for her to play with. Ethan wondered if Rafe would want them for his own children.

Or maybe he'd make another set. Maybe his toy-whittling days were over. Instead, the ranch, Ethan's ranch, had Rafe's mark all over it. One more thing that kept Rafe in charge of this place.

Ethan was real tired of being a poor example compared to Rafe.

"Dinner!" Audra's pretty voice called. Then she used a metal bar to clang the three sides of an iron triangle. From Ethan's earliest memory, that triangle had been hanging on the back door of the house, calling his family to mealtime.

Ethan smiled at the sound of his wife's voice, as musical as the ringing triangle. He didn't mind Rafe's work so much, knowing it made a nice home for Audra.

"We can leave the mare for a while," Rafe said. "Let's go eat."

Rafe's eyes shifted to Ethan as he left the stall a few steps ahead of Seth. He whispered, "We didn't exactly come for a visit."

Ethan arched a brow.

"Julia wants Seth." Rafe glanced behind him and moved a bit faster so they could talk without Seth hearing. Seth was slow in leaving the mare, so they had a minute to themselves.

"No, she doesn't." Ethan thought she'd made that really plain.

"She wants him to help her explore the cavern."

"Rafe!" Ethan stopped walking. He saw Seth move faster to catch up.

A pained expression flashed on Rafe's face. "I promised her."

The smile on Ethan's face got a lot bigger as he tried to cover up how he hated that cavern. The smile felt phony, but lucky for him, Rafe was worried about Seth, so maybe he didn't notice.

Audra chose that moment to swing the kitchen door open and yell again, "Dinner's on, Ethan."

The three brothers went inside. To cover how unhappy he was about the cavern, Ethan slid his arm around Julia's shoulders and said, "Did you know your ma was such a fine cook?"

"My ma?" Julia stared at him, her brows lowered in confusion. Then she smiled. "Oh, right. Audra's still my ma. I keep forgetting. You know, she's my sister now, too."

Ethan laughed.

Rafe, on Julia's other side, shoved Ethan's arm off her shoulder. "Go hang on to your own wife. Leave mine alone."

He pulled Julia close with rough affection. She smiled up at him in a way that made Ethan's heart ache. Rafe and Julia really were in love.

That was something he lacked, and he liked lacking it. Love always ended up hurting more than it was worth.

Until he saw the affection pass between his brother and his sister-in-law. Then maybe he wanted it a little. He smiled bigger. "Hey, you know what that means, Julia?"

"No, what?" Julia sounded suspicious of his high spirits.

"Since I'm your ma's husband, that must mean I'm your father." Ethan grinned.

At Julia's flabbergasted look, he smirked. Audra snickered. Seth laughed out loud.

"And," Rafe added, "Audra's babies are my sisters-in-law and my nieces, and if they're my sisters, then they're your sisters, too, right?"

"So I'm my daughter's brother?" Ethan shrugged, his smile a bit forced, mainly because he was still thinking about that blasted cavern. "Sounds about right."

"And if Julia's married to the children's father's brother, then, Julia, you're their aunt too, and I'm their uncle." Rafe frowned in mock concentration as if he was trying to work it out. Rafe's teasing smile was different—easy, relaxed.

All in all, his brother had the look of a happy man, despite his contrary wife. Or rather, because of her.

Which reminded Ethan that he had a contrary wife of his own. Which drew his eyes to the shining smile on Audra's lips. She had a steaming pot in her hands.

Julia noticed at the same moment.

"Audra, you shouldn't be lifting that heavy pot!" Julia went straight to being in charge. She wrestled Audra for the pot of boiling potatoes. Ethan saw the flash of irritation in Audra's eyes, but Audra let Julia win.

Seth picked up Maggie where she stood beside a chair. He sat down at the table, on the side that was closest to the wall. With Maggie on his lap, he began feeding her bits of bread.

"Let me take her, Seth. Thank you for watching out for her." Audra let go of the pot, then bustled around, setting a thick book under Maggie's diapered bottom at the corner, with a chair between her and Seth. She wrapped a towel around the little girl's belly, threaded through the back of the chair, tied tight to keep her from falling.

While Ethan washed up, he noticed Lily lying in the drawer he'd brought downstairs. He was working on a cradle, but for now, the drawer, padded with a blanket, was more than big enough.

"Seth, will you come home with us for the day and help me—?"

"Us." Rafe cut Julia off. "Help us."

"Yes, help us explore the cavern some more." Julia gave Rafe a disgruntled look. "I'm not planning to leave you behind, Rafe."

"Seth might be."

"Sure, I'll come with you." Seth's eyes took on a wild look of joy. Ethan didn't like it.

"No, he can't go." Audra tapped a metal ladle on the side of the potato pot she'd just emptied into a bowl. Her sharp voice turned everyone in the room to look at her.

Ethan wondered at her tone. She spoke her mind with him, but when it came to Julia, and Rafe for that matter, Audra mostly just said "yes" and "I'm sorry."

"I think Seth should stay with us a while longer," Audra said. She blushed and turned her attention to setting the bowl on the table.

"I need him, Audra," Julia said. "He knows that cavern better than any man alive. I mean, better than any man."

What did she mean by changing from the words "any man alive" to "any man"? Ethan wondered that as he moved close to sit between Seth and Maggie to watch her grabbing fingers. Audra hadn't needed to tell him. He was learning.

"I don't want him down there. At least not yet." Audra's

chin had a stubborn set to it, but she was talking straight at the platter of tender roast beef as she placed it on the table. She added a thick gravy and a bowl of carrots she'd dug up from their garden. Rafe's men had tended the garden while Rafe had been busy getting himself married, and now Ethan and his family were eating like kings.

"Audra, this isn't your decision—it's Seth's." The last of the food was served and Julia sat next to Rafe, who was at the head of the table.

Audra looked at Seth, her eyes wide with regret. "I'm sorry. I don't mean to sound that way."

Seth was busy eating, so he didn't say anything. He acted like he was ignoring the whole conversation and he probably was. In the end he'd do as he wished. And Ethan knew well that Seth usually wished to go into the cavern.

Ethan scooped up some of the perfectly mashed potatoes and did his own tapping to get the food on a tin plate. He blew on the steaming potatoes and touched them with his fingers. When he was satisfied they weren't too hot, he spooned them into Maggie's wide open mouth.

He'd like to stuff a spoonful of something in Julia's mouth, so Audra would be happy and Seth would be kept aboveground.

"Seth needs to face that cavern." Julia had Lily in her lap, bouncing her with one impatiently tapping toe.

"Julia, please. It's too soon." Audra finally sat down to eat her own meal, with Maggie between her and Ethan, but she kept that unusually stubborn look on her face.

Ethan knew she was trying to prove she could be strong. She didn't seem to have that much of a problem standing up to him, but he admitted that Julia was quite a test of a sturdy backbone.

"He needs to learn to handle his fears if he's ever going to stop having nightmares." Julia seemed to be bouncing Lily faster all the time.

"It's probably not good for her to be bounced quite that hard when she's so young." Ethan relieved his sister and daughter, Julia, of his daughter and sister, Lily.

"The cavern might make the nightmares worse." Audra bit her lip, and Ethan found himself watching her every move. Which, considering he was feeding Maggie and holding Lily, was something to be proud of.

"I don't mind going." Seth was still shoveling roast beef into his mouth.

"You don't know that, Audra." Julia ignored Seth. And why not? It was Audra who needed convincing. "And I need him. But I wouldn't ask him to go if I thought for one minute he'd be harmed by it."

"He's not going." Audra finished eating, then turned her attention to Maggie and wiped her little chin. Audra's words were stern, yet her touch was gentle.

"I kinda miss the cave." Seth might as well have been talking to himself.

"He is too going." Julia cut the tender beef with way more energy than was called for.

Audra untied Maggie's little towel and stood her on the floor. Maggie toddled to Ethan with her hands outstretched. She bounced, her little knees bending as she reached for him, squealing to be picked up.

Ethan slid Lily into one arm and scooped Maggie up with the other. He needed her to be quiet so he could jump in and protect Audra if Julia got too bossy. Then he wondered where he'd find the fortitude to control Julia. He kind of liked watching them fuss at each other. Even Audra's mild stubbornness was a big change from his ma's quiet sadness. Ethan wondered if Julia had even noticed that Audra wasn't taking orders as well as she used to.

Finally, when the meal was finished and the women began clearing the table, Rafe said to Seth, in a low voice that carried under the women's chattering, "So what do you think? Will it bother you to go into the cavern again?"

Seth shrugged. "Don't see why."

"Now, don't just say it without thinking," Ethan said. He decided menfolk ought to take over this decision, and he wasn't giving Rafe a clear hand. Rafe relieved him of Lily. Ethan felt the need to back his wife. Although . . . Ethan froze as he thought of something else. If Seth rode off, he'd have his wife and children to himself for the afternoon.

Maybe Seth could stay for a couple of days. A week even. Permanently maybe. Why not? Those nightmares were getting real old, Julia wanted him, and Seth loved the cavern. Suddenly Ethan liked the idea so much, he tried not to encourage Seth just because he wanted to get rid of him.

"You've been having a lot of nightmares lately." Ethan could really stand a good night's sleep. Real selfish. And while he was being selfish, it wouldn't break his heart to be alone with his wife for a while.

Maggie bellowed and swatted him in the chin.

Alone with the two young'uns, that is.

"Part of it is the laudanum Tracker was feeding him." Rafe leaned closer to stare at Seth as if he could see inside his head and judge whether there was a steady well-settled brain in there.

"I think it takes some time to get that stuff out of your system. If that's right, maybe you should wait awhile."

"Rafe!" Julia broke up their little discussion.

"I'm just saying, honey, if it'll hurt Seth, we should wait." Rafe didn't want to go hunting around that deadly cavern. Ethan could see Rafe didn't have his usual cool control anymore. Married life had warmed him up.

"Seth," Julia said, leaning down and looking him in the eye, "how are you feeling?"

"I'm fine. I like that cave. I miss it. Let's go."

Audra came up beside Julia to face Seth. "It could give you worse nightmares."

Seth shrugged. "I doubt they can get any worse."

Ethan had to give him that.

Rafe shoved his chair back and said, "It's settled then."

Ethan had kinda stopped listening, so he wasn't sure just what was settled.

"What's settled?" Julia asked.

Ethan wasn't the only one who'd lost the trail of this argument.

"Seth is going with us."

"Now, Rafe . . ." Audra was doing her best to unsettle things. "I don't think—"

"I said it's settled." Rafe glared Audra into silence. "We said we'd let Seth decide." Rafe's glare didn't have any real fire to it. Ethan knew Rafe could do much better. Still, Ethan felt his fists clench. Rafe wasn't going to talk to Audra like that.

"Audra, you know leaving the cavern behind was as much for you as for Seth, because we were worried about the children." Rafe's tone eased, which kept Ethan from stepping in. "When we first found him, I admit I thought he might vanish back down that hole and not come out."

"I'll come back, Rafe." Seth was talking with his mouth full. He'd loaded it up when the women started taking the food away. It gave Ethan a lot of pleasure to watch his skin-and-bones little brother pack away the food. Of course, he was probably hurrying to clean his plate so he could leave for the cavern. "Why would I stay down there when Audra and Julia are the best cooks in Colorado?"

Rafe smiled and clapped Seth on the shoulder. "See what I mean? He's a lot better. And if you're still having nightmares, then I don't see how it could hurt to go down. With Audra and the babies all the way over here, he can't take them down. So there's no reason Seth couldn't wander in that cavern all he wants."

Ethan swallowed hard to keep from mentioning floors that broke like eggshells.

"I'd really like to show Maggie the cavern sometime," Seth said, then scooped up his potatoes with lightning speed.

Rafe's smile faltered. He looked at Julia as if he wished he could kidnap her and forget this whole cave mess. Ethan could sympathize.

Then Rafe squared his shoulders and said, "Let's go, Seth."

Rafe had always been like this. Ethan knew his big brother hated that cavern. Hated it almost as much as Ethan did. But he'd faced it. He'd been brave enough to go back down. Not Ethan. Going in after Maggie had been terrible. Before that, he'd gone in once, just a little, when Rafe called out for a lantern. That was it. He'd stayed far away, even though he knew that made him a coward.

Now Rafe, hating the cavern as much as ever, was going down, facing it. Under control. It made Ethan ashamed.

"We need to see to the foal, but even so we can be back to our cabin tonight, and we'll explore come morning. Maybe you can stay a few days, Seth."

Rafe deposited Lily in Julia's arms. Julia smiled as she took Lily, and Ethan wondered when his big brother might end up with a baby of his own.

"We'll take care of him, Audra. I promise." With his arms empty, Rafe came around the table and swept Audra into a hug, which Ethan found annoying.

His voice soft, Rafe said, "Thank you for caring about Seth. If I get any idea that his nightmares are worse because he's been down there, we won't try this again. I promise."

Audra's brow was furrowed, and for a second Ethan thought he saw a shimmer of tears.

"Let's go see how your mare is doing." Rafe clapped his hat on his head and led the way outside. In charge as always.

As they left, Ethan thought about his wife's tears for Seth. Ethan wasn't sure he liked his little brother being such a favorite of Audra's. Sometimes it seemed as if she liked Seth more than she liked him. And on that thought, Ethan found his smile.

Somehow smiling helped him turn off all the things he fretted about. It had always been that way for Ethan.

When something bothered him, he smiled and thought about something else. It usually worked, and right now it was working just fine because he realized he was going to get his pretty wife all to himself for at least one day.

And night.

Maybe it was time for his wife to find out what it meant to be a wife. And he could find out what it meant to be a husband while he was at it.

CHAPTER
9

Jasper Henry, hearing footsteps rushing up behind him, ducked into an alley. He drew the little derringer he always carried and cursed himself for leaving his guards behind in his office. Especially at night. But he wanted to check the telegraph station by himself. He didn't completely trust the men in his employ, and if the news was bad, he'd have to deal with it secretly.

Anyway, he hadn't been able to stay in that room for another second without exploding. And if he did explode, he didn't want any witnesses.

He had the name of a little Colorado town now. Beyond that, Mitch and Grove hadn't found the money. Time was running out. Jasper had figured himself to be a thorough man. But despite a lifetime of plotting and planning, suddenly he realized his life was built on sand in a fast-emptying hourglass.

The footsteps came closer and his heart pounded. He felt feverish, his stomach unsettled. It was fear.

His hand clutched the derringer as if it were the only hold he had on life, and it just might be. Fear made him furious; it made him sick. Jasper Henry didn't fear anyone. People feared him. He was the strongest man in the underbelly of this wide-open western town of Houston, and the town worked smoothly as long as everyone remembered to fear Jasper Henry.

"Jasper, honey, come on out."

Trixie.

He sagged against the wall in relief. Trixie Bouvier was an old friend from back in their early days in New Orleans, when he poured drinks behind a bar and she worked upstairs. They'd both survived. When Jasper had gotten his own saloon, and a taste for having money, he found out that the way to money was through power. He began a step-by-step plan to gain both, and if a man had to die to clear Jasper's path, Jasper had been willing to do the clearing.

He'd brought Trixie along.

Now she owned a saloon and had a string of girls, and Jasper had the rest of the town.

"You come in here," he said.

Lights from the buildings on both sides of them poured enough light into the alley that he could identify Trixie and see she was alone.

If the men he owed money were angry enough, they'd use anyone, including Trixie, who was the closest thing to a friend he had. He stood straight before she could see his slumped shoulders and weak knees. She had on her usual red dress. Her cheeks were red with rouge, and even in the darkened alley in the late evening, her lips glowed vivid painted-on scarlet.

He saw the wrinkles, too. Trixie had been a beauty in her youth. She was still pretty when she was dressed right and had rouge on her cheeks. But now in the shadowed alley with a dim light coming from a nearby window, all her artifice was gone. All he saw was an old worn-out dance-hall girl.

Yet he was her age, which meant he was old, too.

Cringing in an alley seemed real worn-out.

"I heard talk, Jasper."

"Talk?" Jasper's stomach dived. Had the word gotten out about the theft? Jasper thought long and hard, hating Wendell for being at the wrong place at exactly the wrong time and walking away with Jasper's money.

"About somebody taking what was yours," Trixie added.

"What did they say exactly?" Jasper knew the rumors that ran through Trixie's saloon were wild and undependable. But even a whisper about Jasper not being able to pay his bills would quickly reach the Hardeseys.

"I heard you were cheated. Cheated big. That's why I came. The fact that you got robbed at all is big, Jasper, honey. I'd say you've got until the payment is due at the end of the month. If there's trouble then, Hugh Hardesey will start listening closer to the rumors."

His men should be hot on Wendell's trail. If the system he'd worked out with Tracker Breach held up, they'd find Breach real fast. And Breach disappearing would mean he'd either run afoul of Wendell or the law, keeping Breach from coming back—or Breach had found what Jasper sent him after, had grabbed it and run. Jasper couldn't blame the man; it would take someone strong to resist.

But not blaming Breach wasn't the same as letting him get away with it.

A cold chill slid like a knife into Jasper's gut. Equal parts terror and determination. He had three weeks to either get that money from Wendell or die.

Or run.

Wendell had run and Breach hadn't found him.

Breach had maybe run and Mitch and Grove hadn't found him.

The West had a way of swallowing a man up. He heard that sand running through the hourglass. Heard the minutes of his life trickling away.

He suddenly knew he had no choice. Even if Mitch and Grove found Breach, they weren't going to be able to get to Wendell in time.

Jasper had to go and stay gone until he'd found his money.

Opium.

The Hardeseys were brutal, vicious killers. He should never have gotten into the drug trade. The money hadn't lured him. He'd already had enough money to last him a lifetime—at least until Wendell had crossed him. But the crime element that went with drugs was the kind of thing a man either got out in front of or got run over by. And Jasper had waded into the filthy waters of dealing in opium to keep his place on top of the criminal world.

"What are you going to do?" Trixie faced him in the alley and ran a hand up his arm, then rested it on his shoulder.

Jasper leaned back against the wall and looked at Trixie. Strange to think he'd miss her. She was his oldest friend. His only friend.

As he studied her, the aging courtesan, he remembered how they'd teamed up so long ago. She'd fed him rumors that helped him move up the social ladder. When he'd moved up, he'd turned around and helped her. Even bought her the saloon, then helped her gather the girls.

Why hadn't he gotten her out instead? At the time he'd thought he was doing her a service by setting her up in this way. Making it possible for her to get out of making her money through living that dismal life, but only if she lured other women to take over the same duty. Pouring whiskey for men who should be home sleeping, when instead they were draining their pockets of money while she plied them with booze and women and poker.

When he'd finally gotten established, why hadn't he married her? They'd always been close. Jasper had even been faithful to her, as he suspected she was to him. Why hadn't he made an honest woman of her?

Honest. There was a word he didn't deal in much.

Why hadn't he gotten her into a life that was . . . was just as sordid.

Jasper hadn't felt shame in about forty years, since about the age of ten. He'd felt shame that almost destroyed him when a cigar he'd snuck into his bedroom caught his house on fire and killed his ma and little sister.

His pa, once Jasper confessed, had kicked him out.

The shame had hurt worse than the beating Pa had given him. As Jasper scrambled to stay alive, he'd done things that numbed a boy to shame.

He was a little bit surprised to recognize it.

Lifting his hand, he wove his fingers through hers. A tiny gasp barely sounded as Trixie widened her eyes.

Odd to think he was about to give Trixie the power to become very rich, very fast, by selling him out to the Hardesey clan. And he didn't have the tiniest shred of doubt that he could trust her.

"Here's what we're going to do," he said.

It only made Jasper more ashamed when Trixie didn't even hesitate.

Sweet mercy, he finally got rid of his brothers. "I thought they'd never leave," Ethan said.

Audra nodded. "I can't believe they left."

She had Lily, and Ethan had Maggie. His family. Alone at last.

The foal had been slow in coming, so the day was getting away from them.

Ethan turned to face her. "Seth'll be all right, honey."

"No, he won't." Audra looked down to find Lily asleep, which made Ethan look at Maggie. She was passed out against his chest. He smiled down at the sleeping toddler. She was a ringer for Audra, except bald.

"Let's get 'em to bed." Ethan led Audra up the stairs. The babies were limp as Ethan rested Maggie on the bed and Audra put Lily in the drawer. As they walked out, Ethan said, "I need to get the cradle finished and build a bigger crib."

Audra went ahead of him to the stairs and he followed her down, bracing himself to listen to her start in fussing about Seth.

When they were well away from the babies so their voices wouldn't bother them, Audra looked up at Ethan, her hands clutched at her waist, her brow furrowed. "I think Julia is so bent on finding the fossils in those caverns that she's not thinking of what's best for poor Seth."

Ethan smiled, but it wasn't that easy. He was mighty tired of hearing about poor Seth.

A sudden desire to make sure Audra knew just whom she belonged to prompted Ethan to pull her into his arms and hold her tight.

"Rafe won't let anything happen to Seth," he said. A slight tremor shook Ethan as he thought of how badly Seth could be hurt in the cavern, no matter how close to hand Rafe was.

"Tell me what happened down there," Audra said.

"No, I'm not talking about that stupid cavern."

"I know you hate it."

Ethan laughed, but it was a coarse laugh, no humor in it at all. "Noticed what a coward you're married to, huh?"

"Being afraid of something you know is dangerous isn't cowardice, Ethan." Audra's voice was sharp, and Ethan had the notion that she wasn't talking about him or the cave. He wondered what danger she'd faced and feared.

"It is if your brothers went through the same thing and both of them could get over it and go back in there."

"What happened?"

"Please, let's just forget it."

Audra lifted her arms to wrap them around his neck. "If you feel like what happened down there paints you as a coward, then maybe what happened makes Seth behave so recklessly. Maybe while you avoid the cave, which is good judgment in my eyes, Seth feels like he has to defeat it. He probably sees himself as a coward just like you do. Maybe Rafe, too. But they're just reacting to that in different ways. All three of you were scarred by it."

"Not me. Seth is covered with scars, and Rafe has one on his forehead, but I walked away without a scratch."

"I think you have some scars, Ethan, but they're inside where only you can see them."

She might be right.

"If you'd tell me what happened, we might be able to help Seth. Maybe we can help all three of you."

Ethan swallowed hard. "Maybe if we talked to Seth. But what's the point of telling you the story?"

"If I knew what happened, I'd understand better. There might be a better way to treat him. And that could help him get over his nightmares." Audra tightened her hold, and Ethan realized the warmth of her body was strong enough, steady enough, he could talk about what had happened for the first time in his life.

"I doubt anything can end those ugly dreams. Seth's had times when the dreams would come less often, but he's never gotten over them completely. Not in all these years." Ethan had never admitted his part in what happened to Seth. Rafe hadn't been there. Seth too probably didn't know what all had happened in that madness.

"I know Seth was hurt in an accident. He fell in a hole and his terrible scars are from burns."

"I did it."

"Did what?"

"I burned him." Ethan started to tremble. It was shocking how powerful the words were when spoken aloud. "I dropped my lantern and burned my little brother almost to death."

Audra felt it, because she hugged him tight, then drew him to the nearby kitchen table and sat him in a chair. She stepped away and Ethan reacted without thinking. He grabbed her around the waist and pulled her on his lap.

Somewhere inside he knew he shouldn't touch her. When she heard the whole story she'd stand and put space between them. She'd probably move out of their bedroom and start sleeping with the children.

Audra held Ethan closer. It was shocking how pleasant it was to be in her arms, especially when he knew it might be the last time.

Audra shivered in his arms as she thought of that dark pit. She'd stepped inside the cave entrance, but she'd never gone farther in until the day Seth had taken Maggie down there.

"We ran around down there all the time as kids and never quit finding new tunnels and caves," Ethan said.

"It's that big? Really?" Audra felt Ethan's strong arms flex as if he were hanging on for his life.

He nodded. "We explored a lot and never found the end of it."

Audra pulled away from Ethan. "We could have lost Maggie down there and never found her again." It terrified her to think of it. "But you can't blame yourself for dropping a lantern, Ethan. It was an accident."

"The lantern was bad, but that wasn't what I hate about that day. The burns"—Ethan shook his head silently—"they were awful. He was so badly hurt. For weeks after, we thought he'd die. He had ugly sores that took forever to heal."

Audra reached over and ran her hands through Ethan's hair, wishing she could snatch that memory away from him and throw it down into a bottomless pit.

Under his hair, Audra found a rough patch. Ethan pulled her hand away.

"What's that scar?" she asked.

"I cut my head that day. I just sat there while Rafe tried to save Seth—while Seth screamed and burned. I did nothing."

"You do have scars, then." Audra caressed the raised spot.

"Rafe hit me."

"What?" Audra was suddenly furious.

"He was trying to get me to help. He punched me in the jaw."

Audra's hand left the scar on his head to cup his face. "Well, he's just a big old skunk."

Ethan smiled over that. "He hit me and it did bring me out of whatever was wrong with me."

"You were hit on the head—that's what was wrong with you, for heaven's sake."

"Then Rafe told me he was going for help. The fire that caught on Seth's shirt was out. When Rafe left, I thought he was going all the way back to the ranch. I thought he was leaving us for hours. It turned out Rafe had gone to get the lariat tied on his horse. He was back pretty fast. We got Seth out of that pit, but he was so burned. His skin was black in places. Every time he moved it bled. And when we got home, Ma was horrified by the burns. She cried the whole time she was trying to help him. Pa was furious at us for letting Seth get hurt. Then the nightmares started. Ma just seemed to cry herself to death. She lived for a couple more years, but she was never the same after I hurt Seth. And Pa just as good as quit the family. The nightmares wouldn't end. One night Pa suddenly went into a rage and stormed out of the cabin. We didn't see him again for months."

Audra held him so tight she hoped to crush such memories out of him.

"The only way I could stand the screaming nightmares was to not care. I'd grouse about missing out on sleep and laugh at Seth and smile at my ma, even when she was crying, and smile at my pa when he'd yell about us being in the cavern to begin with. I didn't care about any of it." Ethan inhaled slowly, then raised his eyes to meet hers. "And I've never really cared about anything since. Except I guess hating that cavern is caring. But I fix that by staying far away."

"Ethan Kincaid, I'm a bigger coward than you'll ever be," Audra said.

"You?" Ethan smiled, but it wasn't that shallow smile he usually wore. No, this one looked genuine. "You're the bravest person I know."

Audra snorted.

"You are," he insisted. "You argued with Julia and Rafe to try and keep Seth here. That's mighty brave."

"I didn't argue enough and you'll notice Seth is gone." Audra's hands caressed his hair, running over the tiny scar no one else even knew was there.

"Well, usually no one argues with Rafe at all. He gives orders and we obey them."

"I don't think he orders Julia around. I mean, he might try, but I don't think he has much success."

Ethan's smile widened. She didn't fool herself. He still believed he was a coward. She knew how hard it was to stop that kind of thinking, but for now she was surprised at how pleasant it was to cheer him up a bit.

"Remember the first time we met?" she asked.

"The day Rafe found Julia in the cavern." Ethan shuddered.

"Yes, when Wendell was so sick. Do you remember I told you I knocked him down?"

Ethan quit shuddering and rolled his eyes. "You did not."

Huffing out a breath of annoyance, she said, "I did too."

"Hit me."

"What?"

"Right now, uh, you're a little close. Maybe you should stand up and just punch me right in the face."

"I will not!"

"Bet'cha can't knock me down."

"Well, you're quite a bit larger than Wendell, but that's not the point. Whether or not I knocked him down or he fell, the point is I made a promise to myself that night that I wasn't going to be the quiet little girl who obeys orders anymore."

"I've never met that little girl." Ethan smiled, knowing exactly what she meant.

"You sure haven't, because I changed before you got there." Audra thought of how she'd meekly let Julia take Seth. Audra had argued a lot more inside her head than she had out loud. And Audra had little doubt that staying away from that cavern was in Seth's best interests.

"Well, good for you."

"What I'm trying to say, Ethan, is that I've been a coward all my life. When I thought Julia might never come back home, I realized just how worthless I was."

"You're not worthless, Audra."

"If my normal life had gone on without Julia, I'd have been alone in that rickety cabin with Maggie and a baby on the way. It would have taken every ounce of strength I possessed to survive. When I thought Julia might not come back, I realized I'd gotten myself into a terrible mess. I swore I'd take charge of my life and get myself and my children somewhere safe. I told Wendell I was going, even if I had to walk. He started ranting. I didn't realize he had a fever. That's when he told me he'd stolen from a dangerous man. He told me we couldn't go anywhere because that man would never stop looking. He shoved me and I hit him. I knocked him down."

"So you took charge of your life?"

"Right before you showed up. I decided all the people who'd been running my life had done a poor job of it—my father, who as good as sold me to Wendell to pay off a gambling debt." She saw Ethan flinch at that. "And my husband, who'd brought me to that dreadful, lonely place. I decided to take over and run my life myself."

"And that's when you went to punching Wendell?"

"I didn't exactly punch him. He put his hands on me in anger, and I . . . I put a stop to it." She jerked her chin. "But I suppose it wouldn't have gone as well if he hadn't most fortunately been deathly ill."

"Most fortunately?" Ethan grinned.

Audra narrowed her eyes. "I should think you'd be just the tiniest bit frightened of me, Ethan Kincaid. I can do some damage."

"I'm shakin' in my boots, darlin'." He kissed her.

"Glad to hear it." She spoke against his lips, loving the taste of his smile. The conversation ended for a considerable length of time as Audra contemplated what an improvement her new husband was over her old one.

"So it sounds like you've cured yourself of being a coward." Then Ethan's smile faded. "Now we only have me left to cure. Then maybe I can learn to . . . to . . . care again."

Sympathy like none she'd ever felt before welled up in her. "You care about your brothers."

With a shrug he said, "I rode away from here five years ago and only just came back. My pa and ma are dead and I haven't visited their graves since I've been home. I never wrote a letter or even thought much about it."

"You care about Maggie."

A smile crept back onto Ethan's lips. "I reckon I like the little ones good enough."

"And you know what, Ethan?" Audra kissed him. Ethan had kissed her on a few occasions, but how often had she kissed him? She thought it was her turn to start something. Audra realized she knew more about being married than Ethan, and maybe it was time she showed him what it all meant. She took her own meager courage in both hands. "I can show you something else you'll care about."

"What?"

She deepened the kiss, and unlike the other times, she pulled him closer instead of pushing him away. This time she didn't tell him they mustn't. It had been long enough since Lily's birth, far longer than she'd been able to make Wendell wait.

"You didn't answer me. What is it you think I'll care about?" Ethan asked.

Audra smiled as she realized Ethan was far more of an innocent than she. For some strange reason, that pleased her deeply.

She rose from his lap and reached out her hand. "Come on upstairs to bed and I'll show you."

His eyes got wide. He clearly had some idea of her intent. He stood, so much taller than Wendell, so much stronger, so much kinder.

"We pledged before God to be man and wife." She took his hand. "That vow is about a spiritual union and a lifetime commitment, but there's more to it than that."

Ethan tugged her forward. Arm in arm they went upstairs.

Audra couldn't be certain, but as they took the final step to being fully married, she thought Ethan acted like a man who cared very much.

CHAPTER
10

"Seth and I will go on into the cavern while you check your cattle." Julia wasn't sure quite when she started trusting that loco Seth Kincaid. About the same time he'd moved out probably. Absence definitely made her fonder of the man.

Rafe narrowed his eyes. "No. If you go, I'm coming with you."

"We'll just go in a little ways. I want to take Seth to the place where he brought us out, after the cave collapsed. He thinks there's another entrance to that one cavern he liked so much." She'd spent a good part of the ride home quizzing him.

"Yeah, but it's not very big," Seth said. He looked toward the cavern, craving the dark tunnel. "I crawled through it on my belly and it was a squeeze. That's why I don't go that way."

Julia swallowed hard at the thought of being squeezed—maybe

stuck—in a tunnel that small. She'd never been in anything like that. But she only needed a back way out of the cavern Seth wanted to show her. Just a back way, in case the roof fell in. She didn't need to use it, only know it was there.

God, why am I afraid? Don't you want me to explore in there?

She'd never feared a cave before. Of course she'd never run into trouble like she had in this cave. It flickered through her mind that maybe the fear was a warning. Maybe God wanted her to abandon the idea. . . .

Then why did you put this desire in my heart to study fossils and stones, and why did you put me here beside this beautiful cavern?

"Rafe." She went up to him and took his arm.

He frowned down at her. Then, as he looked in her eyes, he relented with a rueful smile. "I know, I'm just trying to put it off." He leaned close to whisper, "I don't know if you've noticed, but I don't like that cave very much."

"No," Julia said in mock surprise, "I had no idea."

"Let's go. One hour, then I've got to check the cattle."

"Thanks." Julia turned to Seth. "I just want you to show me the tunnel that makes a second exit." *So I can quit being afraid.* "We won't do any more than that today."

Seth shrugged. "I thought I might sleep in there tonight."

Rafe slashed one hand sideways. "No."

"No, Seth." Julia spoke at the same time as her husband. "We're worried about you having nightmares. I don't think you should stay in there."

"I have nightmares no matter where I sleep."

"But we're here to wake you up. Otherwise the dreams might torment you for hours." Rafe took Julia's hand and drew her along out of the barn. He came even with Seth and rested a strong hand on his brother's shoulder. "I want you to stay in the house with us. Promise me that."

Rafe's words could qualify as a request, but his tone was pure command.

"Okay. Sure. Let's go." Seth said it so casually, Julia didn't believe he took his promise seriously.

They went to the cave entrance in the valley. Rafe had a lantern handy for each of them. The man was a fanatic about lanterns, which Julia appreciated.

Seth led them down the steeply declining tunnel. He scampered along the narrow ledge of the hole. Julia followed much more cautiously.

They moved quickly through a series of caves and tunnels, the tunnels seeming to get progressively tighter, though the caves they opened up to came in all sizes. Seth stopped at an entrance and looked inside. Julia saw her markings.

"This is the cave that collapsed when Tracker was shooting at us." Seth frowned as he stared at the nearly destroyed cave.

"Rafe and I climbed over that low spot." Julia pointed at a pile of stones that didn't quite reach all the way to the cave ceiling. "We can still get into the tunnel you wanted us to use, but I don't like the looks of the walls in here. See the cracks? I decided we should talk to you before we go any farther. I'd like to make sure there's a second tunnel. So if this room caved in any more and blocked us off inside, we could still get out."

Seth tore his eyes away from the barrier of rock. "This was a pretty room. Tracker shouldn't've done what he done. He ruined something beautiful."

For one long moment, Julia and Seth were in complete harmony. Despite the fact that he brought out a bossy side of her, right now they were in agreement on how wrong it was to damage such a beautiful part of God's creation.

"The tunnel we need to use if the other one gets blocked is up there." Seth stopped and pointed to a fissure in the tunnel that Julia would have walked right past. It looked like a slightly larger crack in the wall, one of hundreds down here.

Julia studied the spot about a foot above her head. Her throat went dry as a fossil.

"That's the other tunnel you found?" Rafe's voice dragged her out of a terrible flight of fancy. "That little hole right there?"

"Yep." Seth smiled.

"You've crawled through there?" Rafe sounded incredulous.

Seth nodded. "Sure, a few times. I don't like it, though. It's so tight I was afraid the first time. Afraid it would end and I'd have to back up. I wasn't sure I could." Seth shrugged. "But I have before. I can always figure something out."

It was then that Julia realized Seth wasn't just a touch crazy. Her brand-new brother didn't care if he lived or died.

She reached up and patted him on the shoulder. Seth had gained weight since they'd found him hiding in this cavern. And he was as tall as Rafe and almost as strong. But he wasn't strong inside his head. Julia said a quiet prayer for him, then gave him a few more encouraging pats.

"Let's go back to the house now," she said. She saw a look of disappointment on Seth's face, and a look of relief on Rafe's. Both made her smile. "I promised we'd only stay in here an hour and it's been at least that long. We can come back tomorrow after breakfast and finally you can show me that cave you love so much."

Seth smiled. "Wait'll you see it—it's like it was created in layers. The rock is striped, and you can tell each layer is a different type of stone. And one of those layers had a lot of fossils in it. Fish, like you said, and leaves and other things. The ceiling has pointed rocks coming down."

"Stalactites."

Seth tilted his head. "Stalactites . . . I need to learn these words."

"Let's go for now," Julia said. "We can talk about rock formations and fossils tonight if you want. I've found several fossils and chiseled them out of the rock since Rafe and I moved here. I can show them to you and teach you what they are, as best I know."

"You lead us out, Seth." Rafe pressed his back against the wall to give Seth room to pass.

"Okay." Seth passed them, heading out. He acted pleased to be asked to lead, but Julia knew Rafe wasn't worried about finding his way out. Julia's charcoal marks showing the way out were clearly visible, and this was Rafe's third time down here. But Rafe didn't want to turn his back on Seth, even for a moment.

Seth had nightmares. Rafe hated this tunnel. She was scared.

Again Julia wondered if her drive to explore this place was a terrible mistake.

"We'll spend the night here in Rawhide," Mitch said to his partner Grove. He felt an itch between his shoulder blades and decided he wanted people around him tonight. Stupid, since it was usually people who caused all the trouble. He looked over at Grove. "Ride around town, get a feel for the jail. If there are windows, try and sneak a look inside without drawing any attention—just in case Breach has run afoul of the law."

Being locked up would explain why they hadn't heard from Breach. Up to now, they'd checked the jail in every town they'd passed through.

With a grunt Grove headed out, both men riding into Rawhide—a place that barely counted as a town—but each moving in a different direction.

Besides the jailhouse, there was a general store, what looked to be a saloon, and a few cabins and barns with lanterns shining in the windows, tucked up near the woods on the edge of the ragged town.

Leaving the jail to Grove, Mitch rode toward one of the dimly lit barns. It had double doors that swung inward. He heard the clank of iron on iron ringing out into the dusky night.

He dismounted and led his horse inside, where he saw a man with massive arms pumping the bellows of a forge.

The man set his hammer down and ran an arm across his sweat-soaked forehead. "Looking for a place to board your horse?"

Mitch nodded. "Can I get a bit of oats and hay?"

The man jerked his head toward an empty stall. "Turn him loose in there. Plenty of feed and water. It'll cost you two bits to leave the horse till mornin'."

Mitch pulled some coins from a pouch in his saddlebag, counted out the correct amount plus a little more, and handed the man the money. "Been riding the mountain trails a long time," he said. "I haven't talked to anyone in days." He began stripping the bridle and saddle from his horse while he spoke. "I'd buy you a meal, mister, if you'd just come and keep me company for a while."

The man looked up and smiled, white teeth flashing in his

soot-blackened face. "Let me wash up and then we can go to the back room of the saloon. Folks can get a meal there most days."

Before the evening had turned to full dark, Mitch and Grove had met most everyone in town and learned a lot of news, all of it bad. Tracker Breach was on his way to prison, too far down the trail to bother trying to catch up to him and break him free.

A man named John Gill, who by his description had to be Wendell Gilliland, was dead. And he had a wife. A wife with a couple of little children. Mitch felt a surge of excitement. A mother would do anything to protect her children. Pay any price. Tell any secrets.

CHAPTER
11

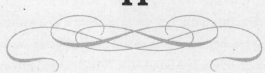

"I reckon when Rafe ran this place, he always kept the horses in the corral to the north side of the barn," Ethan said.

Ethan rose from beside the little colt, a real beauty. Ethan had already decided to keep him for a stallion. Turning to Steele, he was tempted to swing a fist. Instead, he smiled and refused to care.

The trouble was that Rafe did most everything for a reason, and a good one. So going against Rafe's way just to be in charge made a man do stupid things. But Ethan had his own ideas, and he'd like to give a few of them a try. He'd do it too, starting now. He hesitated over that. He hated caring enough to get mad. Maybe he'd start tomorrow.

"North side's fine then." Ethan's smile held, but he heard his teeth grinding together.

Steele led the pinto mare out of the barn.

Ethan followed, thinking it was time to go wrest a noon meal out of his sweet little wife. It was early, but he'd be willing to drink a cup of coffee and watch her hurry around the kitchen. Since Seth had left, Ethan had found out the pure magic of having a wife.

Thinking about it made him stir restlessly right now, in the middle of the day.

He'd also gotten through two nights in a row without having a screaming brother disturb his sleep. The baby had awakened him briefly, though that was Audra's job. Which suited Ethan just fine.

Maybe while he was in there, he'd see if she'd let him give her a few orders. He could practice up on her, then try the cowhands.

As he stepped out of the barn, two men rode up the trail from Rawhide.

Ethan stopped and watched as they approached.

The men stayed a respectful distance back. "We heard in town you were taking on hands," the taller man said.

Ethan nodded. "You heard right. It looks like you've come a long ways."

Their horses were thin and looked worn down. Their clothes were stained with sweat and trail dust.

"I'm Mitch Smith." The taller man sat in the saddle a pace ahead of his partner. Ethan noted that, while his clothes were filthy, the man was clean-shaven, his saddle and gun well cared for. Smith jabbed a thumb at the man on his left. "This here's Grove Johnson."

Mitch Smith wore western clothes, but he didn't look comfortable in them. A city slicker playing cowboy? But maybe he'd be able to play it well.

Johnson had the look of a hangman. Grim and quiet. Ethan was cautious of him on sight. He looked over his shoulder to see Steele walking toward them, leading the horse. Steele had seen the men ride in and had turned back. Ethan was glad of it.

"This here's the foreman, Steele Coulter." Ethan tipped his head toward Steele. As much as Steele was one for quoting Rafe all day long, he was an experienced cowhand and Ethan was glad to have him here to size up these men.

"I'm ready to eat," Steele said. "Why don't you men come and eat at the bunkhouse. We can talk about what'll be expected of you and decide if the job and you are a good match."

Ethan noticed Steele hadn't offered them a job. There'd been a few other new hires, and Steele had looked them over for a few seconds and hired them with no fuss.

It made Ethan even more cautious. He pointed at the corral by the barn. "Put up your horses. We can give 'em some hay, and after you've eaten we'll talk. Have you handled cows before?"

There was some grunting that told Ethan no, they hadn't. But everyone had to start somewhere, and there was plenty of unskilled work on a ranch to keep a man busy. He'd yet to meet a man who couldn't master a pitchfork. Still, they weren't youngsters. Usually a cowboy started young or he didn't start at all. To Ethan, that meant some kind of trouble had pushed these men west.

Neither one did much talking. But Ethan watched them strip the leather from their horses and pitch hay without asking which end of the pitchfork to hold. Steele came up beside Ethan, and the two of them leaned on the fence while the newcomers worked.

"Think they'll shape up, Steele?" Ethan asked quietly. Steele did his share of pushing when he and Ethan worked together, but Ethan realized right then that Steele rode for the brand in a way Ethan could respect. Worrying about the way Rafe did things—and how eager Steele was to mention them—didn't seem all that important as they faced the newcomers together.

"Looks to me like they know horses, which usually means they've been riding the grub line awhile. I'll talk to 'em over a meal. If we hire 'em, we'll keep a close eye on 'em. We can use at least five more men so we have enough to send Rafe. More than that when we get Seth set up in ranching."

"I've got a woman here now." Ethan didn't bother smiling about that. "I don't want a man around who'll bother her or the children. And Rafe'll feel the same, so we'll watch 'em awhile before we decide to hire 'em permanent."

Steele nodded.

The men finished with their horses and walked toward the fence just as the cook stepped from the bunkhouse and shouted that dinner was ready.

"I'll show 'em where to wash up," Steele said. "You stay close to that wife of yours until we're sure there ain't gonna be trouble."

"Sounds good. Maybe they can ride herd for a time after the noon meal. That'll test 'em a little."

Steele jerked his chin. "I'll make a point of testing them a lot."

Jasper grabbed Trixie's arm and pulled her behind a moving wagon. "Keep even with the buckboard. I just saw someone who knows me. We don't want anyone to be able to say we were in this part of town."

Jasper lifted his head to glance over the top of the wagon as the man entered a seedy diner Jasper knew had an opium den on the second floor.

"We're leaving town right now." Jasper looked back at Trixie. "I've got some money. Enough for two train tickets and a bit more laid by. I want you to come with me. We can catch a carriage a few blocks over and head for the train station."

"No!" Trixie jerked on his arm.

Trixie usually did whatever he asked. He was so surprised that he didn't even get mad, and he always got mad when someone told him no. "Why?" he asked.

"The train will be the first place they look once you turn up missing. If there is any suspicion about you, they might be watching it already."

"We need to get out of town fast, before anyone gets a hint that I'm thinking of it. If rumors have started, then I need to go."

"We'll ride horses instead." Trixie was dragging him along, heading the direction he wanted to go anyway.

"But I don't want to ride a horse halfway across the country." He could only think of heading toward Colorado. The last telegraph he'd gotten had come from there, from Mitch. He was on Tracker's trail and that gave Jasper a direction.

She embedded her fingernails into the silk fabric of his shirt. "You think I haven't dreamed about leaving my life behind?"

"You mean . . . you've planned this out?"

"For years I've been getting ready. I have enough money to buy a little house and live quietly, plant a garden, maybe get some chickens and a milk cow. I could get by even if I never work again."

"That is a fantasy, darlin'. What you're talking about is hard work. Backbreaking work."

Trixie pulled him down a narrow street that left behind the crime-ridden part of town. Only a few blocks and they'd be in a safer area where they could find a carriage for hire.

"It's honest work." Trixie stopped and turned to face him. They had half a block to go before they came out onto a street well-lit with lanterns. She dragged him around to face her.

Jasper tried to remember the last time he'd been pushed around like this.

"It's hard work, but it's decent. I'd be decent. I've always hoped to live long enough to make the break and find a clean life. But there was no way to do that in Houston. I'm too well known. I could never just sell the saloon and retire. The stink of it would stick to me here."

"So why didn't you go?" Jasper hated to think she'd lived in a way she hated. Trixie was his friend, his partner. She was almost his wife.

"Because you were here, you fool. I stayed for you." Her eyes blazed. With love. For him.

He swallowed hard. He didn't want anyone to depend on him. At the same time, he knew she'd been depending on him for years. Just as he'd been depending on her. He nodded, afraid to speak the words she no doubt wanted to hear.

"So . . ." He cleared his throat. "You have a plan, then?"

She looked disappointed. Worse, she looked like maybe she felt a little sorry for him that he couldn't admit any feelings for her.

That annoyed him. He'd asked her to come along, hadn't he? True, it had been at least partly because he hoped she had some money. His wouldn't take him far.

"Yes, I've got a plan. I've got plenty of cash money that no one knows about, because I've been rat-holing it for years. And I know the name of a man, an honest man with a livery who sells horses. He doesn't know I know him. I just did some quiet checking. We'll buy two horses and ride out."

"We'll need a change of clothes." He looked at his silk shirt and broadcloth pants. They marked him as wealthy. They drew the eye just as he wanted. But now he didn't want anyone to look twice, and Trixie's flashy red dress was even more noticeable.

"I've got enough money to take care of all that."

"I need to go to my bank and get the cash I've got on hand." It wasn't much.

"No, we walk away now. We get my money because we can pick it up without anyone knowing. We buy a change of clothes and two horses, then we leave town. No stopping at any bank or anyplace we might see someone who knows either of us. Once you leave, the wolves will dive on the remains of your business. You can't come back and reclaim it without starting from the ground up."

Jasper nodded. "We can go west. I can set up business, buy a saloon and—"

"No! If you run from the Hardesey clan, you need to change your life."

Gardens and chickens didn't appeal to him.

"Think, Jasper."

He didn't mention that he'd hate being a farmer. Other than that, he liked her plan. Especially liked her cash on hand. It was going to much improve his chance to survive until he got his money back from Gill.

"If you do this right, live honest, they'll never find you. Never. The West swallows up men every day."

The scratch of a footstep brought Jasper's head around.

"Someone's there," Trixie whispered. "Probably just a pick-pocket, but let's get out into a better-lit street."

Jasper grabbed her wrist, and they began walking steadily, quickly. But when Trixie seemed set to run, he tightened his hold to slow her down. Running would only draw attention.

Just a few more steps and they'd get out of this dark, narrow street and onto a well-lit one. From there find a ride to Trixie's cash and—

A bullet whizzed past Jasper's ear, so close he could feel the heat. He threw himself down on the hard wooden boardwalk, scraping his hands. He clawed at his jacket and pulled out his derringer. It was only useful in tight quarters.

With a firm grip on Trixie, he rolled off the edge of the boardwalk and fell to the dirty street with a thud.

More shots fired. A woman screamed from the street ahead. A man shouted. Witnesses, hopefully to scare their assailant away.

Trixie shoved him, and Jasper saw they could crawl beneath the boards. Scrambling, Jasper took cover. "Crawl," he whispered.

The boardwalk was high enough that they could move quickly. Trixie had trouble with her dress, but she was somehow managing.

They made it to the corner and rounded it just as another bullet fired. The sound of a fast-moving horse echoed from the street ahead. Jasper could look out and see the flashing hooves.

They rounded the corner of the building, still crawling. Jasper slammed his back against the foundation and waited, gun ready.

Staring forward, Jasper considered climbing out onto the street. Whoever was after them would know he couldn't get away with cold-blooded murder in front of dozens of witnesses.

Another bullet whizzed past them across the busy street. Someone cried out in pain. The recklessness of it brought Jasper's jaw into a tight line. There would be no running from this. No hope of safety in numbers.

He struggled to silence his breathing and aimed his derringer at whoever was pursuing them. The scratching in the dirt told him someone was crawling straight for them, coming fast. Then he heard more, two people at least. These weren't pickpockets, not even hardened thieves. Thieves struck, and if they missed, they ran.

Jasper knew it because he'd been one.

The scratching was the sound of someone crawling on his hands and knees straight for the corner that concealed Jasper. He'd have two shots. A move to his right drew his attention for one second. Trixie with her own derringer, and a knife in her teeth.

That was the kind of woman he wanted to run off with. He looked back as the scratching got louder. He heard someone breathing hard.

An extended arm, pointing a gun, rounded the corner. Jasper grabbed the arm and shoved up. The gun fired and fired again. Splinters exploded from the wood overhead. Jasper yanked hard and the man fell forward. A neat round circle appeared in the man's forehead. Jasper hadn't shot him.

It had to be Trixie. The man slumped forward, and Jasper braced himself for the next attacker, only to hear pounding footsteps running away, back down the narrow street.

"We have to get him or he'll report that he's seen us." Jasper shoved the dead man out of the way, but Trixie's nails sank into the neck of his shirt.

"No! We go. We run. Now! The opposite direction that man went. And we don't look back." Trixie's face was ashen white.

Whether it was panic talking or horror at what she'd done or good sense, Jasper knew she was right. The man was gone. If he worked for the Hardeseys, then he probably had friends close by. And Jasper had none.

"You're right," he said. "Let's go." He crawled straight out ahead into the busy street. People had started to gather. A man lay on his back groaning. Several people crouched near him, giving aid.

"That man under there tried to kill us." Jasper pointed under the boardwalk and kept moving. They all turned to look at the dead man. Once they were diverted, no one considered grabbing Trixie or him. They rounded a corner, where Jasper spotted a passing wagon. Jasper had no money and Trixie had lapsed into silence. From her grim expression, Jasper knew she was just starting to realize she'd killed a man.

Jasper needed her to be thinking. She was proving to be better at it than he was. But right now, he didn't have time to calm her down. He grabbed her and dragged her onto the back of the open wagon.

The driver didn't notice because he kept moving forward. "Where'd you hide your money?" Jasper whispered once they were in motion.

Trixie roused herself enough to tell him, and Jasper realized their luck as they were heading in the right direction. He sank back against a wooden crate, pulled Trixie close to him, and braced himself to expect another attack.

CHAPTER 12

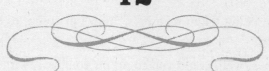

"We hired two new men today," Ethan said.

Audra looked up from where she was washing the dishes. She was a good little wife. The food was hot and plentiful, the house was clean, and his clothes were washed and mended.

Ethan was a contented man.

Lily lay kicking her feet on a blanket on the floor. Maggie sat on the floor beside Ethan, trying to eat her own toes.

"I heard you say you need more men so some of them can go hire on with Rafe, and later with Seth." Audra set the last pan on the counter to drip dry and opened the drain to let the water flow out. Rafe had built himself a modern wonder of a kitchen.

Ethan came up behind her and wrapped his arms around her waist. "I'm just telling you so you can be mindful." He kissed her neck.

She squirmed and grinned over her shoulder at him. "Behave yourself, Ethan Kincaid."

He stole a kiss, since her lips were right there handy. "The other men have been here awhile and they're steady. But whenever someone new joins up with us, we watch 'em close for a time."

Audra wrung her dishcloth and draped it to dry over the edge of the sink. Then she turned in his arms with a frown. "I don't like being taken care of, Ethan. I'm trying to stand on my own."

"Uh . . . well, could you stand on your own while staying inside the house?" Ethan could tell, despite her efforts to be fierce, she was fighting a smile. "Please, let me gather eggs and tend the garden for the next few days." He should have made it an order. He'd been planning to practice on her, but she was so sweet, surely saying please didn't hurt anything. "I don't want the men to even lay an eye on you. They may know I have a wife, but they don't need to see how pretty she is."

"I know you're trying to take care of me, but I've made a mess of my life up until now by turning everything over to others. I'm trying to grow up and turn into someone I can respect."

"I respect you, Audra." He kissed her again. "In fact, I respect every inch of you."

"Okay. For a few days, I'll stay inside."

She smiled and Ethan was overcome by a restless need to get his wife alone. And there were two wide-awake babies making that impossible. Then Maggie yawned and rubbed her eyes. "Maggie looks plumb sleepy," he said.

"I fed her early because she was fussing. I think she's ready for a nap."

162

Ethan crouched and gently slid his arms under Lily and lifted her blanket and all. He handed her to Audra. "I'll bring Magpie."

He picked little Maggie up, and she gave him the sleepiest smile Ethan had ever seen. It hit him hard how lucky a man was to have children to his name. He was surprised how easy it was to care about them. He cradled the little girl in his arms, and she moved her cheek against his chest to snuggle closer. His heart ached with the sweetness of it, and he didn't like it, that ache. It felt too good and it threatened too much pain. Life was so fragile, and Ethan wasn't a man to count on in times of trouble.

There were a lot of Bible verses about the good fortune of having many children. His eyes lifted and he watched Audra as she carried Lily upstairs.

Many children.

Many seemed like more than two.

He watched her gently swaying skirt for far too long, then followed quickly. In the time it took to walk upstairs, Maggie had dropped off to sleep. He laid her down on the bed while Audra settled Lily into her recently finished cradle. He gave Maggie a kiss on her mostly bald head and watched her heavy eyelids sink closed.

He exchanged a look with Audra and the two of them slipped out of the room. She turned for the stairs and he caught her arm. "What?"

"Shh." Ethan jerked his head toward their bedroom. She was obedient enough to come along and be quiet. Two orders, both followed. A rare woman. Of course any woman was rare. But Ethan had noticed Julia didn't have a lot of obey in her. That suited Rafe right down to the ground, but Ethan was finding he liked a biddable type of female.

He pulled her into the room and closed the door quietly. Then he turned her to face him.

"What did you need, Ethan?"

The question made a shiver run up his whole body. He bent and kissed her.

Long moments passed before Ethan raised his lips from hers. "I think, honey, that more than I need to eat a meal . . . I need to be . . . married."

Their eyes met. He slid his arms around her waist to head off an escape attempt. Instead of running, she smiled and rested one of her soft, sweet hands on his cheek. "I think I need to be married, too." She guided his lips back down to hers.

Ethan thought she was turning out to be about the best little wife a man could ever have.

And then he didn't have another clear thought for a long, long time.

Audra woke up and listened. Since Seth had left, the night hours were much easier. That didn't mean she didn't get disturbed by one of the children. Then she realized it was the sound of Ethan's heart beating, right under her ear.

She turned her head and saw that he was awake. It was probably some stirring, some faster pace of his heart that had awakened her, because she thought she'd been sleeping on him for quite some time.

She hadn't given any thought to practical things while he'd been making love to her, but now her mind was clear.

"You know, Ethan, we'll probably be adding to our brood before long."

He smiled. She purely loved his smile, and it was a good thing, because he did a lot of it. In fact, it seemed the worse things were, the more he smiled. As handsome as that smile was, it didn't tell her much. It certainly didn't tell her if he was happy.

"I've been thinking of a psalm," Ethan said. " 'Children are an heritage of the Lord: and the fruit of the womb is his reward. As arrows are in the hand of a mighty man; so are children of the youth. Happy is the man that hath his quiver full of them.' "

"Um . . . how many arrows are there in a quiver exactly?" Audra was sorely afraid there were quite a few.

He smiled and said, "Audra, honey, have I mentioned lately that I am finding married life with you to be a pure pleasure?"

It wasn't I love you, but it was nicer than anything Wendell had ever said to her. Which was no great contest to win, considering Wendell had the temperament of a rabid skunk. With a mental shake of her head, she turned her thoughts from Wendell, refusing to allow him in her head when she was with Ethan.

Then Ethan leaned over and kissed her, and she didn't have one bit of trouble concentrating solely on him. Ethan pulled her closer—which wasn't really possible—just as a soft whimper sounded from the next room.

"Lily," she whispered.

"I'll get her." Ethan gently drew one callused finger down her cheek, then swung around to rise from the bed. He pulled on his pants, grabbed a shirt.

"Hurry so she doesn't wake Maggie." With a pang of regret, Audra watched her very handsome husband leave their room. She didn't know much about love for a man. She loved her children fiercely. She loved Julia as the true sister of her heart. She loved her little brother and sister.

Her mother was a quiet woman who had little to do with the children, leaving that for servants. But Audra had loved her desperately until it had gotten too painful. And when Mother had stood by while Audra was forced into marriage, that love had died a dreadful death.

Her father had only been a man to fear and avoid.

She remembered a few beautifully romantic poems in her school days, and they'd spoken to her and seemed to promise her happiness in married life. But she'd never come close to feeling any love for Wendell. Now, with Ethan, she thought . . . maybe.

The warmth in her chest as she watched her husband hurry to fetch the baby might be close.

Love.

She remembered the pain of realizing her mother didn't love her and felt a terrible fear for what would lie ahead if she loved Ethan and he didn't return that love. Instead, he only smiled in his shallow way. But what if he learned to love her? When his touch was so generous and passionate, she dared to think it just might be possible. She sat up and put on her nightgown, preparing to take Lily when Ethan returned. While she nursed the baby, she'd find a way to lure a few words of affection out of her always grinning husband.

She stood and looked out the window across the moonlit ranch yard.

A man darted out of the barn.

"Ethan, come quick!"

She saw the man vanish into the woods, heading away from the bunkhouse.

Ethan came in and ran to her side. "What is it?"

"I saw a man running from the barn."

And then she saw a lick of flames coming from the barn's hayloft.

"Fire!" Ethan whirled away.

"Ethan, the foal!"

Ethan still had Lily, and he took her with him as he snatched up his boots and hurried down the stairs. Audra rushed after him. When she got outside, he turned back and thrust Lily into her hands, then picked up the iron triangle and banged away at it. Steele came charging out of the bunkhouse.

"Fire in the barn! The hayloft!" Ethan yelled. "Audra, you know the trapdoor in the kitchen floor?"

"Yes, of course." She'd seen it there in the kitchen, but she'd never opened it before.

"That's the cellar. Get yourself and the children down there right now." He pulled on his boots as he talked. "Fire can't get at you in the cellar."

"Ethan, I don't want to hide underground." Like a frightened animal.

Ethan took her by the arm. "Please, Audra. Or I'll have to divide my attention between the fire and worrying about you. Listen, there's a separate room at the back of the cellar. It's stocked with a lantern and a few supplies. I've checked it since I came home and everything's there. The room has a door with a bolt on it. Throw it."

"Lock the door?" She shook her head, hating the idea of being locked up in a dark cellar.

He leaned close. "Audra, we don't know who that man was. Chances are he set that fire. If he's up to setting a fire, then he's capable of all sorts of trouble. Get down there and lock yourself in and don't come out until you hear me or Steele call you."

Audra knew protecting her children had to come first. "I'll do it."

"I'll get Maggie." He turned to go back inside.

Audra slapped a hand on Ethan's chest. "No! I'll get us down there. We'll be safe. Go."

Ethan heard the mare whinny in panic from the barn. He glanced at the wooded area surrounding the house. "If the trees catch, this fire could burn for miles. The house could go, but you'll be safe in that room in the cellar. It's dug back so it's not under the house. Stay there!"

Their eyes met. "Trust me, Ethan. Now go!"

Ethan jerked his chin, turned, and ran. It struck Audra that the trust Ethan had just put in her to take care of herself and her children was the finest moment of her life.

She looked down at Lily, awake and waving her arms, but content. Turning, she ran upstairs to the girls' bedroom. She slid an arm under Maggie. No need to wake her if it wasn't necessary.

Audra rushed back down and stopped, frozen, in the kitchen. She couldn't get the trapdoor open with her hands full of babies.

After a moment's hesitation, she knelt and laid little Maggie down on the hardwood floor. She pulled up the trapdoor. It was so heavy she wished she'd laid both girls down. Lily was wide awake, though, and she'd squawk if she was set down.

Audra shoved the trapdoor up and it tipped back so it hit the wall beside the kitchen sink. With an uncertain glance at the black hole in the floor, she decided she couldn't make the descent with both girls at once. There was a slanted ladder, which nearly qualified as a stairway but was very steep, and the steps were about four inches wide. She crouched to hold tight to the sides of the gaping hole and went down the steps, mindful of her dangling nightgown. She reached the bottom, and the hole was lit only from the square overhead.

She peered through the darkness, looking for the deeper part of the cellar. He'd said it was at the back. She faced that direction and carefully began heading toward the back wall. Running her hand along the smooth wooden wall, she found a door, then a latch. Lifting it, she smelled the dank air and stepped in.

"I'm going to have to lay you down." On the dirt floor. Lily had a small blanket around her, but it wasn't much protection. Heaven only knew what kind of crawling critters were down here. Shuddering, she only had to imagine the house on fire and Maggie still upstairs. The horror of it made it easy to set the baby on the floor.

"I'll be right back, Lily." She needed Lily's drawer. That would get Lily up off the floor. She kept it in the kitchen. And she needed another blanket for Maggie.

The infant whimpered as Audra turned to leave. She hated doing such a thing. "Don't cry, honey . . ."

Audra kept talking to Lily as she hurried back to the ladder. Speaking aloud to comfort Lily also bolstered her courage. Lily's cries gained strength.

Audra scrambled up the ladder and, with a pang of fear, saw she'd left Maggie asleep so close to the hole she could have rolled right off the edge. Sickened by her lack of clear thinking, Audra snatched the little girl up and descended the ladder. She turned and stubbed her right foot on what felt like some kind of sack. She didn't have time to even guess at what it might be. A few seconds later she hit something on her left side, stumbled, and nearly fell.

Lily's cries had reached the screaming stage. Audra dashed

into the little room. She laid Maggie down on the damp floor. "A blanket," she muttered. "I have to go get one."

What about that man she had seen? Could he still be lurking around? Could he have started the barn on fire, then come to do the same to the house?

With Lily awake and crying, and Maggie on the floor, sure to be awakened soon, Audra had to do something. Going back to the trapdoor, she abandoned her children, feeling like a monster. "The drawer Lily sleeps in. A blanket for Maggie. That's it." The drawer was close at hand. She grabbed it, and although it wasn't large, it was big enough that she needed to carry it down on its own. Yet another trip down and up the ladder.

She hurried into the cellar's back room and picked up Lily to comfort her. A quick adjustment moved Maggie onto Lily's blanket. But now the room was too cool for Lily. "Oh, God, what should I do?"

Audra wanted so much to prove she could take charge of her own life. "And now Mama has her chance, little one," she said to Lily.

"I have my chance, don't I?" She talked and listened and tried to decide. She'd need to run all the way upstairs to get a blanket for Maggie.

Pray.

The thought came to her so strongly she knew it was put there by God.

As she prayed, instead of lessening her fear, it grew.

The fear built as she prayed aloud, bouncing Lily on her hip. It seemed as if fear became a restraining hand that blocked the door. Audra fought it, hating her cowardice, hating herself.

Upstairs and back. One minute and she'd close this door and throw the lock.

She'd have to lay Lily down and leave both girls, but not for long.

She braced herself to do the brave thing for once in her life.

Ethan charged toward the barn.

He hated leaving Audra, but she was right. She could handle whatever happened back there.

He raced into the barn and climbed straight up to the burning loft. Hay blazed in front of him, but it was manageable if they moved fast. Steele was up the ladder in a flash, two other men with him. Ethan grabbed a pitchfork.

"Steele, tell some men to put out the burning hay when I pitch it out. Someone get the mare and her foal out. The rest of you men work up here, get buckets of water."

Steele started shouting orders, then rushed down the ladder.

Ethan stabbed the fork deep into a flaming pile of hay and carried it to the window. He took a quick look below to make sure his men were alert, then threw it as far as his strength allowed.

Thuds from behind him assured him that his men were battling the fire. Without a pause as he pitched fire out of the loft, Ethan noticed that a cowhand carrying a bucket of water climbed up, handed the water over to Steele, and then disappeared for more. Another hand on the ground below doused the flames that rained down into the yard.

Ethan heard his mare scream with fear. He hoped Steele had someone who could handle the crazed horse. Ethan trusted Steele to know his job.

The flames danced high, licking at the rafters. If the roof went, they'd lose the barn. And if that happened, the woods would catch fire. They'd start a nightmarish blaze that could dole out destruction for a hundred miles.

Ethan jammed his pitchfork into the next clump of blazing hay, and the flames whooshed up, singed his face and hair. His shirt sleeve caught fire!

"Do it," Audra goaded herself. "You want to be treated like a mature woman. You want to make your own decisions. Now you've got your chance."

Lily stirred, and Audra realized she was holding on too tight. She was such a coward, she'd almost hurt her baby.

Audra needed that blanket. She squared her shoulders and took a step out of the cellar room. Then she stopped. As she tried to make herself move again, her heart pounded with fear. Finally, hating herself, she went back inside the room.

She couldn't overcome the fear. Instead, she let it control her. She'd wait, for now, put it off for a bit. She turned to Lily and whispered, "Your pa said there was a lantern down here. Wouldn't a little light cheer us up?"

Lily's crying eased as Audra bounced her and talked with her. Turning to the back of the room, Audra fumbled her way along the side. It was tiny. Audra could have touched both walls with her arms stretched out. It was about twice as deep as it was wide.

"Now where is it?" Audra's hands brushed against glass, and the rattle of metal against glass told her she'd found the lantern. She looked back at the wide open door. A rectangle only visible because it was a slightly lighter shade of black.

"The room has a door with a bolt on it. Throw it."

Ethan's order came to her so vividly it was as if he was here. "Your pa said to close it and throw the bolt." Audra swayed with Lily and wondered how to get the lantern lit with no matches and only one hand to spare. Now that Lily was calm, Audra hated to get her wound up again by putting her down.

She looked at the door again. The fear was almost a physical grip on her body. Such cowardice! Praying, whispering to Lily, Audra wasn't sure she could force herself to go back upstairs. But could she close herself in this tiny room in the pitch-dark? Her throat threatened to swell shut from the force of all her fears.

The door taunted her, called her a coward.

Children were afraid of the dark, not grown women.

Open, the door gave her light.

Open, it stood as an invitation to danger.

A creaking sound overhead stopped her fretting. A leg appeared on the ladder.

"Ethan, you're back!" Audra took two quick steps toward the cellar room door. "Is everything all right?"

The man, barely outlined in the dim light, turned and she knew. The dark form wasn't her husband, nor her husband's foreman. She lunged for the door, mindful of where Maggie lay. Praying for speed.

"I've got you!" The man jumped the last few feet to the cellar floor.

Frantic, Audra pushed the heavy door to close and lock it, but it dragged on the dirt floor. She couldn't get it shut!

The man lunged toward her.

She'd waited too long and now she and her girls might die.

CHAPTER
13

Ethan ripped his shirt off, the memory of Seth's blackened bleeding skin as wicked and hot as the fire. He threw the shirt on the floor. He felt hands on him, slapping at the fire. He was too busy stomping his shirt out to notice who was hitting him.

He got the flames out. Glanced at Steele. "Thanks."

"You okay?" Steele looked worried in the flickering firelight.

"We'll see. No time to check now." Ethan turned back to the flaming hay.

He hurled fork loads of hay out the window from the worst of the fire.

Steele and the rest of the cowhands battled the smaller blazes.

Tongues of flame licked up the side of the barn. "Steele, don't let the wood catch." Suddenly they were losing the fight.

Fire in front of Ethan too big to quit on. Fire in two corners of the hayloft. If that barn wall caught, they'd have to get out, let the barn go, and turn to keeping the fire from spreading to the nearby woods.

Jabbing with his pitchfork, Ethan saw Steele charge the barn wall.

Back to the main fire, Ethan pitched and stabbed, pitched and stabbed.

Repeating the moves, he lost track of time as he and his men fought for their own lives, the life of the ranch, and the woods that surrounded it.

Suddenly a bucket of water splashed heavily on the stack of hay he'd kept from spreading but hadn't managed to defeat.

The flames leaped high, hissed like a beast being defeated in battle, then vanished.

Panting, looking desperately for the next place to fight, Ethan saw Steele holding a dripping bucket. There were no flames anywhere.

"That's the last of it, boss." Steele, his face blackened with soot, jerked his chin in satisfaction and slapped Ethan on his bare back. Steele pulled his hand away quickly. "You get burned?"

It took Ethan a second to even remember his shirt.

"I don't think so. Nothing serious anyway." Ethan couldn't fail to notice he'd been called boss. "How about you and the men?"

"I didn't see anyone catch fire but you." Steele sounded exhausted but whole.

Another cowboy poked his head up to the top of the ladder. "I've got more water."

Steele turned and relieved the man of his burden. "That

oughta do it. But no one sleeps until we're sure there aren't any hot spots."

Ethan pointed at the wall. "Make sure that wall isn't smoldering. It was on fire for a few seconds." Ethan paused and looked at Steele. "Until you put it out."

Nodding in the darkened barn, he added to his men, "Thank you. Thank you all."

"We ride for the brand." Steele doused the wall with water, then turned and went down the ladder with a bucket in hand, shouting orders—orders that Ethan had given first.

The man tripped over something and fell facedown as if God himself had flattened him.

Audra used strength she didn't know she had. She slammed the door shut and with fumbling hands slid home the heavy wooden bolt. A split second later she heard the man's body crash into the door.

Maggie woke up with a frightened yelp and started crying. Lily, who'd nearly gone back to sleep, wound up again, crying louder than ever.

"You can't hide from me!" The door shuddered under the assault. Audra turned, pressed her back against the door, and prayed.

The man pounded on the door, trying to smash open the locking bolt. Audra leaned harder against the door. She knew her weight alone couldn't keep the man from breaking in, yet it might be enough to keep the lock from giving way.

Lily screamed at the commotion.

Audra held her in one arm and held the bolt latching the

door with the other. Then she saw she could drop the bolt into a little notch that locked it tight. She quickly slid it into the notch.

"I'm not leaving without you!" Fists pounded. Then came a harder sound, lower in pitch. The man was slamming his heavy boots into the thick wood door. Again, Audra threw all her weight against the door.

God, please protect us. Protect my baby girls.

It took Audra a few moments to realize all his assault on the door wasn't budging it. The lock held. The man's blows came slower as if he'd exhausted himself.

Maggie hugged Audra's leg. Audra crouched and picked the toddler up. Maggie clung to her neck and sobbed.

One last blow to the door was followed by a vicious shout. "I'll be back, Mrs. Gill. You've got something I want, and I won't quit coming. And others are coming after me. Next time I'll make sure and bring an axe along so you can't lock me out of anywhere."

She heard the man stomp away, grunting with effort as he scaled the ladder. Seconds later a door slammed.

"Hush, honey. Don't cry. Don't cry."

Both girls disobeyed her thoroughly, and Audra decided it was an idea with merit and she began to cry herself while she cuddled them.

It was a good time for tears, now that she and her babies were safe.

Ethan turned to sift around, hunting for smoldering hay just in time to see right out his barn window. A dark form dashed across the yard.

"Someone's been in the house with Audra!" He dropped the pitchfork and jumped for the ladder.

Steele was one step behind him. "You men keep hunting for any sign of fire," he shouted.

Ethan charged into the house, terrified he'd find it on fire, too. Terrified he'd find his wife hurt, or worse. How long had that man been in here with her? Had there been time for her to get in the cellar?

He saw instantly the trapdoor laid open. He raced for it and heard crying, and not just little babies.

"Steele, check the house."

His foreman raced past the kitchen.

Ethan slid down the ladder with reckless speed.

"Audra! It's Ethan." He tripped over something that stuck out from the side of the little space. He staggered deeper into the cellar until he found the door to the room at the back. "Audra, are you there? Let me in!"

"Ethan? Is that you?"

He'd told her to lock herself in down here and only open the door to him or Steele. She'd remembered. She'd taken charge and protected herself and the children. Ethan hated that he'd left her on her own.

"Yes. It's me," he said.

"We're safe in here. Go . . ." Her voice broke. "Go fight the fire."

"The fire's out. Let me in, honey."

"Be careful. There's a man out there, and he might hurt you. He beat on this door. He was after me."

"I know—we saw him run away. He's gone now. Please, unlock the door."

There was what seemed like far too long a time while cries of Ethan's daughters echoed out of the dirt cellar.

The scratch of wood on metal told him she was finally unlocking the door.

The door opened a crack and Ethan reached for it. "Step back, honey. It's heavy. I'll get it."

A light shone in the little room. Lantern light. She'd kept herself and her children—no, their children—safe. She'd found the lantern. As he swung the heavy door open, he saw that she'd even brought down Lily's drawer for her.

Ethan wrapped his arms around Audra, holding two babies, and drew them out of the dungeonlike room. Audra trembled violently, but she had a firm hold on the little ones.

"You're all right, aren't you, Audie?"

Her chin rose and she stood straight. "Do not call me Audie."

Ethan smiled. That put some fight in her.

He glanced over his shoulder when Steele called down through the trapdoor, asking if everything was okay.

"We're fine," Ethan shouted back. "Post a guard. And I want the men all accounted for, especially the new ones. Scout around and see if you can find whoever did this. Watch for strange tracks. The sun is about to rise, so we'll have light to work with."

Steele took the orders and vanished, leaving Ethan alone with the bravest woman he'd ever known.

"I'm such a coward." Audra broke into more sobs. She felt as if all she'd done since she'd seen that man run from the barn was shake with fear or cry like one of the girls.

She hated herself.

180

"You did fine, Audie."

She slapped his arm. "I hate that name. Don't you dare start calling me that." Then she touched him again. "Where in heaven's name is your shirt?"

"It burned off my body."

"What!" She stood away from him.

"I thought that might distract you from beating up on yourself."

"I'll beat up on myself if I want to, and what do you mean your shirt burned off your body?"

Ethan coaxed her forward. He lifted a sobbing Maggie out of her arms. "If you can't climb the ladder, I'll take Maggie up, come back for Lily, then come back for you."

"I carried them both down here, didn't I?" Audra had been scared right down to the bone, but that didn't mean she couldn't climb a stupid ladder. "I can climb out with Lily," she said.

"That's good, honey." Ethan's hands left her, and she realized when they did that he'd been supporting her since she'd let him in the cellar room. She missed his hands desperately. The lantern light from the cellar went out.

Then his hands were back. With one strong, steady hand, he urged her toward the ladder. "You go first," he said.

Climbing up was harder than she'd expected, considering she'd flown down and up several times with her hands full. He was only a step below her, his hand still on her back. How could he hold Maggie and her and climb at the same time?

But he did it.

Her husband.

She didn't deserve him.

But she knew.

Suddenly, in that moment, she knew she was completely in love with him.

She didn't deserve a man so strong and kind. But she had him and she wasn't letting him go.

As she reached the kitchen, she saw that the sun was turning the sky to lightest gray. Another night had passed.

This time they couldn't blame Seth for their exhaustion. He wasn't here to scream and wake them up. But between the fire and . . . and the way they'd passed the earlier part of the night, Audra had barely slept at all.

She climbed the ladder and turned around to tell Ethan she loved him, and saw his burns.

CHAPTER
14

"This is where we get out." Trixie grabbed Jasper's hand.

They waited until the wagon slowed for a turn and then jumped.

Jasper vibrated with nerves. Now that he'd decided to run, he wanted to run fast and far. Trixie caught his hand and dragged him back the direction they'd come.

"Why did—?"

"Keep quiet . . ." Her voice broke.

It was dark enough he couldn't see her expression, but she'd killed someone. That knowledge was in her voice. He knew she wanted to clean up her life.

Now, on day one, she'd shot a man.

"Don't do anything to draw attention," she whispered.

The street was mostly deserted, but there was an occasional

lit-up building. Voices could be heard wafting out the swinging doors along with tinny music and the smell of whiskey. Jasper wouldn't have minded wetting his throat and steadying his nerves with a swallow or two.

They walked so far that Jasper had to fight to not complain. All he could think was Trixie had planned this—apparently for years.

So, since his only plan was to run for his meager bank account, hope he could empty it without the Hardeseys spotting him, then make a dash for the train—a series of actions that would almost certainly get him killed if the Hardeseys were looking for him—he'd let her lead.

They came to a dry-goods store, and Trixie pulled him into an alley. "Go in there and buy us some things."

She then gave him a concise list and the money to pay for what she wanted. He listened to the drab clothing she wanted and hated it. But he followed the only plan they had.

They changed into less eye-catching clothes in a little entry built onto the back of a store.

The store, the lean-to, even the clothing was all part of her plan. She'd left nothing to chance.

They got rid of their old clothes and kept on walking. The night began to give way to dawn. They needed to get out of town before daylight, when he'd be much more likely to be spotted. Trixie left him behind at their next destination. She went into a derelict building and came out with a reticule that hung heavy on her wrist.

"My money. I had it hidden under a floorboard in there. Now we buy horses."

Before the sun was up, they had two horses from a hostler, who was just opening in the predawn hours, along with saddlebags stuffed with provisions. Once they cleared the edge of Houston, he decided it was finally time to talk.

"Stop," he said.

"No, I want more miles between us and that awful town."

It wasn't the town that was awful; it was the life they'd chosen. Jasper grabbed her reins and pulled both horses to a stop.

"Jasper, let go!" She yanked against his hold, but he dismounted and dragged Trixie off her horse.

Looking at her in the full light of morning, he could finally see what was in her eyes. Devastation.

He wanted to demand details, but instead he pulled her hard against him and kissed her.

She struggled long enough that he knew she wasn't thinking. Trixie never struggled. At last she went limp. He expected the next move to be her throwing her arms around his neck. Instead, she began to cry.

He was manhandling her, yet when the tears came he softened the kiss, deepened it.

Then he quit altogether. This wasn't a time for kissing. He slid his arms more securely around her waist and pulled her head into his neck and cradled her while she wept.

"I'm sorry." He rubbed her back.

"I—this is stupid—I didn't—I've never killed anyone."

"You had no choice, darlin'."

"Of course I had a choice." She gave a violent shake of her head and shoved at him.

He held on doggedly. "Not if you wanted to live."

Her hands came up to cover her face, and she sobbed until it wrenched her body. He held on tight. "That's just it, Jasper. I could have died. Both of us could have died."

"That's no choice."

"It is. I want to change my life. I've known for years I needed to change, to get right with God."

Jasper couldn't control the shock. His hands tightened with a spasm on her waist. "Get right with God? Trixie, women who own brothels don't . . . don't . . ."

"Don't believe in God?" Trixie's head came up. "I do."

"Well, yes, I'm sure there is a God, but—"

"Then what, Jasper? Women who own brothels don't go to heaven? Is that what you're trying to say? There's a heaven, but we don't get to go there? I'm getting older. Women in my profession don't live to a ripe old age. I spent time with . . . with men doing things that make me believe I know what hell will be like."

"Trixie, I'm so sorry." And he was. He should have taken her out of that unsavory life and given her . . . another unsavory life . . . with him.

"I don't want to spend eternity there." She gripped the collar of his shirt. "I've had enough of it in this life. I've been looking for a chance to get out for years, and now I've done something that will put me beyond the grace of God."

"No, I don't believe that."

"Jasper Henry, you don't believe in anything except your money and your hired thugs." The venom in her voice shocked him. She loved him. She'd as good as admitted it. And yet now she sounded like she hated him, held him in utter contempt.

So which was it? Hate or love? And could it possibly be both?

"Don't waste my time telling me what you believe, because it means nothing."

Their eyes locked. Jasper saw things in her eyes he'd never

noticed before. Her wish to change her life told him a lot of what she was saying had been her true feelings for years.

Which, since he'd never noticed, meant he was as unfeeling and cruel as any man who'd ever lived. But he didn't have to stay that way. "What do we do now?"

"You mean now that I'm a murderess?"

"It was self-defense."

"He's just as dead, and at my hand."

"To keep me alive. You saved me, Trixie." Jasper didn't want to think about heaven and hell. He had managed to live this long by not thinking of what kind of afterlife he was fit for. But right now, Trixie needed him to say the right thing.

And he had no idea what that was. How dare he speak of what is right? It was so far from his life, he couldn't quite imagine it. So he said, "Let's get married."

Her jaw dropped. Well, at least he'd distracted her from this self-flagellation thing she was doing.

"It'll be a good cover. No one will imagine us as a poorly dressed"—he flicked the ruffled neck of her blue gingham dress—"married couple. They'll be looking for a wealthy criminal and a . . ."

"Prostitute? Light-skirt? Streetwalker?"

Jasper stared at her, then felt a smile creep across his face. "Whatever you were, now you're a frumpy frontier woman."

"Frumpy?" Trixie's eyes flashed with indignation. She was weary and hard-living, but she'd always been attractive.

He kissed her. "Only the dress, darlin'. You're still the prettiest thing I've ever seen."

She swatted his arm and some of the tight grief eased from her expression.

"Killing a man is a terrible thing." He held her upper arms and rubbed, trying to help her feel anything but guilt. "But it happened. If you want to change your life, instead of starting last night when we decided to run, start now. From now on, you're as sweet and innocent as a newborn baby."

Trixie shook her head, a rueful expression on her face. Her hand let loose of the choke hold on his collar and came up to rest against his cheek. "You always were a sweet-talking devil."

He bent to kiss her again.

She ducked. "Now you behave yourself, sir. I am a proper woman, and I am saving myself for the man I marry."

Jasper jerked back and frowned. "Really? We've been up all night. I sort of thought we could find a place to camp now and, well, considering the trauma you've just experienced, maybe you'd allow me to . . . to comfort you."

Trixie snorted. "You aren't going to comfort me until we find a preacher man and say some vows before God and man. Until then, you just behave."

"You wouldn't consider changing your ways a couple of days from now, would you?"

Trixie laughed.

The sound gave Jasper hope that she'd be all right. But there were still shadows in her eyes. Killing a man would haunt her. The memory would jump out and slap at her at odd moments for the rest of her life.

He knew it for a fact.

It would be a ghost that followed her like the ghosts of men who had dragged her into a life she considered a lake of fire.

Jasper had more than a few ghosts, beginning with his mother.

"I know a little town that's a hundred hard miles from here."

Jasper decided it was his turn to plan. "We can make that in a day on a fast horse, if we push. By nightfall we can be in Bryan, a town big enough to have a parson. And we can make this trip our very own honeymoon."

"Riding hard away from Houston suits me." Trixie nodded.

They lit out for the West. They'd gone through all the steps of her plan apparently. Changing clothes, getting her money and horses, leaving town and leading a respectable life.

The where didn't matter.

So she let him pick the direction.

All he could think of was the last message he'd had from his men about a little town called Rawhide, Colorado.

He spurred his horse toward the northwest.

"Ethan, sit down!" Audra grabbed his arm. She acted as if she needed to hold him up. Which was ridiculous. He'd been holding himself up just fine.

"What's the matter?" Ethan let himself be dragged to the kitchen table. He started to sit when Audra said, "Wait!"

She turned the chair around. "Straddle it."

"Why! Audra, I have work to do. I need to track the man who did this, and the barn needs to be checked real carefully for sparks."

"Your arm."

Ethan straddled the chair, with Maggie wriggling in his arms, all tears forgotten now. Audra's mention of his arm made him look down, and what he saw on his left arm made his stomach lurch. Ugly. Red. Blisters from his elbow to his shoulder. As soon as he saw the wounds, he felt them and they were agonizing.

In fact, as soon as he realized what he was feeling, he knew they'd been hurting for a long time.

He thought of Seth's ugly scars. He'd have them now, too. Audra wouldn't be able to stand to look at him.

"Set Maggie down. She's not crying anymore."

Maggie was on his lap. Happy. The little imp needed to be asleep, but it wasn't her fault she'd been thoroughly disturbed.

He set her down and she giggled. "Make sure and close that trapdoor. Before Maggie takes a tumble."

Audra shoved the trapdoor forward carelessly so it slapped shut with a loud bang.

Lily jumped in her arms, but Audra bounced her and rushed for the basin.

"We'll get cold water on the burns while I make a poultice." Audra was suddenly crackling with energy and purpose. She bounced Lily while she grabbed a washcloth, doused it in the water basin, and wrung it out. The woman was truly an expert at handling children.

"Just get me a clean shirt." His arm burned, and if he wasn't mistaken, his back did, too. "That's all I need. I've got work to do."

He remembered how sick Seth had gotten with the burns. Ethan had been sure Seth would die. The way he'd treated his little brother had made it worse, had hurt Seth on top of the burns.

A sudden sick fear that his burns might be that bad almost made him act like the coward he was. He found he couldn't summon a smile.

"No time for fussing, Audie, darlin'."

"If you call me Audie again, I will pour a whole cup of salt on your burns."

"No you won't."

"I might. I hate it. It sounds like odd. Like you're saying I'm odd. My little sister used to call me that." She sounded fierce, but she cast him a worried look that took the danger out of her voice.

"I need to get to work."

"I'm calling Steele in here and sending him for Rafe if you get out of that chair."

Ethan scowled, but he didn't want her to tell Steele. It sounded like a threat to tattletale to his mama. And he didn't want Rafe here. And he didn't want Seth to see the burns.

He stayed in the chair.

Audie. He decided he'd call her that all the time. Except maybe he'd wait until he had his shirt on, to avoid being salted.

She rushed over and gently, so carefully, pressed the cool cloth on his shoulder.

It felt like heaven.

"I didn't realize how hot it was. Cold really takes the pain out."

Audra gave him a smacking kiss on the top of his head, then whirled away to grab the basin and carry it to the table beside Ethan.

"I'll get more cloths. We'll cover all the burns and keep them cool until I get the poultice done." She deftly laid a bigger cloth on his back.

All the burns?

"How bad is my back?" Ethan didn't really want to know.

"Big blisters down to the middle of your back, mainly on the left side. It's red all over. The blisters haven't popped. I think that's a good sign the damage isn't too bad."

Ethan tried to not let his sigh of relief move his shoulders. He remembered the blackened skin on Seth's back.

Feeling encouraged, he waited until she'd covered his back and shoulders with cold, dripping rags. Chilly water slid down and soaked his pants, but the cold on his burns was worth the discomfort. Then, when she straightened away from her doctoring, he caught her free arm, the one not holding a baby, and pulled her back to kiss her thoroughly.

The kiss went on a lot longer than Ethan had planned, and he only let go when he got kicked in the face.

By Lily.

He backed up a bit to look his little wife in the eye. She didn't notice because she was focused on his lips. "Thank you for taking care of me, darlin'. It is a wonderful thing to have the soft hands of a woman around when a man is in need."

She moved first. Back toward him. This time Lily had to kick him and Maggie had to yank on his pant leg and scream quite a while before they were pulled out of the moment.

When Audra straightened, she looked so sweet and kind and worried. "Who was that man, Ethan? Who did that? Who would set a fire and break into our house and bang on that door the way that man did?"

That took Ethan's mind off the sweet affection of his wife.

"We need to find out if we've got any cattle missing. Find out if any wanted men have been spotted in the area." Ethan raised his hand and drew one finger down her cheek. Amazed that he'd managed to get himself married to the prettiest woman in Colorado.

Now it was his job to protect her. And instead he sat here, burned, with his wife doing the caretaking when he ought to be hunting tracks. He was good at tracking. Better than most men. And he knew all the tricks to tracking a man in the woods and over rocky ground.

"I know you're worried about my burns, Audie."

"Stop that, Ethan. I'm warning you." She slapped him, but she hit his right shoulder, the one that wasn't burned, so there was no real venom in the attack. "Of course I'm worried about your burns."

"But I need you to really look at them. How bad are they? If they're so awful you're afraid I'll die or end up real sick, then fine, I'll be careful. But honey"—Ethan scooped Maggie up in one arm and hooked the other arm around Audra as he stood—"I need to track that man. If you're just worried because you know it hurts and you've got a heart as soft as a feather pillow, then I need you to tell me. I'm the best tracker in these parts. And it's my job to protect my wife and my ranch. I don't trust any of the men to be as thorough as I will be. I need to take charge of this hunt."

Audra's pretty, smooth brow furrowed as she looked at his arm. "It looks bad, but I'm sure you'll be okay. It'll hurt to wear a shirt, Ethan. And if you break those blisters open, they might get infected. I lost one husband already to a minor injury that turned septic."

"Not much of a loss." Ethan only kept from grinning because Maggie picked that moment to wrap her arm around his neck and touch his burns. He flinched and let go of Audra and pulled Maggie away and hated doing it. He liked having the little one hanging from him.

"No, he wasn't." Audra leaned forward and kissed him. "But I don't want anything to happen to you. I like being Mrs. Kincaid a lot more than Mrs. Gill."

Audra straightened with a little squeak as if she'd gotten jabbed by a pin. "That man, he called me Mrs. Gill."

Ethan's eyes narrowed. "That's what your husband called himself in town."

"Yes, and he called himself Mr. Wendell in Houston. When I married him the parson said, 'I now pronounce you Mr. and Mrs. Wendell.' As far as I know—and heaven knows I could be ignorant of many of Wendell's lies—he only went by the name of Gill in Rawhide."

"So whoever came out here, it had something to do with Wendell?" Ethan just wasn't quite sure what that meant. "If they found out you were here, it's because they found out I married you. That's the only trail that leads here. So why did he call you that?"

"That awful man could have destroyed your entire ranch." Her whole face crumpled. "And it has something to do with me. I'm the cause of this night's madness."

"Not the cause, darlin'. The cause is laid right at the feet of whoever lit the match."

"Ethan," she said, resting a hand on his wrist, "I'm afraid." His wife, who'd spent pretty much every minute since Ethan had known her trying to prove she could take care of herself, said, "I don't want you to leave me alone."

And that's when Ethan knew he was going to have to do something that burned him worse than fire. Something that made it almost impossible for him to smile. That ate at his gut until he wanted to kick something.

CHAPTER
15

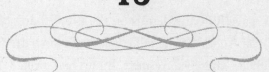

At the sound of pounding hoofbeats, Rafe whirled around, his revolver drawn.

"Ethan sent me, Rafe," Steele shouted as he rode up to Rafe's cabin. "We need you to come home. Ethan's hurt. We had a fire. His shirt caught. He's all burned up."

Rafe was dragging Julia toward the horse before Steele had finished asking him to come home. Julia didn't need to be dragged, though. She was in fact passing him.

"Seth, you come, too. With Ethan hurt, we'll need extra hands over there," Rafe said.

Seth was already rushing for the horses, as well. Something eased in Rafe. Seth had been eager to explore the cavern today. His brother wasn't too loco to know they had to get to Ethan fast.

Steele came prepared. He'd brought mounts for all of them. Left them on the east side of the stream, crossed it on foot, caught one of the horses Rafe kept pastured near Julia's old cabin, and rode on to the ranch Rafe had claimed.

Fording the stream, which was impassable on horseback, cut hours off the distance between Ethan and Rafe.

Rafe had plans for a bridge, but he hadn't quite found the time for that yet.

Steele gave Rafe the details on the fire, Ethan's burns, and the attack on Audra. Steele talked about Ethan with more than just tolerance—there was respect. Ethan had proved up for the old cowpoke.

They rode into the ranch yard in the late afternoon to find Ethan standing at the cabin door with Audra wedged between him and the outdoors, Maggie in her arms.

Ethan looked up, saw Rafe, scowled, then immediately replaced his frown with his more usual careless grin.

Audra turned to see what Ethan was smiling at, and Ethan slipped past her.

Audra was squawking. Rafe wasn't sure just what the woman was squawking about, but she came along right behind Ethan as the two followed Rafe, Julia, and Seth into the barn.

As Rafe dismounted, Audra came rushing into the barn after Ethan. "You need to stay inside until your burns have healed."

"Hey, Rafe, Seth. Glad to see you."

Stripping the leather off his horse, Rafe listened while Ethan and Audra fussed at each other. He also heard something more. Audra's concern. Ethan's placating wish to make his wife happy. They cared about each other. When he came out of his horse's stall, he saw Ethan giving all the horses a bit of grain.

"Let's see the burns, Eth," Rafe said.

"I'm not taking my shirt off in front of your wife, Rafe. It's just blistered, nothing serious."

"It is too serious." Audra jammed one of her little fists on her hips. Rafe wondered why on earth Ethan couldn't control this quiet little woman Rafe had given him. She was by far the easier woman to handle. Sure he couldn't control Julia, but Julia was . . . was . . . well, she was Julia, no more needed to be said.

But Audra was Audra, for heaven's sake.

Shaking his head, Rafe said, "Let's go inside."

"No, not yet." Ethan didn't ask and he didn't try and sway anyone to his way of thinking. He didn't even have a smile on his face. "I want to show you and Seth what we found."

"Ethan, no. I don't want you to go."

"Audra Kincaid!" Ethan turned and glared. "You stop your fussin' right now, woman."

Audra's mouth gaped open but no words came out.

Frankly, Rafe was speechless himself. He'd never heard Ethan sound quite so . . . in charge.

"You go on in with Julia and the girls." Ethan jabbed an impatient finger at the house. "I want to talk with Rafe and Seth about what went on here. It won't hurt my puny burns to walk around in the woods and show them the tracks we found."

Audra finally managed to get her mouth shut. Then her eyes went wide and sad and it looked like she was going to start in crying.

Rafe grabbed Seth by one arm and Ethan by the other. "We won't be gone long. I'll make sure he doesn't hurt himself." He dragged his brothers out of the barn at a near run, and he didn't have to drag much at all, because they were all too willing to hightail it. When they got outside, he looked back to see Julia pick Maggie up with a sweet look of love in her eyes. It made him restless to have young'uns of their own.

"Thanks for getting me out of there, Rafe," Ethan muttered.

Rafe laughed. Seth gave Ethan a wild grin.

The three of them walked along, Ethan in the middle but leading the way because he was the only one who knew it.

Ethan in charge of the situation and Rafe's ranch. And Rafe in charge of running away from the wives.

It wasn't Rafe's ranch anymore and that pinched. But there was also a flash of respect for his brother that he'd never felt before.

"The man who was in the barn ran into the woods right here." Ethan should probably be ashamed of himself for snapping at Audra that way, but she'd obeyed him. The feeling of power made his heart pound and his poor burned shoulders square. Pride. Male power. It was such a great feeling, Ethan knew for sure it was a sin.

Of course she'd been about to cry.

At which point he might have agreed to do anything to get her to stop.

So that was cowardice . . . which might be a sin, too. Honestly it seemed like a man sinned nearly every time he drew a breath.

But Rafe had saved him.

Big brother came through.

Ethan shook his head at the strangeness of being married. Then he remembered the nights. Holding Audra in his arms. The wonder of what passed between a man and wife. That was strange too, in a mighty fine way.

He led the way into the thick woods surrounding the ranch and it was like being swallowed up. The forest and scrub brush closed around them and cut them off from any sight of the house or barn. The land was wild and untamed. They had open meadows where their herds grazed. It had taken a lot of scouting to find grassland in this rugged, mountainous place. It was one thing Pa had done well with all his trapping and the extended trips away from home. He'd come back and said he'd found a trail to a grassy valley. Pa would go to town, sell his furs, and buy the land, then come back and they'd spread their herd over an even wider stretch. He'd built a good-sized holding by the time he died.

Ethan crouched by the first track. "I put some rocks around this footprint and warned the men to stay away. It's one of the clearest." The ground was studded with rocks. Between the rocks the land was covered thick with undergrowth and centuries of fallen leaves and limbs. There were game trails in here, but it took a knowing eye to spot them. Once in a while there was a bit of clear dirt, and a running man had landed a foot here, square in the middle of such a spot.

Ethan glanced over his right shoulder. "You're a good tracker, Seth. Not as good as me, but decent."

"I can out-track you with my eyes closed. Always could." Seth knelt beside the track, studying it. "I got better during the war, too. Scouting was my job."

"You might as well look too, big brother." Ethan gave Rafe a big old grin. "Who knows? You might see something useful."

"I was tracking when you two were still in diapers." Rafe clenched his fists.

Since they were about as close in age as three brothers could be, it was a joke. Ethan didn't worry that Rafe's fists would fly. They'd had their share of fistfights as boys, but it had mostly been high spirits. There'd been a punch in the nose and an occasional black eye that had set a temper off now and again, but mostly the trouble passed before they drew blood.

"Now, don't go pounding on me," Ethan said. "You promised Audra you'd treat me real gentle."

Rafe hunkered down straight across from Ethan. Seth was on Ethan's right. Suddenly the three of them looked up from the footprint and started laughing.

Ethan reached out and rested a hand on Seth's shoulder, ignoring the scars he could feel, and the possibility that Ethan might soon have a few of his own. "I've missed both of you. It's great to be home."

"Haven't you always been here, Eth?" Seth asked.

That question surprised Ethan, but then why should it? Seth was gone. He hadn't known what Ethan and Rafe had been up to. "Nope. I guess we haven't much talked about it, but I spent the last few years wandering out West, spent time in California and a fair stretch at sea."

"You worked on a ship?" Seth asked.

"Yep. I sailed around Cape Horn on a clipper ship. We went from San Francisco to Florida. It was during the Civil War, so we didn't go farther north than that."

"I remember you took off before me, but I didn't know you stayed away. I figured you were here at the ranch."

"Nope." Rafe looked between the two of them. "I've been alone here for years. I've been hoping and praying that whole time you'd come back."

"And now we're here and you two are both old married men."

Seth grinned and his wild blue eyes flashed. Then the grin faded and his brow furrowed.

"What's the matter?" Ethan braced himself for more of Seth's craziness. He'd been acting purely sensible for nearly a minute now.

"Shh . . ." Seth put a hand up. "Let me think." Seth shook his head slowly, as if trying to stir his brain around a little. "Something about what we just said almost . . . almost seems like . . . like . . ."

Seth stared off into the distance. Ethan exchanged a quick glance with Rafe and went back to watching Seth. Worried about him. He had so many more clearheaded days than at first. Ethan had gotten to thinking that if the nightmares would just stop, Seth would be okay. But there were still moments when Seth seemed purely loco, right while he was wide awake.

"I don't know what it was, just a flash of something." Seth rubbed his head. "I think maybe I'm a little jealous of my two big brothers. You both seem to like being married. I wonder how I'm ever gonna find a woman out here. You two have married up the only ones there are."

"Colorado is getting to be a settled land." Ethan clapped Seth on the shoulder and felt those old, twisted scars. "When the law comes in, so do women. You'll find yourself a wife, Seth."

Seth shrugged in a way that dislodged Ethan's touch. "I'm a mighty ugly man under this shirt. I don't reckon any woman is going to want any part of me." He rubbed his head again. "These tracks are bigger than my foot and deeper than the track I leave. But it doesn't take much to weigh more than me. Big shoes usually mean a tall man."

"They're not as deep as mine, so he's between me and Seth in weight, I'd say, not heavy." Rafe ran one finger along the edges of the track. "No sign of being worn down at the heel. We're looking for someone with new boots."

"He's got a long stride." Ethan pointed to another track barely visible, close against a rocky spot under a gnarled pine tree. "I'd say that makes him a long-legged man. More proof he's tall. He's running. Audra told me she saw him running flat-out away from the barn, and he looked tall and skinny to her."

"You got any cowhands fitting that description?" Seth asked.

"A few." Ethan rose from where he studied the tracks, and his brothers stood upright, too. "And it includes two new ones who came in yesterday. Steele is keeping an eye on them, and he'll pay attention to where they walk so we can have a look at their tracks to compare. They've both got new boots on, but then several of the hands do."

"He might not be one of your men, either. How carefully have you tried to backtrack him?"

"Steele's sure he slipped around in the woods and came back onto the property. Probably helped fight the fire he started." Ethan's fist clenched as he thought of it. "Which makes him a low-down, belly-draggin' sidewinder."

"Let's see what else we can find from his trail." Rafe jerked his head and they all moved carefully along.

"I'll show you the trail Steele found. If any of you think Steele's got it wrong, speak up. I sure wish the trail'd read a different way. I'd like it better if I didn't think someone on my ranch started that fire."

Ethan enjoyed working with his brothers again, despite the trouble that'd brought them together. When they were young, they'd been a good team. "When are you going to build a cabin, Seth?"

Seth looked up from a heel track. "I guess I've got to have a building up before snow flies, right?"

"That's right." Rafe had gotten ahead and he dropped back. Again waiting on his little brothers, Rafe's take-charge attitude always grated when they were kids. Not enough to keep Ethan from loving his brother, but it was a burr under his saddle, no denying it.

Now it wasn't so bad. It felt familiar. Rafe taking the lead was part of coming home.

"You need to live on the property." Ethan looked through the woods, and an opening in the trees let him catch a glimpse of his tidy cabin. He felt some guilt. He should give Seth the homeplace and do the building. He was better able to do it. "I claimed my acres. Rafe claimed his and bought some more land. We can add that to Pa's holding and now yours. The Kincaid spread is a mighty big ranch these days."

"We'll get your cabin up in plenty of time, Seth. We now hold water rights that will give us control of the whole stretch between here and my land." Rafe paused, nodded. "It's over a thousand acres with the land Pa left us. The Kincaids will be a name to be reckoned with in Colorado Territory before long."

"We can buy more land as we can afford it." Ethan felt the satisfaction of it. Having his own place felt good. Having his brothers close at hand felt even better. The three of them together. A big swath of land. The Kincaid Ranch. They were a team.

"But I don't want to live alone all winter," Seth said.

Trust Seth to not want to be part of the team.

"That won't be very fun." Seth wiped his hands on his pant leg.

Sweaty palms. It was an affliction Seth had brought back from the war. Whatever kind of crazy Seth had been after what Ethan had done to him, he'd been easy with it. A boy who took terrible chances all the time wasn't given to nerves or worry.

"It'll be lonely." Seth stared at his hands as if he wondered why they were sweating. "I miss Callie."

"Who's Callie?" Ethan asked.

Seth wiped his hands again and didn't answer.

"Seth, who's Callie?"

Seth looked up and narrowed his eyes at Ethan. "Callie who?"

"Callie I-don't-know-who. You just said you miss Callie."

"I don't know anyone named that." Seth gave Ethan a look that seemed to question Ethan's sanity.

Ethan tried not to return the favor.

"I just don't want to live in these mountains—snowed in, stuck inside a cabin all alone."

"We'll figure it out, Seth." Rafe frowned. "We'll get the cabin up and you have to live in it about half the time, but the rest of the time you can stay with Ethan or me. Take turns."

"If we build it on the south edge of your property, you could come to my place and sleep at night," Rafe offered.

Seth shook his head. "Snow gets mighty deep in these mountains."

"And we'll get a bunkhouse up. Spread the cowhands between our three places. That helps. I . . ." Rafe's voice faded for a few seconds; then he went on more quietly, "I've lived alone for three years since Pa died and you're right—it's no fun."

"I haven't even been to visit his grave." Ethan tugged the brim of his hat low. "Nor Ma's. They weren't a good pair, those two."

"Nope. He was gone more than he was here, even before Ma died." Seth dropped to his knees beside a new track. "Afterward, we about raised ourselves."

"And after you two left, he barely called this place home," Rafe added. "It's a wonder he's buried here. He came riding in late in the spring, his horse loaded down with a winter's worth of furs. He was so sick with a fever that he fell off his horse in the ranch yard."

"You said earlier he got to spending the whole winter away." Ethan hadn't realized just how much Pa had been gone.

"The ranch was his, but I got to thinking of it as mine. I hadn't seen him in nearly a year when he died. He'd come through in the spring the year before on his way to sell his furs and stayed around for a while, complained about you two being gone when you should have been home running the ranch."

"A man who's never home has a lot of nerve complaining because his sons go a-yondering." Ethan smiled to cover his regret for abandoning Rafe. His regret for the years of living with one parent sick in her head, another as good as gone.

"He was raving when he got here. He kept talking about his fur traps. Crazy, telling me to get them for him. 'Go get them.' He must've said it a hundred times in the few days he spent dying. A man is dying and all he can think about is his traps. When he made any sense at all, he wanted you two to be here. Talked about his family. Talked about Ma, wanted me to get her. Said he wanted us to be together. Told me I should take care of his family."

"Pa always made that your job, Rafe. He put too much on you. Both our folks put too much on all of us." Ethan let his smile fade. "I'd never neglect my little girls like our parents did us. A youngster needs someone watching over them."

Ethan looked from one brother to the other, and he knew

they were all thinking about that cave. How wild they'd run. How Seth almost died.

How Ethan had watched his little brother's mind break. How Ethan had done the breaking.

"It's not gonna be like that for the children Julia and I have. I don't know why Pa even gave us a thought. I suppose dying makes a man consider his life. I reckon he wanted to tell you good-bye, but he was ugly about it. Mad at me for not keeping the family together. There he was dying and all he cared about was trapping and complaining about his children. He said something about wanting a wife or a daughter at his side. Ranted and raved about women taking better care of him than I did."

"I reckon he's right about that. Girls are usually better at caring for the sick, short of doctoring." Ethan had the urge to give Rafe a hug for going through all that. To stop such an embarrassing thing from happening, he shoved his hands in his back pockets.

Oh sure, Rafe had hugged him when he'd first come home, and they'd both hugged Seth. But that was enough of that nonsense. Ethan decided he'd maybe hug his wife just a bit more tonight to get the feeling to ease. He liked that idea. Rafe could get Julia to hug him, too.

Which again left Seth. Seth definitely needed a wife.

Seth wiped his palms again. "Let's get back to tracking. Talking about Pa is about as much fun as living alone in a cabin all winter."

Ethan had to agree. Anything to do with Pa was no fun at all.

"How could you not get her, Grove?" Mitch wanted to come at Grove with his fists. Furiously he said, "Now they'll be on their guard."

"Guard or not, our chance'll come." Grove didn't like to be pushed, and Mitch was in the mood to do some serious pushing.

Grove's icy-cold eyes studied the woods around the ranch.

Impatient and grim, Mitch thought of just how Jasper Henry handled people who betrayed him. Merciless. No one got away.

"Jasper is probably about ready to send someone after us." Grove's icy eyes went downright frigid.

"Yep, he was in a powerful hurry." Fear skittered up Mitch's backbone and it made him mad. He liked dispensing fear a lot better than feeling it. "Tracker was only a day late contacting the boss before he called us in."

Grove pulled his Colt out and checked that it was fully loaded.

Mitch didn't know why he bothered. Grove and his gun were always ready. "We'll never get that woman and find out what she knows about Jasper's money without a fight. And having all three of those Kincaids around makes it harder. We need to thin them out."

"Might be a good time right now. The men are worn down from a bad night's sleep. The Kincaids are off in the woods looking for trouble." Grove swung those eyes to Mitch. "Maybe we oughta let them find some."

Mitch liked the idea. He was in the mood to hurt somebody. "Let's do it before they learn anything from their tracking."

Grove bristled. "I was careful."

"Careful or not, those Kincaids are knowin' men. The folks in Rawhide all say so." They'd all agreed that the oldest, Rafe, was the toughest cowpoke in the territory, maybe in the whole West. A couple of folks in town had been around long enough to remember the younger brothers. Ethan, the middle one, always full of easy smiles but as smooth and fast with a pistol as any man needed to be. The youngest was a wild man, not afraid of anything.

Grove hissed.

Mitch fell silent as the foreman came walking up. "What've you got for us to do now, Steele?" Mitch hadn't meant to sound gruff. He didn't need to give this old wolf an excuse to fire them. "Sorry. Long night. We're ready to work, boss."

Mitch deliberately forced his shoulders lower and tipped his head down. He could feel the need to hurt someone, work off the frustration of failing last night.

"We're all worn out."

Mitch didn't like this one's sharp eyes, and he didn't want to stand around getting to know him, just in case Steele could read too much.

"I showed you a couple of the pastures yesterday. You two ride out and have a look. No one's been out all day." The foreman had a casual tone to his voice, but his eyes were mighty watchful.

Mitch strode alongside Grove on their way to the corral. As soon as they were out of hearing range from Steele, Mitch said, "Once we're away from this place, we'll circle back and thin out the Kincaid brothers."

"I'm ready." Grove slapped leather on his horse, swung up, and spurred the gelding toward the woods directly away from the Kincaids'.

CHAPTER
16

"I feel an itch between my shoulder blades." Seth turned in a circle, studying the thick forest.

Ethan paid enough attention to draw his gun and make sure it was loaded, but he couldn't help but remember Seth was as crazy as a hydrophobic squirrel.

"You hear anything? See anything?" Rafe rose from where he'd hunkered down by another footprint. He yanked his gloves off and tucked them behind his belt buckle, then checked the load in his gun.

"Nope." Seth had his gun out, too.

Should a lunatic carry a gun? Ethan decided to think about that later. Right now he didn't mind having both his brothers ready to fight.

Rafe studied the woods in one direction, Seth in another,

Ethan took a third. There was a sheer wall of rock lifting up on one side, so they were safe from the west.

Ethan got real close to Seth and Rafe and lowered his voice. "If Seth's itch is right, maybe whoever started that fire is out here, listening, to see if we're on to him."

They'd come a long way from the clearing around the ranch. They'd as good as climbed a mountain following a difficult trail. At the top of a rise, the trail had begun moving to the south, then curled around in a line that, if it kept going, would take a body around the ranch and come out behind the bunkhouse. Or if a man went a bit farther, he could get into the cabin without being seen from the barn—where all the men were busy fighting fire. Ethan's jaw got so tight he thought his teeth might crack.

"Spread out." Rafe giving orders. "No sense making ourselves an easy target."

Made sense to Ethan. He dropped back. Seth surged ahead and to the left. Rafe eased off to the right.

"I don't think there's much more to learn from these tracks. Let's head back." Obeying Rafe was as familiar as the sunrise. "We'll see if the men are all accounted for."

His brothers nodded but didn't talk as they fanned out and descended a section so steep, Ethan could reach his arm out straight behind him and touch the ground. Things leveled off and they picked up the pace. Seth, a few yards ahead, stepped into a clearing, Rafe next.

Just as Ethan emerged, the sharp crack of a twig snapping brought his head around to his left. "Get down!"

All three of them were already moving. He dove for cover just as two six-guns opened up.

In the instant he was in midair, Ethan remembered something about the three Kincaid boys.

Sure Rafe was a tyrant.

It was true Ethan refused to take life seriously.

Seth was a crazy man, no denying it.

But they were all wilderness born and bred. They'd endured bitter cold winters and cattle stampedes. They'd lived through run-ins with rattlesnakes and grizzly bears. They'd survived working with longhorns and bucking broncs. They'd hunted wildcats and rustlers and lived to tell the tale. Besides that . . . they'd been saddled with a mighty poor set of parents. They'd raised themselves, and except for being bossy, apathetic, and crazy, they'd learned a lot of hard lessons about survival in a hard land.

It all added up to them being hard men to kill.

Ethan clawed his way to a boulder. A bullet caromed off the rocks two inches above his head. Spinning around on his knees to take aim, he saw Seth, who'd been in the lead, get out of the small clearing on the far side, about twenty feet away. He scrambled behind a narrow oak and vanished.

Good thing the boy was skinny.

Rafe had been farthest from the gunmen, but he was also farthest from safety. He fired with his right arm crossing his body, shooting under his left arm as he ran, crouching low. A bullet slammed into him and his six-shooter flew.

A shout of rage tore out of Ethan's throat.

Rafe jumped over a fallen tree. He landed on his belly just as bullets bit a line into the trunk. Blood glistened on the stump. A thin line of Rafe's shirt was visible. The shooters were on high ground and they had him pinned down.

Ethan opened fire. He sent a rolling crash of lead in the direction of the attack. He couldn't see where the shooters were hiding, but he could make a good guess. Even without a target, he needed to draw the fire away from Rafe.

A glance at the fallen tree told Ethan that Rafe was still flat on the ground, unmoving, behind that meager protection.

Was Rafe still because he had to stay down? Or was he dead?

The smell of smoking cordite burned Ethan's lungs and lit up his rage as he kept up a thundering volley of bullets.

He counted two gunmen, both shooting down from a rocky ledge to the north. Ethan couldn't see the ledge, tucked back in the trees, but he knew Kincaid land, and he knew that ledge was high enough that, from up there, this clearing was easily visible.

Fury welled up in Ethan as he thought about his big brother, who may be lying dead at the hands of cowards. He kept up his shooting, and at last the bullets turned to him.

He pulled the trigger on an empty chamber. With a quick hand he cracked the gun open and shoved in more bullets.

His shoulder-high boulder was one of a heap spilled down from the side of a mountain, and Ethan had thought it looked like solid cover. Then bullets started bouncing off the rocks behind him and he was dodging lead from every direction.

Seth opened fire.

The bullets smashed into the rocks and whizzed past Ethan's face. Bits of granite sliced his skin. He dropped and dragged himself along on his elbows to stay low, trying to get away from the vicious field of fire.

Ethan got another rock between him and the stinging, careening bullets. Once he was clear, he opened up again. Seth was no longer shooting. Afraid he'd find another brother shot and maybe dead, he twisted around until he could see the tree Seth had ducked behind. Seth had quit shooting so he could climb the tree he hid behind.

Like a giant squirrel.

A giant crazy squirrel.

Ethan couldn't yell at him to keep down or he'd give away Seth's position—if Seth was crazy enough to answer. Instead, Ethan kept moving, hoping he could find a spot that was clear enough he could see what he was shooting at. He moved to a spot where he could no longer see Rafe, so he had no way of knowing if Rafe had moved to better cover.

But with Seth and Ethan taking turns shooting, they were drawing the fire away from Rafe.

As Seth climbed, Ethan scrambled sideways, shooting, ducking, dodging bullets, keeping his head down as he crawled forward, then opened fire again.

He had only a few more yards to go to get in a position where that ledge was visible. He could take dead aim. Finish this.

Steele and the cowhands were coming now. Ethan knew it without hearing a thing. When Steele got here, the dry-gulchers would cut out for sure. Knowing Audra and Julia, they'd probably come running, too. Ethan had to end this before the women got involved.

He kept moving.

"Rafe! Ethan!" Steele was charging into the fight at the risk of his own life. His yelling told Ethan he was trying to draw the fire toward him.

There were pounding footsteps behind Steele, so he'd come with help.

The attack broke off. The bullets quit buzzing as suddenly as they'd begun. Ethan heard rustling in the bushes and the sound of running feet.

He jumped to his feet, conscious of the would-be killers, but taking a chance.

Determined to get a least one good look at the varmints.

All a man had to do was run around the edge of the clearing, then come dashing up with Steele and the men to give themselves a perfect alibi.

Ethan sprinted around trees and rocks. Footsteps sounded in the distance, and Ethan charged toward the sound. He heard hoofbeats and knew he was too late. One look, one glimpse of these men, was all he wanted. He ran on until the galloping horses outpaced him in the distance.

He gave up, disgusted, and turned just as Seth dropped down from the tree right in front of him.

Squirrel-Boy was short a furry tail. Then Ethan looked closer and Seth had the look of a hunter in his eyes. His gun was drawn. Ethan fought the urge to back up, get out of the line of Seth's six-guns. Seth's eyes seemed to focus on Ethan. The guns went back into the holster and the predatory gaze faded.

Ethan closed his eyes to keep from cutting a chunk out of his loco brother.

Brother!

"Rafe!" Ethan's eyes popped open and met Seth's. They turned and ran back to the sight of the shooting to see Rafe standing up, shaking his bleeding hand.

"How bad is it?" Ethan asked.

Rafe shook his head. "It's just a scratch. I'll live to be shot at another day."

"I heard them ride out to the north, Steele." Ethan turned on his foreman. "I want to know who's not accounted for."

"I sent half the men out to check the herds because no one had been out all day. I can't begin to account for where everybody is right now."

Ethan clenched his fist and only kept from punching his foreman because it'd be pure stupidity. "Then what horses are missing? You know our stock. See if you can identify the hoofprints."

"I'll try. Bad ground for tracking." Steele shouted a couple of names and headed into the underbrush.

"Seth, did you get a look at them?" Ethan turned to his tree-climbing brother. Maybe the boy wasn't entirely crazy.

"Nope." Seth reloaded his gun, his movements jerky and fast. "They took off running before I could see either of them."

"Let's get back to the cabin, quick." Ethan looked at Rafe's bleeding hand. "The women will have heard the shooting. And you need to get that gunshot looked after."

The mention of the women set them striding down the slope toward home.

Ethan stepped into the clearing around the cabin to see Julia and Audra at open windows, both armed, braced for trouble. They'd gotten to Ethan's rifles and had them in hand.

"Smart women," Seth said. "I sure wish one of them would've married me."

Ethan slugged Seth in the shoulder. "Can't have mine."

"Mine neither," Rafe said, smiling, holding his bleeding hand against his chest.

"Rafe!" Julia dropped her rifle and vanished from the window.

"Should've stopped the bleeding before we came into view." Rafe picked up speed. "I don't like them outside. Those gunmen might still be around."

The front door of the cabin slammed open and Julia shot out of it and down the steps.

"I'm fine. It's just a scratch. None of us got hurt." Under his breath, Rafe added, "Much."

"Let's get inside," Ethan said. They all three hurried forward, and Julia met Rafe only a few steps from the cabin. He caught her in his arms, lifted her off her feet and kept moving.

"Rafe! You'll hurt your hand!" Julia wiggled to get down even as Rafe practically ran toward the doorway.

"Hold still. You'll hurt me more if you're moving around." Julia froze.

A surprise to Ethan. She was actually being obedient. His big brother was a genius.

Audra came to the door. Holding Maggie in one arm with a rifle in the other.

What a woman.

Ethan heard Lily crying in the background and was hard on Rafe's heels as Rafe carried Julia into the house. Audra stepped back to clear the doorway.

"What's going on, Rafe?" Julia slapped at Rafe's shoulders. Ethan noticed she didn't put any force behind it. "Why are you carrying me?"

"I want you inside. That's why."

Ethan pushed past Rafe and went to pick up Lily, disarming Audra as he went by. He stole a quick kiss, too. He scooped Lily up and she slowed down with her bawling. By the time he'd hung his rifle up on the rack near the fireplace, the baby was calm. Ethan turned to see Rafe surrounded by fussing women. He almost wished he'd gotten shot.

Nah.

"Ethan, I want to see your burns." Audra scowled at him as if he were a naughty schoolboy. And since Ethan had never been to school, having never lived near one, it surprised him some to recognize the look.

"This is a crease from a bullet, Rafe Kincaid. You tell me right now what happened." Julia was snipping at him, but she held his hand so gently and her eyes were so kind and worried, Ethan figured Rafe was enjoying himself.

With Maggie on her hip, Audra whirled from Rafe's side, got a basin of steaming hot water, and hurried back to the table with it. Ethan enjoyed watching her move.

"I've got some bandages torn up. I made them for Ethan." She turned to flash a look at him so fiery he wondered if he might have a few new blisters. "But he hasn't stood still long enough for me to wrap him up."

"You can't wrap up my whole back, Audie." Ethan snagged her as she hurried past him and took another kiss, slower this time. They were getting pretty good at kissing with two babies between them. When he eased back, he said, "I'll let you take care of my burns later, sweetheart, just see if I don't."

"Don't call me Audie." That order would have carried more weight if she'd been able to look away from his lips.

Seth laughed.

"I need those bandages now, Audra." Julia was giving orders. Everything seemed normal. Except for Rafe having a bullet wound. "For heaven's sake, stop dawdling and get them."

Ethan snagged Maggie from Audra as she passed. Maggie started bouncing in Ethan's arms, enjoying the commotion.

"I'm going to go help Steele backtrack those horses." Seth left the room. He sounded calm, sane, responsible.

Nothing like a squirrel.

Ethan decided to enjoy it for as long as it lasted. "Be careful.

Whoever was shooting at us wasn't too particular where his lead went flying."

"Start talking, Rafe." Julia could have taken charge of the cavalry with that voice.

Seth ran. Ethan looked after him enviously.

Ethan had enjoyed the sight of his wife with a rifle in one hand and a baby in the other. But now he was left to face Rafe's bullet wound. Add in the burns on his back and the attempt last night to burn down his barn and steal his wife.

Suddenly everything was purely serious. So serious, Ethan couldn't even smile.

CHAPTER
17

Audra held the bandage on Rafe's hand as Julia fastened it in place. When Audra straightened, she turned to her stubborn husband. His wounds were far worse than Rafe's little scratch and he'd been dodging any doctoring all day.

"Your turn now, Ethan." The sun had set. The men had all retired to the bunkhouse. Steele had posted guards. Audra hoped the man had chosen people he could trust.

Ethan gave her that vapid grin, but Audra wasn't having it. "Let's have a look at you. Now."

Ethan's smile melted like soft butter in a skillet, and Audra didn't mind one bit being the one to wipe the smile off his face.

"Yeah, Eth. Your turn." Rafe hadn't been an easy patient. Audra could tell he wanted someone else to suffer. "The women-folk are done tending my scratch. Let's have a look at the burns."

"Sit down here, Ethan. I have the most doctoring experience of anyone here. I've tended my father." Julia pointed at the chair Rafe had just vacated.

"Who died." Rafe patted her on the back. "That's no recommendation, Jules."

"And delivered two babies."

"I appreciated the help, Julia," Audra said with an apologetic smile, "but really, you just caught them. There wasn't much doctoring beyond that."

"Which still makes me the most experienced doctor of the four of us."

"I'm not letting Julia see me with my shirt off." Ethan had a faint blush on his deeply tanned face. Audra couldn't take her eyes off this vulnerable side of her always overly casual husband. The man let almost nothing upset him. Though Audra had seen him get worked up a few times, now he was embarrassed over Julia seeing his back.

"It's not fitting. My burns are fine. Rafe can have a look at them if you're so all-fired worried." Ethan scowled. "Upstairs."

"Now, Ethan . . ." Julia sounded like she planned to coax Ethan into obeying her. That was quite a change from her usual general-on-the-battlefield manner.

Marriage had mellowed her.

"I'll take a look at the burns, honey." Rafe was more begging than ordering. Marriage had mellowed them both. "If Ethan needs you, he'll tell me—right, Eth?"

"Right."

Audra saw Ethan's insincere smile and knew there was no possible situation in which Ethan would ever find himself in need of his sister-in-law's medical assistance if it required him being shirtless in front of her. And now somehow Audra wasn't allowed to help, either.

"I'm going to go see how bad those burns are." Audra looked after Ethan and Rafe as they left the room, anxious to be with them when they talked about Ethan's wounds.

"Help me finish this stew first," Julia snapped. "Rafe and Ethan don't seem to need a woman's help."

Lily lay kicking happily in her drawer. Maggie sat on the floor trying to put her foot into her mouth. Audra wondered if too much chewing could be bad for a child.

Julia grabbed a carrot and started paring it. "We can watch the children, get an evening meal on, and probably build a new room on the house while Rafe doctors your bashful husband."

Julia's annoyance didn't much bother Audra. She was used to it. In fact, having Julia here reminded Audra of all she'd gone through last night and today. "Both of our husbands could have died."

Julia's cranky expression changed to a worried frown. "That man last night called you Mrs. Gill."

Audra nodded. She'd told Julia all about it. "It's got to have something to do with your father."

"And the only thing that could make someone come after my father is that money. We've got to find it and give it back before somebody gets killed. Could we have missed a place when we were hunting through the cabin or that shack in town? Could Father have gold or cash buried somewhere?"

"He could have buried it anywhere," Audra said. "But how did he move it out here?"

They stared at each other. Audra sliced an onion, thinking back over the trip from Texas. "Could he have stuffed gold bars or coins into a . . . a false bottom of a packing crate? Or maybe a hidden pocket of a satchel?"

"Gold is so heavy. He couldn't have carried much. He wasn't a strong man." Julia sank down onto a chair by the table.

"If it wasn't gold, then what else? A fortune in paper money takes up a lot of space." Audra pictured the few boxes they'd brought along. She could swear she'd packed them all with Julia's help and knew what was in each of them.

"Maybe the money he stole isn't that much." Julia began peeling potatoes. They'd had meat simmering before the shooting started. Just because there was a fire, an attack, and their menfolk were hunting for outlaws didn't mean they didn't have to eat.

"Maybe it's only a fortune to the man he took it from." Audra would see one hundred dollars and think it was a fortune. "Maybe a small bag of gold coins was enough to wipe this man out and bring him after Wendell. Maybe Wendell carried it around in his pocket." She scraped the chopped onions into the pot and washed her hands.

"Maybe. But whoever Father stole from is hiring men. He had to have lost a lot for that to be worthwhile."

"Not if he simply wants revenge. Maybe he's vindictive. Maybe he's a man who never gives up." Audra felt tears burn her eyes and wished she could be stronger. Hold up under pressure better. "What are we going to do?"

The dark expression on Julia's face suddenly lightened into a smile. "You really like Ethan, don't you?"

Audra thought of the things that had passed between her and Ethan. She did indeed like him very much. In fact . . . Audra looked over her shoulder to make sure Ethan and Rafe were gone upstairs and Seth hadn't come in.

"I'm falling in love with him, Julia." Audra considered that to be a very foolish act on her part. "I don't know if Ethan can feel such a thing for me. He doesn't seem to let himself feel anything deeply. But I know I would be devastated if something happened to him."

Julia suddenly set her potato aside and threw her arms around Audra.

Audra hung on tight.

"We can't let anything happen to our men," Julia said.

Those words were like an oath spoken before God. "No, we can't. And if this man is after something he thinks we have, then it's our problem. We're the ones who've brought danger to our men."

Julia pulled back and looked in the direction Ethan and Rafe had disappeared. "Which means it's our job to keep them safe."

"Where could that money be?" Audra wanted to be with Ethan. She wanted to doctor him, find excuses to touch him, make sure he knew how much she cared. But to really help him was more important.

"When he was dying, out of his head, what exactly did Father say? It was about the cavern. Is that right?"

Audra tried to remember. "He didn't say anything specific. Ranting, mumbling, he said 'deep.' " Audra closed her eyes to bring Wendell's feverish words into focus. "He'd told me about the money that first night you were missing. All about his gambling and stealing the money and running. But there was nothing about where it was except that he hid it deep."

Audra tried to squeeze out of her memory exactly what Wendell had said. "Later he said he struck it rich. He said he hid a fortune. I was trying to get him to pray with me. I knew he was almost out of time. I feared he was using his last bit of strength on money when he needed to be making his peace with God, so I cut him off, tried to get him to forget the money. But I couldn't get through to him. If I'd been a stronger woman, I'd have stood up to him long before I did, before he was too sick to reason with."

"I think . . ." Julia hesitated. "I mean, I don't judge my father."

"I try not to." Audra was sorely afraid that despite their best attempts to not judge, they had indeed both judged that Wendell was facing a long, hot eternity.

"What I mean is . . ." Julia swallowed hard. "Father didn't live a godly life, but I believe he had his chance. Any words either of us said, we can't waste time thinking they weren't the right words."

"But isn't that a Christian's foremost job? To speak the truth? To spread the word?"

"It is, but we did that with Father. You're upset because you didn't say it with enough fervor, or at the right moment, or you didn't say it often enough or loud enough. I think about that, too. I was so busy trying to keep peace, walking out on him whenever things got too tense. I should have stood face-to-face with him and demanded he listen."

"You mean, instead of leaving, you should have had ugly shouting matches with him in front of Maggie?"

Julia and Audra looked down at the sweetheart who was pulling herself up on the table leg. Finally Julia said, "No, I couldn't do that."

"And it wouldn't have worked anyway." Audra knew Wendell quite thoroughly after three years of marriage. She was sure Julia knew him even better.

"Which brings me back to my point. Father had his chance

to believe. Whether through our words or the words God has written on every man's heart. And now he's gone and we're left with his mess to clean up. And we begin cleaning it up by finding that money so we can return it to whoever he stole it from. That's the best way to get the attacks to stop and protect our men. We have to find that fortune. What else did Father say?"

"He said no one would ever find it. I remember he laughed when he said it. Smug even when he was dying. He said, 'I stuffed it in deep. Down deep and . . . dark.' He said deep and dark. I was barely listening to him, but I remember thinking deep and dark sounded like that cavern."

"But he never said the word cave or cavern! He could have just meant he was burying it down deep."

Audra tried to visualize Wendell as he lay feverish and irrational, and as always, unkind. "Not the word cavern, but he said, 'I put it in a hole.' As far as I know, Wendell didn't even know about that cavern."

"Audra, come on up here and give me a hand," Ethan called down the stairs.

Julia shook her head. "We've got to figure this out. How much time have we spent around the cabin looking for a hole he might have dug somewhere on that rocky ground? Maybe he marked it, left a pile of rocks so he could find the spot again."

"We only really looked in town." Audra rubbed her forehead and felt her furrowed brow. Even dead, Wendell was giving her wrinkles.

"Because we know every square inch of our cabin and there's certainly no fortune stashed anywhere." Julia jammed her hands on her hips and began tapping her toe. "And the ground's so rocky I can't imagine where he'd have buried it."

Despite the seriousness of the day, Audra almost smiled to see Julia returning to her old self. Rafe getting shot had turned her attention from issuing orders for quite a while. But of course it couldn't last. And that was fine because Julia's take-charge attitude was one of the things Audra liked best about her.

"Now you go on up to tend your husband."

"Yes, Julia." Audra wondered if Julia could tell she was being gently mocked.

"I'll get a meal on."

"There's bread in the cupboard. And—"

"I know how to get a meal."

"I know you do, Julia."

Julia quit tapping and waved her hands to shoo Audra away. "Go on up now. I can handle the meal and the children."

"I know you can, Julia. With your eyes closed."

Julia quit shooing, looked Audra hard in the eye, then burst into tears and threw herself into Audra's arms. "I'm so glad they're all right."

Audra held on tight and had a bit of a cry herself. Then Ethan called again and they broke apart and mopped their eyes.

"Before I go, I've been worried about my little brother and sister."

"Yes, Carolyn and Isaac."

"I don't know quite what to do. I'm especially worried about Carolyn."

"Because of how your father treated you?"

Nodding, Audra said, "All this talk of Wendell and this thieving has made me almost frantic to know how Carolyn is. She's only eight years old. So she's probably safe from my father"—Audra swallowed hard when she almost said selling— "marrying her off to some man he owes money to."

Audra thought of how bossy Julia and Rafe were and knew the difference between a well-meaning—though bossy—friend and a cruel, heartless tyrant. "I need to somehow let Carolyn know I'm all right. And if she needs a home, I could give her one. Ethan said I could bring her and Isaac here."

"Of course you can." Julia rested her hand on Audra's arm.

"But how do we get her here?" Audra noticed she was wringing her hands. Not the strong woman she wanted to be at all. Trying to sound more decisive about her inability to solve her problem, she listed off all the things that had been stopping her.

"Even if I asked Ethan for the money for her train fare, and even if she took the train, it doesn't come all the way here and she wouldn't dare travel alone. And going back to get her would take weeks. And what about Isaac?"

"You can't go alone, not with two little ones." Julia seemed full of even worse reasons. "And if Ethan went with you, he'd be gone a long time from the ranch."

"At least now I can tell her where I am. Rafe wanted us to keep quiet about the wedding, but now that a man attacked the ranch and called me Mrs. Gill, clearly my connection to your father is known. If Ethan says it's all right to mail a letter, I thought maybe, since you're so much closer to Rawhide, you and Rafe could see to getting it mailed."

Julia bristled. "A woman shouldn't have to ask permission of her husband to write a letter."

"I'll ask anyway. And Isaac is six by now. Old enough to be learning how to be a man at my father's knee." Audra's heart hurt to think of it.

"We'll talk with the men and see if they think it's safe now for you to write the letter. Maybe Rafe can think of some way to contact your family. Now that you're remarried, your father can't find a new husband for you."

"And that may be the very best thing about being married to Ethan." But as Audra ran up to care for her new husband, she thought of a lot of reasons she liked about being married to Ethan that had nothing to do with her father.

"Hi, honey." Ethan couldn't believe how much he liked being married. "Rafe says I'm going to be fine."

Rafe smacked him on his not-burnt arm. "I did not say that."

"Don't you hit him, Rafe Kincaid." Audra stormed across the bedroom. A cute little storm. Her fiery expression couldn't have raised a single blister on Rafe's tough hide.

Ethan smiled. "I'm fine." His shoulder burned as if his shirt were still on fire. He smiled bigger.

"I said I think you'll be fine if you don't break those blisters." Rafe looked at Audra as if he wanted to team up with her to tuck Ethan straight into bed. Maybe they'd give him a bottle of milk with a nipple attached while they were at it. "I think he's safe from an infection if the skin isn't broken. Once there's a break, I'm afraid of what might happen. Which means"—Rafe glared at his brother—"you need to be careful."

Ethan spared one withering look at Rafe. "I can't sit around worrying about my blisters. I've got a ranch to run."

Audra leaned so close that Ethan could smell her. A woman was a wonderful thing.

"How far down his back are the burns? I couldn't tell if new blisters were still being raised when I looked earlier."

"The big ones go down to the bottom of his shoulder blade. There are smaller ones on his arm. And he only has them on the left side."

Audra rested a soft hand on Ethan's right shoulder while she looked over his left and down his back. She was so close, he could have pulled her into his lap without a bit of trouble.

"Did any of them break?" Audra straightened away from him and glared, yet not a fraction as fierce as Rafe. "While he was out there having a gunfight on a mountainside?" She leaned in and looked right into his eyes. "After you promised me you'd be careful."

"Now, honey, don't go getting all worked up. I'm fine. No broken blisters. And a few broken blisters wouldn't kill me anyway. I've had my share of blisters in my life, for heaven's sake."

"Not like these. Ethan Kincaid, if you won't promise me—"

"I'll stay a week." Rafe interrupted Audra's scolding, which reminded Ethan of how much he loved his brother. "I'll run the ranch while Ethan rests."

Which reminded Ethan of how his bossy brother drove him half crazy.

"But you're not done building your cabin."

What Rafe didn't say was that he'd run this section of the Kincaid property to suit himself. Make sure everything was in order after Ethan had had time to mess them up. All Ethan had to do was agree to be coddled and he'd prove everything his hired men believed about him, everything Rafe believed about him, and worse yet, everything he didn't want to believe about himself.

Audra laid a palm on Ethan's cheek, a worried frown on her pretty face. For him. She really cared about him.

Her furrowed brow distracted him from his annoyance at Rafe. As he smiled at her, he realized it wasn't like his usual smile. Because of what was behind it.

Usually there was hurt behind it, or anger, or fear. All things he didn't want to show to the world. Mostly there was a need to not feel anything deeply. But now, behind this smile was—he shuddered—affection. He cared about his wife. He hated the very thought of something happening to her.

He couldn't even smile.

He would not fall in love with her. That would be just pure stupid. Which didn't stop him from wanting to throw Rafe out and drag Audra into his arms. He thought of that man who'd tried to get to her in the cellar, and he forgot all about covering up the affection he felt for sweet little Audra.

"Rafe, I'm not going to fight with you anymore for now. The day is past anyway." Ethan suppressed the feeling of worthlessness. For some reason the only thing he could think of was reminding his wife who was in charge of this family.

"You go on out and get something to eat. I need to talk to Audra for a while. Get a few things straight."

"Just tell me now, Ethan." Audra crossed her arms and began tapping a toe impatiently. "Tell me right in front of Rafe. So when you start arguing with me about not resting, he can help me keep you inside."

"No. This is definitely not something I want to talk about in front of my brother." Ethan looked at Rafe. "Get out."

Rafe's brows arched. A faint smile quirked his lips. "I'll tell Julia to get the meal on."

"Tell her not to hurry." Ethan followed Rafe and swung the door shut a little harder than he meant to, then turned to find Audra coming toward him, her eyes flashing with her cute little temper.

"Ethan," she said, shaking her finger right under his nose. "I am not going to let you umph—"

She quieted right down and caught on to his intentions almost immediately. Then she went to kissing him like a house afire. Ethan made the barely conscious discovery that he didn't have many burns on his neck because her arms were wound around him there and it didn't hurt one bit.

Once she was as calm as could be, Ethan pulled away from her just an inch. "I will not have you nagging and fussing at me as if I'm a child."

She made a movement as if to push away from him, then pulled back with a fretful glance at his injuries. "Did I hurt you?"

"If you're so worried about hurting me, then you just be careful." He kissed her again and didn't notice one speck of pain when he swept her up into his arms and lowered her to their bed.

Next time he gave her a chance to breathe, her eyes blinked open and she didn't speak. In fact, she dragged his head down so she could kiss him again.

A big improvement over nagging.

CHAPTER
18

Ethan came into the kitchen sorting around in his head for excuses about why they were late for dinner.

His hand rested on Audra's slender waist because it seemed impossible to quit touching her. Before he could start talking, Seth came in the door with Steele right behind him.

A distraction just when Ethan needed it most.

"What do you think?" Steele was talking to Seth.

Ethan heard the serious tone. "Think about what?"

"I can't be sure about those hoofprints." Seth shoved his hands into his back pockets and scowled. "Whoever shot at us tied rags around their horse's hooves to disguise them."

"I looked, too." Steele looked at Rafe, giving his report to the real boss. Ethan did his best not to let that bother him. "They pulled the rags off and tossed them into the weeds on a stretch of ground covered in prints. Didn't even try to hide the rags. There just wasn't enough to pin down who was behind the shooting."

"And I looked at the footprints of every cowhand on the place. I narrowed it down. But not enough." Seth moved to a chair as Julia set a steaming bowl of stew on the table.

The thick, meaty smell of it made Ethan's mouth water. He hadn't eaten much today what with the fire and the tracking and Audra treating him like he was a helpless baby every time he quit running away from her . . . which had made him run all the faster.

"Stay and eat supper with us." Audra waved the foreman to a chair.

"I'm mighty obliged for that, Mrs. Kincaid." Steele's usual deeply lined face lightened. "It would be a treat to eat a meal cooked and served by the two Kincaid women. I'd be honored if you'd ask me again sometime. But for tonight, I'm going to the bunkhouse to eat with the men. I want to keep my eye on them. I've got men standing watch, men I've known a long time. So we shouldn't have any trouble tonight. Seth and I have talked this through, so he can give you the same report I would."

Steele tugged on the brim of his hat and left.

There was the scrape of chairs on the wooden floor as Rafe and Ethan gathered enough seats around the table.

Julia and Audra made short work of putting fresh bread, a ball of butter, and a pitcher of milk on the table.

Rafe moved to the head of the table. He pulled the chair out.

Audra said, "That's where Ethan sits, Rafe. Go ahead and take the chair at his right."

Ethan froze. Rafe's chin came up. Seth stole a piece of meat out of the stew bowl with his bare hands and ignored them.

"It's fine, Rafe." Ethan was afraid he might be turning red. For some reason he found Audra's simple statement of the truth embarrassing.

"No, she's right. You're the head of this house. Your place is at the head of the table. Sorry. Old habit." Rafe sounded like he meant it and he slid around the corner and sat before it could be debated anymore.

"Didn't matter much where I sat when I was here alone." Rafe smiled and scooted his chair in.

"Let's say a word of prayer over this meal." Rafe folded his hands on the table, the bandaged one a reminder of what they'd been through. "Ethan had a mighty close call last night and we all did today. I think we need to say a proper thank-you." Then Rafe gave Audra a very phony look of innocence. "I'll say the prayer if it's all right with you, Audra."

Audra at the foot of the table gave him a saucy grin, and Ethan went from being embarrassed to being proud of his pretty wife, straight down the table from him. Rafe was across from Seth, so the three brothers were together. Julia was beside Rafe. Maggie was sitting boosted up on a chair between Audra and Seth. Julia had Lily in one arm while she dished up food.

After the prayer, for a few minutes there was only the clink of metal forks and spoons against the glass dishes of food and the tin plates.

When everyone was served and eating, Rafe looked at Seth. "Now tell us what you found out."

Ethan braced himself to get a long drawn-out story about where Seth was hiding nuts for the winter.

"Dearly beloved, we are gathered here in the sight of God to join this man and this woman in holy matrimony."

God.

Jasper's jaw tightened and he turned his attention from what the parson was saying. It didn't sit right with him to have so much talk of God in his wedding vows. He'd hoped to find a justice of the peace or a judge or someone besides a preacher. But Trixie had insisted and now here they were. Gathered in the sight of God.

He and God weren't on good terms and hadn't been for a long, long time.

Okay, never. And his preference would be to keep well out of God's sight.

"Do you, Henry Duff, take Beatrice Butts to be your lawfully wedded wife?" The parson was a sawed-off runt of a man. Short, fat, his skin so tan he could have passed for an Indian if it weren't for blue eyes blazing with religion. "Will you love her, comfort her, honor her and keep her—?"

Well, sure he'd do all that. Except he wasn't sure he loved her. And he wasn't sure what the parson meant by honor her. In fact, he wasn't all that sure what honor was. He didn't fail to note the shame of that.

But he intended to keep her. As long as she didn't make him tend chickens. And he'd be mighty glad to comfort her just as soon as the parson finished up and let them out of here and they could find a rooming house.

"To have and to hold from this day forward."

Jasper turned his mind away again. He was marrying a woman named Beatrice Butts. It turned out that was Trixie's real name. Could his life get any stranger? He'd told her they should use fake names to get married. She'd suggested instead using their real names. Which were as good as fake, since no one had ever heard of them before.

Then she'd admitted her name was Beatrice Butts.

He'd have laughed his head off if his name wasn't Henry Duff. Henry Jasper Duff. Jasper had rid himself of that name the minute his father threw him out of the house.

But the parson they'd found in Bryan, Texas, didn't need to know a middle name, and Henry wasn't attention-getting enough to give anyone a hint that a ruthless and infamous criminal was marrying a notorious Houston courtesan.

"For as long as you both shall live."

Jasper was doing his best not to listen, but he'd heard that. Some dangerous men would be coming after him. Living a long time was going to be a real hard thing to manage. But it didn't matter much as far as the vows went, he reckoned. He stood here, taking vows before God after all, and he had a feeling God didn't believe a single word that came off the lips of Henry Duff. Jasper certainly didn't.

"I do."

"And do you, Beatrice Butts, take this man to be your lawfully wedded husband?"

Trixie might have been flinching from the use of her name, but Jasper decided to pretend she was just showing him some affection when she crushed his hand.

"In sickness and in health."

Catching that, Jasper acknowledged to himself that he owed Trixie a lot. He'd be in mighty poor health right now if she hadn't killed a man early this morning.

"For richer and for poorer."

That sent Jasper off into a daydream of catching up to Wendell and changing his poorer to richer. Jasper would head for Colorado City, the closest town to Rawhide that showed up on a map, and hope to find a letter waiting for him from Mitch and Grove.

"As long as you both shall live."

He'd get Trixie to come along somehow. Then they'd get to Colorado City and he'd tell Trixie he wanted to settle there. He might even mean it. If they could get back what Wendell had stolen and kill any witnesses. Why not? They'd have enough money to live out the rest of their lives in comfort. Didn't matter what town that was in.

The smallest twinge of his very hardened conscience reminded Jasper he was planning cold-blooded murder right smack-dab in the middle of a church. Right square in the sight of God. He braced himself for a lightning bolt. None came, but it wasn't for lack of deserving one.

"I do." Trixie squeezed his hand again and it drew his eyes around. She was looking at him with love in her eyes.

Jasper did his best to keep the pity out of his expression, because he felt sorry for anyone who was hobbled with the burden of loving him. Mostly the folks that had done that in his life had died.

The vows were done, and Jasper led Trixie down the aisle at a fast walk. Glad to escape the religious fire in the parson's eyes. Jasper's mind turned to the wedding night.

"We need to get back on our horses and keep riding, Jasper," Trixie whispered. "Bryan is too close to Houston."

"No one will recognize us dressed like this." Jasper looked down at the coarse cloth of his shirt and pants. He studied Trixie in blue gingham sprigged with white flowers. He felt another pang of pity. This time for both of them. He purely missed the feel of silk on his body.

"We aren't staying here." Trixie dragged him to the horses, and Jasper went along. She'd have to stop running sometime, and it was true that there could be people in Bryan who'd know him.

He was getting a little old to be all worked up about the wedding night anyway. Right now, despite the vows and the tradition of a first night together as man and wife, Jasper was more interested in a safe place to bed down and a long night's sleep. And revenge.

CHAPTER
19

"So what did you find, Seth?" Rafe asked as he dished himself up seconds.

Audra enjoyed watching the Kincaid brothers wolf down the dinner she'd prepared. She was amazed at the satisfied feeling she got from caring for her family. True, Julia had helped, but this meal came from Audra's own kitchen.

Seth looked up from his plate. "Just the usual. Carrots, potatoes, beef." He glanced over at Audra. "The gravy is really good. You're a great cook."

"Thanks, Seth."

"I don't want to know what you found in the stew." Rafe set his fork down with a sharp click. "I want to know what you and Steele found."

Ethan exchanged a glance with Audra, then turned his smile

on Seth. "You told us you'd done some tracking during the war. Hunting men, not just following game trails. You should have been able to read a lot from those tracks."

"There were two of 'em, just like we figured."

Audra gave Ethan an encouraging smile.

He shrank away as he looked at his little brother. "We know there were two of them. They were shooting at us. Hard to not count two gunmen."

"They circled around the clearing on horseback." Seth frowned at his plate as if his vegetables were misbehaving. "You heard Steele tell how they'd covered their horses' hooves."

Seth reached for another slice of bread and buttered it as if he were creating a great work of art.

Rafe started drumming his fingers on the table, poorly concealing his impatience. "Anything else?"

"Oh yes, there was one other thing." Seth looked up, suddenly excited, eager. He turned to Julia. "Can we go back to your place tomorrow and get back to exploring that cavern? I want to show you that cave. I know you're going to love—"

"Seth!" Rafe cut him off.

"What?" Seth took a hearty bite of bread and seemed genuinely curious as to what Rafe might want.

"We're not done talking about those tracks."

With a shrug and wide-eyed innocence, Seth said, "Sure we are. I don't know nothing."

Rafe's eyes narrowed and he looked about ready to start barking out orders.

"Why'd you climb that tree today?" Ethan had his smile back.

It was that moment, that question, which diverted Rafe

from his anger and Seth from his craziness, when Audra realized what Ethan's smile meant. He gave a very good show of being a man who didn't care about a thing. But he did care. And what he cared about was peace. He wanted a peaceful life. He had a brother who was a wild man and another who could give Napoleon lessons on being dictatorial.

Ethan kept the peace by changing the subject with a smile, drawing his brothers back from the brink.

Audra wondered just how heavy a burden Ethan carried in trying to keep his family together. And the fact that he'd left, been the first to leave in fact, when he loved his brothers and his home so much, said just how unbearable that burden must have become.

"I went up to the treetop," Seth said.

"Like a giant squirrel." Ethan laughed.

Audra could see the worry behind the teasing.

Shrugging off the squirrel comment, Seth went on, "I learned in the war that men don't usually look up. I could be ten feet above a bunch of Confederate soldiers and just sit there in the tree and listen. I'd do my best to hide, but it got so I wasn't real scared even if I was visible. They'd never notice me sitting up there."

"You said you scouted behind enemy lines, right?" Ethan kept smiling but it wasn't just an effort to head off Rafe's temper now. He was clearly interested to learn more about Seth's war years. She wanted to know, too.

"I did it from the first, but I kept getting promoted, so they let me go out in the field less and less."

"How high a rank did you reach?" Rafe asked.

Seth's brow furrowed. "I went up, then down, then back up again."

"Are we talking about your army rank or climbing trees?" Ethan grinned.

Seth smiled back. "Rank. I was a captain for a while. But I hated it. I didn't want to give anyone orders. I said some things, complained about some stupid orders we'd been given, and went back down. Then I did something some general liked and I went back up. The officers above me would order me to order the troops into battle. Well, I didn't want to send them out somewhere they might get shot. So I was a lousy captain, or maybe a lieutenant . . . I might've been a major for a while. Which of those is highest?" Seth looked at Rafe as if Rafe might know Seth's rank.

"So today you went up in the treetop to get closer to those outlaws?" Audra prompted Seth before he started storing nuts for the winter.

"I think . . ." Seth's voice faded, then he went on sounding helpless. "I hate war. I got so hungry. And it hurts to get shot. Almost as bad as the burns."

"Do you remember where you were when you got shot?" Ethan asked. "We saw the wounds on your back."

Shaking his head, Seth's wild blue eyes seemed to lose focus, as if he were looking at something inside his head. "Just somewhere. Some fight. There was always another fight. Always. That's war. Fighting and dying and shooting and bleeding and burning. Cannons exploding. The horses. The men. Both blown into pieces. I guess—I think a cannon blew a real deep hole in the ground and I fell and caught on fire. My shirt was on fire."

Audra gave Ethan a nervous look. Seth seemed to be back in the middle of the war.

"I couldn't get out. I fell and I was burning. I was on fire and I couldn't get out of the hole." Seth's voice rose. "It was like the devil was dragging me down into a fiery pit and I was on fire and I couldn't get out—"

"Stop!" Ethan's hand landed hard on Seth's upper arm.

Seth straightened and the terror and madness was suddenly gone. He looked down at Ethan's hand on his arm, then looked at Julia and smiled. "When are we going down into the cavern again? I really wanted to go today."

Audra saw the anguish on Ethan's face at Seth's slim grasp on sanity. Audra couldn't stand it. Maggie was done eating, so Audra let her get down and slipped into the chair next to Seth and laid one hand on his shoulder, drawing his wild blue gaze to her.

"Seth, honey, we can talk about the cavern if you want to, but not now. Ethan is worried about you. We all are."

"Why? I'm fine." Seth smiled, but Audra saw a fine trembling in his body that was anything but fine.

Unable to resist the urge, Audra drew Seth into her arms and hugged him.

He froze. "What are you doing?" His head drew back, though he didn't push her away from him.

Audra met his eyes, then pulled him closer. "Just let me give you a hug. Did you know I have a little brother?"

"You talked about wanting to bring him out West. I remember. You've got a little sister, too." Seth's hands hung at his sides. It was an awkward hug, but Audra held on.

Audra looked over Seth's shoulder at Ethan, who was watching them with one brow arched and his mouth twisted in what, for once, could not be considered a smile.

"Yes. I have a little brother named Isaac. I have a sister, Carolyn. When I married Wendell, I got Julia as a daughter, and my sister Carolyn became Julia's aunt, even though she is much younger than Julia. And when I married Ethan, I got two more brothers and Julia as a sister." Audra pulled back so both hands were resting on Seth's broad shoulders.

Seth lifted one shoulder. "I like having a big sister. 'Cept you're a puny thing. Not much big about you."

Audra smiled. "You're part of my family now." Then her smiled faded. "And I'm worried about my little brother . . . you. I hate that you're having nightmares. I hate that you saw awful things in the war and were shot and imprisoned."

"It wasn't so bad."

"You were starved half to death and it took you over a year to get home, a year you say you can't remember. Then you went into that cavern instead of coming to the ranch, when you had to know how to get here. That sounds pretty bad to me."

"I guess it does." Seth was really listening, she could tell.

Seth needed a firm grasp on reality. Audra wasn't sure if listing all that was wrong with him was a good idea or not, so she prayed silently for guidance, then followed her instincts and just spoke honestly.

"We worry about you in that cavern, that it has some kind of . . . of unhealthy hold on you."

"Audra . . ." Julia wanted Seth to help her. Audra knew it.

"Maybe facing the cavern is better than avoiding it. But face it clearheaded. You remember that Tracker Breach, the man who was down there with you, was feeding you laudanum."

"He was?"

Audra sighed internally, wondering just how shaky a grip Seth really had on sanity. "Yes, so a lot of what happened, including the fact that you were in that cavern so long, can be blamed on the drugs he gave you. But now your head is clear and we ask you about the war and you drift into talk of the cavern and the accident you had when you were so young, falling into a pit, being on fire. Ethan's injuries last night only make it worse for you. We love you, Seth, and we want you to be strong and . . . and healthy."

"You love me?" Seth's voice held a note of wonder.

Audra realized that it was true. She did love him, as a little brother and as a child of God. She loved Ethan too, but in a different, more wonderful way. Rafe, well, maybe, sort of, sure. He was scary, though. But he was a great husband for Julia. Perfect, in fact.

"Of course I do." Unable to stop herself, she pulled Seth back close. Strange to hold a grown man. One she wasn't married to. She thought of the completely different feeling she got when Ethan held her in his arms.

When Audra eased back again, she squared her shoulders and looked between Ethan, Rafe, and Julia. "For Seth to heal, we need a more peaceful life. So we need to find out who is after whatever fortune Wendell supposedly stole, and then settle with that man who's after it."

Audra looked hard at Julia. "How are we going to do that?"

"We've talked about it." Julia leaned forward, folding her arms on the table. "We just can't remember Father carrying anything that could have amounted to a fortune. But he must have."

"I think maybe, somehow, Wendell found that cavern and hid the money down there." Audra looked at Seth. "Is that possible? How could he have found that place?"

"The cavern wasn't a secret really," Ethan said with a shudder. "I'd never heard of that entrance in Rafe's mountain valley, but the hole we used to climb down could have been known in town. Your pa could have heard of it."

"But does anyone really know the cavern except you Kincaid boys?"

"I know it quite well," Julia reminded her. "Of course I don't know the depths of it. There is a lot more to explore."

"I don't know it at all." Ethan spoke too quickly.

"You hate it, but that's not the same as not knowing it," Rafe said. "We hunted around down there for a few years before Seth's accident. I kept going down, and Seth explored it more than anyone. But I'll bet you know it better than Wendell could have in the short time he'd've had to explore."

"Which means, Ethan, you know it well enough to help with this." Audra frowned. "In fact, I'm the only one here who doesn't know the cavern well. I've never been in it except for that time Seth took Maggie down there." She resisted the urge to slug him. It made her realize she was starting to think of him as a brother. "So, let's pretend like I'm Wendell. I'm going down to a cavern I've heard a rumor about. We figure he went down that hole where Julia climbed in, because except for Seth, as far as we know, the other exit had never been discovered."

Audra was feeling very much in charge as everyone looked at her and, even more amazing, listened to her. "Tell me what I'd see if I climbed down there. Where would I go to hide my money? Are there crevices? Holes?"

"What about the hole Seth fell down?" Ethan asked. "It isn't very far in."

"That's not really what I was thinking of." Audra tried to imagine that awful, dark pit. It didn't really terrify her so much as worry her because of the danger it presented. But going down, feeling like horror lurked in the depths—that didn't seem to be an affliction she possessed. Something for which she fervently thanked God.

"I was thinking more of a small hole, a place a man could stick a bag of money in and leave it. Someplace easily found if a man went down there for the first time."

There was silence as the four explorers mentally searched in that dark place.

Finally, Audra said, "Just start talking. Tell me about it. Tell me how it struck each of you when you first went down."

The conversation that followed was lively. Seth's obsession with the cavern, Julia's passion for it, Rafe's hardy respect, Ethan's barely concealed loathing. They each described the cavern in a different way, but Audra got a mental picture.

She interrupted their stories. "Now let me ask questions about the cavern."

"Why?" Julia asked.

"Because I'm the one who knows nothing about it. My reaction to it might be similar to how Wendell would react. Maybe my very ignorance can give us some idea of where he might hide the money." As Audra asked her questions, her interest in the beautiful cavern grew.

"I'd love to go down there and see the rock formations and stalactites and fossils."

"I'll take you sometime," Seth said with a wild grin.

"You're not going down, Audra," Ethan said with narrowed eyes. "It's too dangerous."

With a sigh, Audra looked at Julia. "Before we turn our attention to the cavern, let's do the simpler things. Wendell's shop in town and the cabin we were living in when he died. Ethan and I searched that building in town thoroughly, but we didn't do any digging. How closely did we really study the floor in that building?" She looked at Ethan.

He shrugged. "We tore up floorboards, but we could probably stand to do some digging inside as well as out."

"If it really was a fortune, Wendell would have wanted it close." Audra shook her head. "And if he dug a hole somewhere, surely he marked the spot somehow."

"I want to ride into town and talk to the sheriff again anyway," Rafe said. "Julia and I can go tomorrow and search more carefully in there."

"Getting away from here might be a good idea, too." Julia looked with a worried frown from Audra to the baby sleeping in her arms. "Why don't we all ride out toward town in the morning? When we're sure we're not followed, Audra and Ethan can circle around and go to the cabin and hunt."

"Can you think of any possible places to hide the money inside?" Audra wracked her brain, but the house was just too small.

"None I can imagine, yet we need to be sure. Check it closely and look around for spots on that rocky ground where there's enough dirt to bury something. When we've done all that, then I think we have to turn our attention to searching in the cavern."

Ethan's gasp was barely audible, but Audra knew he'd never volunteer for that. But it didn't matter. Between Julia and Seth, there'd be no shortage of volunteers.

"I think we should all ride to town together." Ethan reached up to rub his shoulder and stopped. Audra wondered how much his burns hurt. "For the sake of safety, we should stick together."

"No." Audra shook her head. "I want this over with. We've been attacked twice already. These men are deadly serious, and we're in danger as long as someone's hunting for that money. We have to split up."

CHAPTER
20

Ethan was fuming by the time he got Audra alone.

He shut their bedroom door with a force that was just a bit too stern.

Julia was sleeping in the spare bedroom. Rafe was standing watch with Steele. Seth, currently sleeping on a bedroll downstairs in front of the fireplace, would spell Rafe, then Ethan would take the last watch before sunrise.

And at sunrise, they'd ride out, then split up.

"Why did you say that?"

Audra was running a brush through her hair. Her arm froze in midstroke and she turned to look at Ethan. "You're upset with me."

Striding across the room, Ethan leaned down and spoke through gritted teeth, not wanting his sister-in-law to overhear.

"Rafe came over here with Seth and Julia to help protect this ranch. We can't do that if we're riding all over the countryside."

Audra took a step back, her eyes wide with fear. Ethan felt like the biggest bully in the world. Then suddenly the shy, sweet woman he'd married did that strange thing he'd seen her do before. She faked having courage even when she didn't.

She slammed her brush down on the dresser behind her and lifted her pointy little chin up. "The way to protect this ranch is to get to the bottom of this mess. We need to find that money. We need to figure out who's behind this and give his money back or have him arrested. He sent Tracker and we caught him. Now we're in danger from somebody else. They'll just keep coming."

"This is Colorado Territory. There are always outlaws. We fight the ones who bother us and we go on about running the ranch."

Audra studied him like she'd cornered a rat in the kitchen. Some women might be scared of a rat, but Audra looked like she was ready to go in for the kill. "This isn't about us going off to search my old cabin, is it, Ethan?"

Which made no sense. "Of course it is. And we do need to search, but we need to stick together."

"No, you started to get upset when I talked about the money being hidden in the cavern."

Ethan suddenly found it hard to swallow.

The fire went out of Audra's eyes. She reached for him, slid her arms around his neck, gently, he noticed, thinking about his burns. Always kind and gentle and thinking about him.

"Is the cavern really that dangerous?"

"Yes!" Ethan nearly shouted. He hadn't meant to. He

clenched his jaw so no more words would escape. Finally he felt able to whisper again. "It's not about the cavern. It's about us not taking risks, especially not with you or the children."

"So you think the outlaws will be at the cabin?"

"We can't be sure they won't be searching the same as us. And these are pure yellow coyotes, who will shoot a man in the back or attack a woman. Remember, we'll have the girls with us. We can't be taking risks with them."

"If we stay with Julia and Rafe tomorrow, and search in town together, then we can go to the cabin the next day . . . and if the money still doesn't turn up, we can all go hunt in the cavern after that."

"No!" He caught her around the waist and dragged her hard against him. "You're not going down there. I won't let you."

"What happened that makes you hate that place so much, Ethan? I mean, you said Seth fell. You said it's dangerous, but we will be careful."

"No one can be that careful."

"It's not just you, either. Rafe is so hostile to it. Seth is obsessed with it. What really happened down there that three young boys have grown into men with personalities shaped, maybe even twisted, by a simple cave?"

"What happened is that I found out I was a coward."

"You're the bravest man I know." Audra kissed him as gently as a flitting butterfly. Somehow that kiss was like a lock turning. A lock that sprung open, and words pressed against his throat, trying to escape. Words that were a secret Ethan had carried inside him all these years.

"I said things to Seth that . . . that . . . drove him mad."

"No, you didn't. No one can do that."

"I was cruel. I taunted him. I saw him go crazy right in front of my eyes, and it was my fault."

"I don't believe it." She kissed him more intimately. "You've got a child's memory of that day."

"I wasn't a child. I was thirteen years old."

"You've never talked about it since, have you?"

"There was nothing to talk about. My words broke his mind and it's never really mended. Then the nightmares. He was terribly hurt, but we'd have survived it if it wasn't for the nightmares."

"What does that mean? You all survived it."

"No, Ma didn't. She died." It had taken a couple of years, but she'd begun to decline from that day. And it wasn't because of how badly Seth was hurt, though that was terrible. It was because of the nightmares that tormented the whole family, and those were Ethan's fault.

"You can't believe that."

"It took her a while, but she was never the same. She as good as curled up and cried herself to death. And Pa ran off and left us for so long at a time, he might as well have died." As Ethan said those words aloud, anger welled up inside him. He and Rafe had stayed while Ma and Pa had withdrawn. That was no way for parents to treat their children. He would never do that to his daughters. Then the look in Seth's eyes when his mind broke swept away Ethan's anger, or rather placed it where it belonged. On his own shoulders.

"Tell me what happened—please, Ethan. Tell me all of it. I want to understand."

Ethan looked into her gentle eyes and wanted so much to be worthy of her kindness. "You're right that I've never talked about it."

"Then isn't it time?"

His grip on her wrist softened and he caressed the underside of it with his thumb, marveling at how nice it was to have a woman's hand to hold.

"Seth ran off." Ethan swallowed hard. He hated that day like he hated nothing else on earth. "You're always talking about wanting to be brave, but Audra, honey, you've already got more courage than I ever will." He kissed her, drew courage from her.

"Tell me." She held him, almost cradled him, as if she could hold him away from the nightmare of that day.

"We climbed down and Seth ran off. He liked to hide and jump out at us. I never liked it down there, but it was okay. We had fun."

Ethan remembered every ugly minute as if he were thirteen again.

Seth laughed from up ahead. A spooky laugh that sent a shiver up Ethan's spine. "We need to teach baby brother a lesson, Rafe."

Ethan's voice broke, like it'd been doing ever since he turned thirteen. It was getting deeper and it embarrassed him when he sounded like a squeaky little girl. Hating this cavern only made it worse.

"We oughta leave him." Of course, Rafe kept going. Rafe would never go off and abandon one of them, no matter his tough talk.

Ethan pulled one of the torches from a crack in the wall. "Gimme the lantern, Rafe." Ethan lit it, then wedged it back into the crack. "You know Seth is hiding up ahead to jump out at us."

"Sounds like something he'd do." Rafe used his lantern to light a torch they'd stuck in a different crack in the tunnel wall.

Ethan loved the smell of kerosene and fire; it drove back the dank smell of the cavern. He always carried his own lantern, not trusting either of his brothers to stay close at hand.

"Do you ever wonder if monsters live down here?" Ethan didn't really believe in monsters, but if there were such things, this is right where they'd be. And he liked saying out loud the fears he had, only making it sound like he was trying to spook his brothers. "Or maybe outlaws, hiding behind these tall stones growing up from the floor."

Ethan definitely believed in outlaws.

"There ain't no outlaws, Eth. No one knows about this place but us. This is our own secret hideout." Rafe picked up speed.

Ethan knew Rafe was worried about Seth and so hurried to keep close to his big brother. It occurred to Ethan that if no one else in the world knew about this place, then what if something happened? What if the rope they'd climbed down on broke? No one would ever look for them down here. The torches would burn out. The kerosene would burn away, and the three of them would starve to death in the pitch-dark.

Yeah, he had no trouble at all thinking of terrible things that could happen in this pit.

"I think maybe this hole reaches all the way down to where the devil lives. We've found the entrance to hell, Rafe." That thought gave him more than a chill. It terrified him. Which was the whole fun of it.

Rafe shoved him.

Ethan laughed and swung the lantern at Rafe to get him to back off.

"Let's get on with letting Seth scare us. We can light the rest of the torches later." The torches were just sticks wrapped with oil-soaked rags and dried brush. They lit the place up good. Ethan made new ones all the time so they'd always have plenty. Being trapped down here in the dark was his worst nightmare.

Something snapped in the darkness ahead.

A shout stopped Ethan in his tracks.

"Rafe, help!" Seth's frightened cry was something Ethan had never heard before.

Falling rocks nearly drowned out another scream. "Ethan!" Seth wasn't afraid of anything.

"Let's go!" Rafe ran.

Ethan had to force himself to move.

Seth shouted again. The noise echoed toward them. The sound of stones striking each other like an avalanche rumbled, drowning out Seth's sharp cries for help. Then a terrible scream stopped Rafe. Ethan stumbled into him.

Ethan's hand shook as he pointed at a side tunnel. "He's down there." Ethan forced himself to rush in. What he really wanted to do was curl up and cry like a frightened baby.

"Be careful," Seth yelled. "There's a hole!" Ethan saw it and skidded to a stop. For a second he teetered on the brink of life and death. He could see himself going over the edge and falling all the way to the lake of fire. Burning for all eternity.

Rafe yanked him backward, and Ethan shook off the image of that horror.

Ethan dropped to his knees and yelled down, "Seth!"

"Back up." Seth sounded terrified. "You're on ground that won't hold."

"Won't hold what?" Ethan stretched his lantern forward to light the hole. Seth sounded fine. Strong. Scared but not hurt bad.

Rafe dropped beside Ethan and leaned forward, then suddenly

was gone. "Back up, Eth. The ground is cracking." He grabbed Ethan's shirt and pulled, raising his voice. "We'll get you out, Seth!"

Ethan still didn't get what Rafe meant, but he started back, crawling on his knees. One hand busy with the lantern. The rock under him broke and his arm fell through all the way to his shoulder. He smashed his face on stone as he landed flat on his belly.

Ethan yelled and jerked his arm loose as the edge crumbled away from his face.

"Get your weight off this thin rock." Rafe was moving back fast.

Ethan heard his own cry of terror and hated himself for it. The floor cracked again. He slid backward on his belly. The ground seemed to chase him, crumbling under him.

Every solid thing collapsed. He plunged forward.

And stopped.

The lantern slipped from his hand and it fell and shattered.

Ethan dangled in midair. Flames shot up nearly to his face. The heat and the smell made him lurch back. He saw kerosene flow over stone. The fire chased the fuel.

"I've got you," Rafe shouted from behind him. Ethan realized he was hanging from his rope belt. Rafe had caught him.

"Fire!" Seth shrieked from below them. Ethan looked down into the pit. Seth was on fire!

"Rafe, help me!"

One hard yank on his belt and Ethan popped up out of the mouth of Hades, flew backward and hit his head so hard, stars exploded. He was barely aware of an ugly crack from Rafe hitting the other side of the tunnel headfirst.

Ethan tried to surge forward to help Seth, but he couldn't. His vision wasn't right. It was narrow and kept getting worse. He saw blood streaming from a cut on Rafe's head.

"I'm on fire!" Seth's screams grew louder.

Ethan couldn't move. His arms and legs wouldn't work. It was as if he'd been burned onto that spot. Doing nothing while his brother died in a fire Ethan had caused.

Rafe threw himself forward. All Ethan could do was sit there, worthless, stopped by fear. He prayed no more rock would break. He prayed desperately that God would save Seth and protect Rafe.

"Get your shirt off, Seth!" Rafe leaned forward and shouted over the crackling flames. "Get it off, throw it away."

Ethan couldn't even help. He felt something warm wash down his neck and was able to tip his head forward and see blood trickle down his neck and disappear into his shirt, flowing down his chest.

"I'm burning!" Seth screamed.

"Your hair's on fire, slap at your hair!" Rafe was screaming now too, but still thinking, still in control.

Ethan could only listen. He tried to lift a hand and it wouldn't move.

"You got it, Seth. You're all right. The fire's off you. We'll get you out."

"My arm is burned, Rafe. My head. My shoulders hurt."

Ethan could still see flames dancing up from the hole.

"Just be careful of the fire. Stay back."

"I hurt. I don't think I can climb up, even if there is a way."

Rafe turned to Ethan and ordered, "Go get one of the torches."

Ethan couldn't respond. His mouth didn't work any better than the rest of him. He saw blood pouring down Rafe's forehead, coating the whole side of his face. The dancing flames lit up the crimson stain and it seemed as if life was flowing out of his brother. He was hurt worse that Ethan, but Rafe kept working, kept trying, kept facing the danger.

"Ethan!" Rafe lunged at him and grabbed his arm and shook him. Ethan could see it, but he didn't feel a thing. Rafe shook his head in disgust. "All right. I'll go for a torch."

"What?" It was all Ethan could manage. He knew what Rafe was saying. He was leaving them.

"We're going to be down here in the pitch-dark in a couple of minutes. I'm going for a torch while the fire from down there can still give me a little light. Talk to Seth. Make sure he knows we haven't left him."

Another of those muffled sobs sounded from below. Seth was tough. Ethan couldn't imagine what would make his little brother cry. Only agony.

The light diminished. Rafe shouted right into Ethan's face. "Talk to him!"

Ethan shuddered to think of being left alone down here in the dark. With only tormented cries and fiery flames from the deep.

"Talk to him, Ethan. Do something."

Ethan still couldn't move. A blow knocked Ethan sideways and he realized Rafe had punched him in the face.

"Hey!" The blow unlocked whatever had pinned him down. Suddenly he could lift his hands, move his legs.

"Talk to him. Talk to Seth. I'll be right back."

"No, don't leave us!" Ethan grabbed at Rafe.

Rafe shook his head and dodged Ethan's hands. "I'll be right back. Talk to Seth." Rafe jumped to his feet and ran into the dark.

Ethan sat and trembled like a coward while one brother worked to save them all and another sobbed in pain. He felt such overwhelming worthlessness, it was unbearable. For a few awful seconds, tears burned his eyes.

Seth sobbed. Ethan fought his own weakness, grabbed ahold of that sound, and used it to force himself to move. As he tried to stand, his cowardice knocked him on his face. He grabbed the edge of that pit as if he held on to life itself.

Dear God, it's too much. I swear to you I will never come down here again.

Seth cried, "Don't leave me, Rafe!"

Ethan focused and saw his little brother. Burned. One arm blackened. Horrible, ugly burns.

The damage broke off Ethan's prayers, and instead he felt something that was more like an oath. He made a vow to never let himself be terrified like this again. And that vow went so deep, it ripped his soul wide open. What he'd done to Seth was unbearable, and like all unbearable things, it broke him inside. He found a crazy sort of calm and he could function again.

All his fear died along with every other thing a boy could feel.

He leaned forward. Seth was twenty feet down, curled up on his right side, sobbing. There were ugly burns on his left. Ethan could see them in the dying kerosene light. The flames dropped lower by the second. Soon they'd be in total darkness.

Ethan wanted to apologize and beg Seth to forgive him. But that would mean Ethan would have to feel something and he didn't dare. He pulled himself to his hands and knees in the dim light, let go of all his fretting and said, "Quit your cryin'. Rafe'll be right back. He's going to get you out of there."

"He's . . . gone." The word barely got out between the moans of pain and the tears. Seth crossed his arms on his chest. He bent his head and drew up his knees until he'd nearly rolled into a ball.

Those words gave Ethan a terrible jolt. Rafe was gone. The only rope they had was for climbing out. He couldn't use that because they'd be trapped down here.

Right then, footsteps pounded behind Ethan. He looked back to see Rafe running toward him with a burning torch and two unlit ones.

Ethan had a jolt of relief so strong he was glad he was on his belly.

"Hang on, Seth. I'll be back." Rafe dropped the two unlit torches and thrust the burning one into Ethan's hands, then turned and raced away.

"No! Rafe, wait!" Seth's cry was for nothing. Rafe was already gone.

Ethan only kept from begging Rafe to stay because of the strange calm that had him in its grip, and even that might not have held if Rafe hadn't dashed off again. Ethan looked at the two unlit torches. These torches burned for a long time. An hour or more. Did Rafe think he'd be gone that long? Ethan let the fear slide off him. He could stand this if he didn't feel. And if he could keep from feeling, then he could help Seth.

"Hey, little brother, can you sit up and talk to me?" Ethan knew it must hurt Seth terribly to move.

Well, that was just too bad for Seth.

Seth's eyes blinked open and he turned his head and looked

up at Ethan. Slowly, Seth sat up. Ethan saw the blackened burns on Seth's arm and neck, part of his back.

Ethan studied the pit. There was a dark corner that looked as if it might go on down forever. But where Seth was, there was jagged stone and it sloped up. It looked like something a boy might climb. He considered climbing down and raised up on his hands and knees only to have his head swirl around and his vision start to go black. He lay back down on his belly before he passed out.

"You know what'd be great?" Ethan said calmly.

"Wh-what?" It seemed as though Seth was trying to match Ethan's light tone. Maybe Ethan could teach his little brother not to feel anything either. Like pain.

"You oughta try and climb out of there. I mean you haven't really tried, have you? It's not that deep, and we climb that far lotsa times down here." Ethan looked at the rock wall under him and had enough control of his arms to point. "Look at this wall. Now that the fire is dying down, it's easy to see the handholds. You could climb without much trouble if you weren't so busy crying."

Seth's head came up. Something flashed in his eyes, set off by the fading fire. Seth was always reckless, but for the first time he looked more than reckless. There was a flicker of madness in his eyes. Seth rose to his feet, his teeth gritted.

"Maybe I oughta come down there and help the little crying baby." But Ethan knew he couldn't. He knew his grip was shaky and he might pass out and fall.

"I'm not a baby." Seth's voice carried a load of pain and fear. And something else, something nearly loco.

"You just stay down there and cry, baby brother." Seth hated being youngest. Ethan knew it.

263

"I'm not crying." Seth pressed the flat of his palm against one eye with his right hand. He moved his left to do the same, and Ethan saw—in the ugly, dying fire—the blackened skin on Seth's arm, split and bleeding.

Seth cried out and grabbed at his arm, then stopped, afraid to touch it.

Ethan refused to voice his horror of seeing crimson pouring out of the burn. "No sense trying to save yourself, baby. You just wait for Rafe. Even though he'll be hours huntin' up a rope." Ethan had a terrible thought then, and said it out loud. "If he comes back at all."

"No, I-I'll try and climb up." Seth began moving, his left arm held against his stomach.

"Go around the fire this time, baby brother."

Seth looked up and glared, then started forward, one unsteady step at a time, climbing over the uneven rubble-strewn floor, skirting the fire. The crying had stopped. Normally, Seth could climb right out without a bit of trouble. Now, though, the pain made it a chancy thing. Ethan should go down. He should help, get behind Seth and catch him if he fell.

Instead, Ethan remained lying on his belly in the dirt.

Seth whimpered a few times, and each time Ethan called him a baby.

Seth kept climbing.

When Seth finally reached the top of that busted-up hole, he looked straight into Ethan's eyes and Ethan saw crazy.

"I saw his mind break. I saw my words drive him mad. And I didn't even care."

"No, you got him out." Audra hugged him so hard that it drew him out of the ugly memories.

He noticed she hugged him low on his back, mindful of his burns.

"He got out and we started walking to the entrance. We met Rafe coming back. He'd had a rope on his horse. I'd forgotten about that. I could have kept my mouth shut, or just been kind, even crawled down there and stayed beside Seth. None of what I said to him was necessary. Rafe was coming. Rafe would have saved him without hurting him the way I did."

Audra touched his face.

"We all had to live with how terribly he was hurt and the nightmares he had after that." Ethan ran his hands deeply into his hair. "Rafe and I had a few too, but ours faded away. It destroyed our family. Ma just turned into a ghost in our house, a quiet, weeping ghost. She never had much to do with us anymore. And Pa took off. He couldn't stand the nightmares. Finally one night when Seth started screaming, Pa slammed out of the house and didn't come back for months."

"While Seth was still so badly hurt?"

"Yep. I still thought he'd die. Those burns were so ugly. If you'd seen them, Audra, you'd know what I got today are nut-hin'." Ethan shuddered to think of it.

"You didn't drive Seth out of his mind, Ethan. You saved him."

"No, I didn't."

Audra slid her hand up into Ethan's hair and stopped to touch the scar no one could see. "You got hit so hard in the head, you're lucky you were awake. Not being able to move like that, it sounds like maybe it hit your backbone, or maybe you got knocked unconscious for a while."

"I wasn't knocked out. I remember everything."

Audra moved out of Ethan's arms, and he wondered if this was it. If she was sickened. If she'd leave and sleep in Julia's room or with the babies.

She took his hand, and tugging at it, she led him over to the bed. He sat down and Audra sat right down on his lap.

"You were a hero that day."

"I was a coward, a cruel coward." He couldn't let her believe what wasn't true. He'd finally spoken the truth and now he demanded that she admit he'd done all the ugly things he was confessing. "And I quit caring about him, about everyone. I've never really cared about anyone again."

"You saved Seth. He was hurt. Rafe was gone. You kept thinking. You were thinking, weren't you? Why didn't Rafe think of just climbing down? Why did he run off to get a rope? You were thinking more clearly than your bossy big brother."

Ethan shrugged. "Once I stopped caring, I got real calm. I could think clearly again."

"You knew you were too badly hurt to climb down there. That's not cowardice; that's good sense. Besides, if you had gone down, you couldn't have carried Seth up, and neither could Rafe. Even if Rafe had found a rope, Seth would've climbed out of there mostly by himself."

"But I didn't have to mock him the way I did. Taunt him, call him names when he was already knocked down so hard."

"You needed Seth to help. You needed to clear his head. You didn't taunt and mock and bully. You goaded him into helping himself when there was no one else to do it. And you didn't drive him crazy because he's not crazy."

Ethan arched a brow at her.

She smiled. "Well, not all the time. And we'll take good care of him and the crazy days will come less and less, you'll see. The war and the laudanum that awful Tracker Breach gave him deserve most of the blame for the way Seth's acting. He's had a hard time of it. Poor guy."

Ethan suddenly didn't want to hear his wife talking with quite so much sympathy about his brother. Not while she was cuddled up to him. He caught her chin and turned her to him and kissed her.

"And you do care about people." She spoke against his lips. "You care until it's almost too much to bear."

"No, I don't. I'm . . . I'm selfish." How could she still want to be close to him?

Audra pulled back, her hands resting on his face. Her light blue eyes shining in the dusk of a Colorado evening. "You care about your brothers. I could see how hard you worked to keep them from being upset tonight."

"That just means I get sick of them always fighting."

"And you're wonderful with the girls. Maggie adores you."

With a sheepish shrug of a shoulder he said, "I'm just takin' care of 'em like a pa had oughta."

"Their father didn't. I know what it feels like to be with a man who doesn't take care of his children or me. And this feels nothing like that."

Audra wrapped her arms around his neck, pulled him tight to her and kissed him. When she came up for air, they were lying down, as close as two people could be.

"Does this feel like you don't care about me, Ethan? Really?"

It was with a sense of wonder that Ethan realized just what she'd forced him to admit with her words and her warrior's grip and her kisses. "I do care about you, Audra. And the girls, and my brothers, and even Julia."

"What do you mean by even Julia?" Audra looked disgruntled.

Ethan smiled; then his smile faded and he ran a knuckle gently down the side of her cheek. "You could have been hurt last night. Audra, I . . ."

Ethan kissed her again to stop himself from saying he loved her. He pulled her to him and did his best to show it.

But to speak of it out loud would force him to admit that if he lost her, it would destroy him.

"It doesn't matter where we settle, Jasper." Trixie leaned her head on his shoulder as they sat in the hard seat of the stage-coach, bouncing along, dropping into every rut in existence. "I wanted to get away from Houston, but we don't have to go clear across the country."

It was so hot that her being draped on him couldn't make it any hotter. Thankfully the sun was finally setting. The stage-coach driver had warned them he was pushing on into the night, aiming to make it into Colorado Territory. Soon they'd be in Rawhide. He'd tell Trixie where he intended to stop once they were closer to town.

Trixie. His wife.

It gave him pause to remember he'd married her. A month ago, he'd have bet all he had—if he was a gambling man, which he wasn't—on being single for the rest of his life.

"That attack in Houston means the word is out."

Which caused Jasper to reconsider whether he gambled or not. He'd always considered gamblers to be fools. Fools who helped him get rich. But every day he did business with the Hardeseys was a gamble. His whole life was a gamble. He'd as good as spent his life digging his own grave, and now he was running from judgment day. A judgment day that was bound to go badly.

Now Jasper saw his future. Evade the Hardeseys and the devil himself. And he needed his money to evade them in any kind of comfort, for he was a man who liked comfort. He had no intention of spending his life raising chickens.

"We rode plenty far before we got on the stage," he said. "The Hardeseys may be powerful in New Orleans and Houston, but they got no reach way out here. We can stop anytime. Buy a place under a different name and live our lives quietly." Jasper would go where he needed to go with or without Trixie, but for now, rather than fight about it, he'd like her to come along willingly. Especially since she was the one with the money. "Wouldn't you like to get out of this heat, Trix?"

"Houston gets mighty hot, no denying it."

"I want to see the snow this winter." Jasper hated the cold. "I'd like to have a season or two where we aren't burning up." When he got his money back, he decided he'd head for California and year-round summer. Trixie could come if she wanted to. "Colorado sounds nice." He did his best to make it sound casual, like he was thinking of it right this minute.

"Colorado Territory?"

Trixie had saved him. She'd killed for him. She'd financed their getaway. And she provided him cover, because the two of them being together—a married couple, Mr. and Mrs. Duff—wouldn't draw the attention of men hunting Jasper Henry.

"Yeah, why not?" he said.

Trixie nodded. "But I don't want Denver. I want a smaller town. Less chance of seeing any old customers for either of us."

That had been what he'd planned to say next. Jasper patted her hand, and their skin nearly stuck together in the heat. Only years of practice kept his lip from curling in distaste.

"Sounds good, Trix. We'll look for a likely place and then see about buying you that house."

CHAPTER
21

The whole family rode out the next day. Rafe in the lead, of course.

Audra had never gone to her cabin this direction before. She'd gone to Rawhide to marry Ethan. They'd ridden from town straight to the Kincaid Ranch and she'd never returned to the cabin she'd shared with Wendell.

This time, to throw off anyone who was watching, they headed for Rawhide on the trail the Kincaids had always taken. It was heavily wooded, a twisting, turning rattlesnake of a trail that went up and down through the rugged land that stood between the Kincaids and town.

Ethan and Seth dropped back and got off the narrow trail to watch for pursuit.

Rafe stayed in the lead. Julia had Maggie on her lap. Audra

had Lily in a little leather pack on her back that Ethan had made. The women rode side by side, talking about the possible hiding places for Wendell's money.

They reached a fast-moving creek, where Rafe pulled up. "This is the same stream that runs behind your cabin. It's a lot wilder by you, but it's still deep. Let me carry Maggie." Rafe reached for Maggie, who screamed and grabbed at Julia.

Rafe looked a little hurt. "She usually lets me hold her."

"We can keep the babies. Just lead the way." Julia patted him on the shoulder. He looked at Audra as if judging whether she'd melt like spun sugar if she got a drop of water on her, then turned and waded his horse into the water.

The crossing was a little deep for Audra's taste. She had to pull her feet up to keep her boots from getting wet, but the horses didn't have to swim.

By the time they reached the other side, Audra heard splashing behind her and turned to see Ethan and Seth fording.

"No sign of trouble." Ethan came up beside Audra. "We separate up here, just around the next bend in the trail. Hand Maggie over, Julia. I can take her now."

Audra smiled at Ethan.

"Are you riding to town with us, Seth?" Julia asked as she slid Maggie off the saddle in front of her. Maggie reached for Ethan with a squeal of pleasure. Audra couldn't help taking a quick glance at Rafe, who was clearly aware that Maggie liked her daddy a lot more than she liked Uncle Rafe.

"Nope, I'm going with Ethan and Audra to the cavern."

Ethan drew in a breath so sharp, Audra worried he'd choke. "We're not going to the cavern." He glared so hard at Seth, Audra worried her husband might leave new scars on his brother.

"Oh, well, that's fine. I'll go with you anyway. I don't like it in town."

Audra looked between Ethan, Rafe, and Julia. None of them wanted to even ask what Seth had against town.

"Good, that's settled." Audra looked at Ethan. "Lead the way. I've got no idea where my cabin is from here."

"You'll ride right through the land Seth claimed," Rafe said. "You'll pass a wall of red rock on your left as you're heading south. That's the border of his property. You can see if any place looks good to build a cabin."

Seth frowned. "I don't want to live alone. I want to live with Audra or Julia."

Ethan rolled his eyes. "We'll talk about it later. Let's go."

They headed south while Rafe and Julia were swallowed up on the wooded trail west to Rawhide.

There was no real path this way, but Ethan followed the base of a mountain, curving around, making decent time. When they reached the red rock, Ethan looked at Audra and she shook her head to silence him. No sense discussing Seth's future home right now.

They were a long time reaching Audra's cabin, and when they finally galloped up to the pathetic shack, Audra felt her stomach lurch. "It's awful. I can't believe we lived in there all that time."

The cabin was so poorly built she could see through the walls. It sagged to the south as if a strong wind—of which the Rockies had many—could blow it over, and was half done doing just that.

"Where could Wendell have hidden money in that tiny cabin?" Audra swung off her horse with Lily fast asleep in one arm. She handed her reins to Ethan and reached for a sleeping Maggie.

"I'll carry her in for you." Ethan moved to keep Maggie out of Audra's reach.

"I can carry both children." Audra's temper simmered, but rather than snap at her husband, she felt calm enough about her capabilities to simply be firm. "Did I or did I not protect them both from an intruder the other night?"

Ethan studied her. The smile that bloomed on his lips was gentle and genuine. "That you did, wife. You can handle anything that comes your way, I reckon." Ethan handed Maggie over.

"Thanks." Audra probably shouldn't thank a man for treating her with respect. She should demand it, and when he gave it, she should take it as her due. But instead she had to fight down the urge to apologize for her crankiness.

"Go on in." Ethan looked at the cabin and shook his head. "Put them down and take a good look around. We've got to check everything carefully, but I agree with you, there're no hiding places in that little shack."

"If the girls are asleep, I won't be able to help you search out here."

Ethan looked around at the vast expanse of woodlands, mostly so rocky there was no place to dig a hole. "We'll save you some places to hunt."

She smiled at him.

Seth came up beside Audra, leading his horse. "I'll help you get the horses stripped of leather, Eth, then we'll start looking around. We'll see if we can find any evidence of digging or markers that look man-made."

"Thanks, both of you." Audra kissed Ethan to show him she was especially thanking him.

Ethan watched her walk into the cabin. He could watch that woman walk for the rest of his life.

A slap on his burned shoulder drew his attention to Seth, who was smiling like a mule eating saw briars.

"Like your wife, huh, big brother?"

Ethan shoved him. "Watch where you're hitting me. I'm injured, remember?" Ethan smiled to think of how gently Audra had tended his burns. "But my woman is taking good care of me."

"A wife to tend your wounds is a wonderful thing." Seth turned to look at the cabin. "I suppose you want to keep yours."

Ethan shoved him again. They both laughed. "Let's get these horses put up."

They walked toward the corral, one of the few clear spots in this wooded, mountainous area.

Seth shook his head. "I wonder how Wendell ever found this cabin."

"Audra said he left them outside of town, a long way outside of town, camping, while he went into Rawhide. She said he didn't come back for a week. When he showed up on Saturday night, he'd bought a cabin."

"This place?" Seth looked back at the ramshackle building with a scowl.

"Yep." Ethan opened the corral gate and let Seth pass through leading his horse. Ethan followed with his and Audra's.

"Well, they're right about him not spending much of his fortune on it, nor on that building in town." Seth took over and swung the gate shut.

"They spent one day, a Sunday, moving out here." Ethan began stripping the leather off the horses while Seth worked alongside him. For a crazy man, Seth was a mighty fine cowboy. "Wendell spent the whole time telling them how dangerous Rawhide would be for women and children and that they had to stay well away."

"So it's a dangerous area, but he leaves two women and two babies out here alone." Seth hung his saddle on the corral fence and went to Audra's horse.

"His way of telling it was that the danger was only in town." Ethan had to hustle to keep up with his little brother.

"Yep, a wild town is always surrounded by a peaceful countryside. Everyone knows that."

"Julia always lived like this. She was used to it. Her father left her alone for the week while he worked in town. And he was such an old grouch she looked forward to him leaving. That's when she got so interested in hunting around in caves and such."

"I never knew Wendell Gilliland, but it doesn't sound like I missed much."

Ethan looked over the back of his horse to see Seth working. They smiled at each other. Then Ethan felt the ache in his shoulder from Seth slapping him, and his smile faded as he thought of Seth's burns.

"I don't know if I've ever told you how sorry I am for the way I treated you when you had that accident, Seth."

Somehow, talking it through with Audra made it possible for Ethan to finally speak of that day.

Seth looked up from tending the horse. "What do you mean, Eth? You're the one who figured out I could climb the edge of that pit. You stayed when Rafe ran off."

"Ran for the rope, you mean."

"Yeah, now I know he was going for the rope, but back then, well, I sort of thought he was just plain running. He sure took off fast."

"He ran and got a torch, brought it back, and told me to talk to you." Ethan thought of how he hadn't been able to move. Was it possible he hadn't been frozen with fear but had instead been hurt so he couldn't move?

"I didn't know much of what went on up where you were. I only remember you talked to me, told me to quit crying and move, climb out of there. Rafe was nowhere around until we'd walked most of the way to the cave exit."

"I was cruel. Rafe just wanted me to keep you calm, to make sure you knew we didn't leave you. But there you were in such terrible pain, and, Seth"—Ethan wasn't sure he should even say these words—"I said things, ugly things. I didn't care about you or how badly you were hurt. I saw you try so hard to get all that pain and fear under control."

"I'd have never done it if you hadn't goaded me. You saved me, Eth." Seth hung the last saddle on the corral fence and draped the bridle over the pommel and turned to watch Ethan do the same.

"No, I can't let you believe that." Their horses began grazing, their teeth tearing grass up with a dull crunch.

"It's the truth." Seth came close, almost like he wanted to help Ethan, when Ethan didn't deserve anything.

"No, you saved yourself. Maybe you climbed out because of what I said."

"That's saving me."

Ethan shook his head, hating this, but for once he felt as if he had the guts to reach out and grab ahold of the truth. He could finally take the blame for all he'd done to hurt Seth. "It was too much for you. You were in such pain and I . . . I pushed you beyond what you could bear."

"No, you didn't, Eth. I did bear it. I made it."

"I saw . . . I felt like I saw you . . . you . . . lose your mind." Ethan looked at Seth, not so sure he should've said that, even if it was true. "It happened right in front of my eyes."

"For that to be right would mean I'm crazy, Eth. I'm not crazy." Seth's wild blue eyes looked into Ethan's. "Am I?"

Crazy eyes, but maybe not as crazy as he'd once been. Maybe his little brother was finding his way back.

"Maybe not. At least not now. But back then, right while it was happening, you went a little crazy."

Silence stretched between them. Finally, Seth said, "I reckon maybe I did. I was so sick from the burns, and I don't remember much for a while except nightmares. And then I felt like that cavern was calling to me. Begging me to come and be inside it, be part of it. I hunted until I was so at home in that cavern that I loved it below ground almost more than above." Seth's eyes seemed to tame down a bit. "I reckon that does sound a little crazy."

"But not anymore, right?" Ethan could only hope and pray because his little brother had always had a wild streak in him. But wild wasn't crazy, and maybe now Seth had found himself again.

"Nope, not anymore." Seth smiled and turned to get the corral gate and let them out. "I still do dearly love that cavern, though."

Seth swung the gate shut, and the two of them walked toward the cabin, with no idea where to begin searching. They threaded through a stand of trees that ran along a steep ledge.

Seth looked at Ethan. "Maybe I love that cavern too much. But so does Julia, so I guess I'm not any crazier than her."

Ethan exchanged a long look with Seth; then both of them laughed. It felt good. Then he thought of Audra and looked at the cabin as it came into view. "Let's go ask Audra if she knows where to look."

A grunt from Seth turned Ethan back just in time to see his brother falling sideways right toward the steep ledge.

"No! Seth!" Ethan took one step to grab Seth. Something moved behind him and he grabbed for his gun as he whirled.

A blow slammed into his head and sent him falling forward after his brother.

Audra stepped into the cabin to find . . . nothing.

Searching was a waste of time. The cabin was empty. There was a wooden floor made of split logs rather than floorboards, so there was no space beneath them. Log walls weren't tight enough to stuff something in a crack. He'd never been in here alone that Audra could think of—unless he'd come out here when he bought it. Maybe?

With a sigh she looked in both tiny bedrooms. Nothing. She put the girls down to sleep and went back out into the main room determined to look harder, closer. She wasn't just going to assume there was nothing.

The fireplace was open and the stones were a single layer. She'd checked the stones to see if one of them would move and reveal a space crammed with gold.

She took one step toward the fireplace when a man stepped through the door. His gun cracked as he cocked it and aimed it at her heart.

She recognized him from the ranch. Worse yet, by his build, she was sure she recognized him from her cellar.

"Howdy, Mrs. Gill." The man was bone-skinny.

"It's Mrs. Kincaid, Grove." A voice from behind the man caused him to step to the side. "Try and remember that."

"Both your first and second husbands are beyond helping you." The skinny man stepped too close to her in the tight cabin. The other man came through the door dragging Ethan, blood flowing from a cut on his head.

"No, Ethan!" She took a step toward her husband. The skinny man wrapped an arm around her waist and pulled her hard against him, the gun showing as he held it where she couldn't fail to see.

"My name's Mitch, and you're Mrs. Kincaid now. Grove got that wrong the night of the fire, and I knew that gave us away enough that we'd have to move fast." This man looked far more civilized than the skinny man, except for his eyes. They held the threat of death, more chilling because he did everything politely and with a hint of a smile.

"The fire gave us away, Mitch."

Mitch had Ethan under his arms and came on inside, still dragging him. For one crazy second she considered attacking. Grabbing for the gun he held close to her face. That would be the brave thing to do. If she could get his gun and . . .

"Don't even think of it, Mrs. Kincaid. You wouldn't have a chance against me, not even if I was alone. And Grove"—Mitch jerked his head in the direction of the man who had her in his clutches—"he has a particular taste for hurting women. I'd hate for him to get upset with you."

Mitch got Ethan all the way inside, then dropped him so carelessly his head hit the hard floor with an ugly thud. Ethan didn't show one sign of reacting to the pain.

Mitch drew his gun with such smooth precision that Audra knew he'd done it before, plenty.

She wanted to ask what they'd done to Seth, but maybe they hadn't found him. Maybe Seth was out there, poised to attack.

She expected Mitch to start shooting and said a prayer for the safety of her babies and Ethan, for all of them. But instead of aiming at her, he aimed the gun straight at Ethan's bleeding head.

"The money, Mrs. Kincaid. Where is it?"

She wanted to be brave. She was desperate to fight these men and win. She needed to do it for her children and her husband and her crazy brother-in-law.

But what was brave, really? She had no chance in a fight. That gun was steady on Ethan.

Fighting was brave, absolutely, but Jesus's true courage came not from fighting but from sacrifice. From giving His life. Audra felt her heart lift. For the first time ever she felt true courage. No, she couldn't overpower two evil men. But she could lead them away. Give Ethan a chance. Maybe even find the money and send these men on their way. Audra had listened long enough that she knew exactly where she'd look.

She sent a prayer heavenward and carried it in her heart as an idea came to her that she knew came straight from God.

"He hid it in the cavern." She remembered how Julia had twice saved herself by using the darkness and silence. In that cavern, Audra had a chance and she was brave enough to take it.

"What?"

The look on Mitch's face told her he knew nothing about the cavern at all. Had never heard of it.

Which gave her an even greater advantage. Thinking fast, she considered all she'd heard about that dark pit.

"My husband hid it there. We were heading for the cavern right now. But we have to ford the stream behind this cabin, on foot, which is why Ethan was putting the horses up. I was going to show it to him for the first time. I'm the only one Wendell confided in when he was dying, so you need my help." She hoped that sounded like she was pleading for her own life, when she was, in fact, thinking of these men trying to force information out of Ethan.

Where is Seth?

"My husband—that is, my first husband, Wendell—told me where he hid it. I'll take you there. Give you the . . ." Audra hesitated. Gold? Paper money? What? She didn't know, but maybe these men didn't, either. Or maybe they didn't expect her to know. "I'll give you everything Wendell stole, and you can take it and leave. We were coming here today to get it, planning to return it to the man my husband stole it from. We knew the fire and the shooting yesterday had to be about that . . . m-money."

She braced herself for them to accuse her of lying if it was gold. There were no accusations. Audra added, "We've had nothing but trouble since Wendell stole that money. I only want to get it back to the man he stole it from and be allowed to live in peace."

Mitch looked down at Ethan for a long moment. Mitch could kill him and turn his threats to the children. For their sake, even if her precious husband was killed at their hands, Audra would still be forced to help these villains find that blasted money.

With a sudden crack of metal on metal, Mitch released the hammer on his revolver and aimed it at the ceiling. "Let's go then. If you're lying to me, we can always come back. You've got a lot to lose, Mrs. Kincaid. Far more than we do."

Mitch looked at Grove. "Tie him up. Tight. We want to have someone around to put pressure on the little lady." Mitch grabbed Audra's arm and dragged her away from Grove. "I'll keep an eye on her until you're done."

Audra looked out the door and couldn't see Seth anywhere. "If you're looking for the other Kincaid brother, he's dead." Audra gasped. "No, he didn't know anything."

"We didn't need two men to threaten you with. So we made it easy on ourselves." Mitch laughed and used his gun to point to a ledge near the horse corral. "We knocked him cold and threw him over that cliff."

Tears burned her eyes as she thought of that awful ledge. Steep, but not a sheer drop. Could Seth have survived it? He'd been through so much. He'd finally gotten home and had a chance at a peaceful life. And now these men said he was dead. She prayed as she waited for Grove, thinking of Ethan in there, defenseless with that evil man. Her prayers continued even as Grove came back out.

She thought of her babies, sleeping. They were defenseless with Ethan tied up and their mother gone. She had to fight down the urge to start screaming. But she dare not mention the children. Wiping the tears away as they rolled down her face, she knew that prayer was the only thing that was going to give her the courage she needed.

"Take us to the money." Mitch looked at the cabin with a cruel smile, as if he wanted an excuse to hurt Ethan some more. "Right now."

"Yes. You have no need to hurt my husband or anyone else. I'll take you to where Wendell hid it in the cavern right now." Audra crushed down the sobs that wanted to escape and prayed for calm, for her mind to work. She remembered Ethan's story about Seth and the fire. Audra had told Ethan that he'd kept his head. He'd been thinking even in the midst of terror. She had to do that. She had to use her head.

It came to her like a whisper from deep inside.

"Fear thou not; for I am with thee: be not dismayed . . ."

Dismay wasn't a sliver of what she was feeling. Fear not. She clung to that.

Then she remembered the rest.

". . . for I am thy God: I will strengthen thee; yea, I will help thee; yea, I will uphold thee with the right hand of my righteousness."

Peace washed over her as she accepted that there was no way she could defeat two strong well-armed men. Not alone.

But with God upholding her, she had a chance.

She squared her shoulders and looked Mitch in the eye. "Let's go."

She led them around the cabin and up the hill. She'd never been this way, but she'd heard about it. She'd seen Julia coming home after that awful night when she'd gotten trapped in the cavern, when Rafe had saved her and brought her home.

Audra had listened to all the stories and it was exactly as they'd said. She climbed down the steep gorge to the rushing stream, then picked her way across on the protruding stones. Facing a sheer rock wall, she knew Julia had climbed it regularly. So it could be done. Audra began as if she knew what she was doing, reaching up for the most obvious handhold. They were there. It all worked. She soon climbed to a less treacherous level.

At the top of the gorge, she saw the hole. The only time she'd been in the cavern was the day Seth had taken Maggie in. She'd gone in through the simpler entrance in Rafe and Julia's mountain valley.

Pointing to a heavy boulder that was right where she expected, she said, "We need to move that. The ladder is under it."

She thought of Ethan's story, of how they'd explored down in this cavern, climbing in and out using a ladder. And Julia had gotten out the time she'd been stranded by Breach, when Rafe had lowered the ladder and found her.

Mitch and Grove threw their backs into moving the rock. When the ladder was there, in a small depression, Audra heaved a silent sigh of relief.

These men still believed she knew what she was doing. They lowered the ladder with its dull clinking metallic rungs.

"I'll go down first," Mitch said. "We want someone ahead of her and behind her at all times."

Audra knew it was as dark as pitch down there. If one of them had matches, they'd use the torches and her chance of escape would be much lower. But with light or without it, she'd find a way. God would strengthen her. She prayed and the prayers gave her the strength to remain calm. To keep thinking.

When Mitch dropped out of sight, Audra didn't look at Grove. Mitch's words about Grove liking to hurt people were clamoring in her head. She moved to the ladder, but Grove caught her arm before she could begin her descent.

"You're a pretty little lady." Grove's eyes crawled over her. "You might need some protection before we're done here. I can make you real comfortable if you stay with me."

Audra jerked on her arm, but Grove hung on. She met his eyes defiantly.

"You're brave enough right now, but later, when there's trouble, you come to me and let me take care of you. You'll have to pay a price for that, but you'll pay it if you want to live."

Though her stomach lurched until she was afraid she might be sick, she held his gaze. He had to feel her shaking, yet she

285

wouldn't assure her survival by submitting to any demand he made in exchange for safety.

"Your turn." He dropped her arm with a smug smile.

Rushing to the ladder, she began her downward climb and felt as if she was leaving the world behind. She fumbled for solid footing as she descended. The cavern was dimly lit from the sun shining down in the hole, but it was murky and she knew from listening to the Kincaids and Julia that as soon as they left this first cavern, they'd be plunged into complete darkness.

Before she'd gotten down, Mitch said from below her, "The ladder isn't long enough. There's a long way down from the ledge."

Thinking frantically of what she'd been told, she said, "We climb down rocks the rest of the way. We don't need the ladder. Move to the right and you'll find where the ledge has good handholds and footholds."

"It's too dark to see anything down here."

Audra kept her mouth shut about the torches, hoping Mitch and Grove would let her lead them in the dark. But if they were going to give up, she'd admit they were there rather than go back to the surface where Ethan and her children were so vulnerable.

She heard the scratch of Mitch moving below her and felt the jiggle of the ladder as Grove began his descent. She reached the ledge and followed after Mitch. His movements were enough of a guide that, with the light reaching down from above, she found her way.

Before her feet hit solid ground, she heard a small scratch from behind her and a flare of light told her Mitch had matches with him.

"Hey, good. Torches." A flickering light grew as Audra turned to face Mitch.

Losing these men in the dark had just become a lot more difficult.

Looking frantically around, Audra saw what had to be the cavern tunnel the Kincaids had always taken. And as she looked she saw a line drawn with charcoal. It wasn't terribly noticeable, but Julia had told her about marking her trail carefully.

"The treasure is this way." She started forward just as Mitch found another torch, lit it, and handed it to Grove. Audra realized how completely in their power she was. Alone down here. She prayed that their quest for the money would keep them from hurting her. Until they found out there wasn't any.

Within a few seconds, Mitch caught her by the arm and said, "Don't even think of leaving us behind in here. The minute we lose you, we turn around and go right back to where we left your husband and finish what we started."

And that destroyed her last chance. Unless maybe, just maybe, an idea came to her. She couldn't win in a battle of strength, but she could outsmart them.

She could get these two into some tight spot they couldn't get out of. And her inspiration told her exactly what that tight spot might be.

Seth struck the ledge, rolled, and slammed into a rock. His leg twisted as it caught in a crevasse. He hung by his leg for sickening seconds, then he fell again. He stopped, dazed, rolled onto his back, and almost fell off a cliff. Throwing himself back, he realized his head hung over the edge of a stone outcropping.

Ethan! He reached to pull himself up and his leg caught fire. He glanced down, expecting to see the flames.

Flames. War. Death.

Shaking his head, Seth fought off memories exploding in his head. Cannon fire. Men blown apart. Screaming men on fire.

Seth forced himself to focus on his leg. Stare at it. There was no fire.

"I'm hurt. It's broken or sprained." Then he shut up before he could give away the fact that he was down here. Whoever hit him might stick around to make sure he was dead.

Think! C'mon.

A tiny flex of his foot shot fiery pain up all the way to his brain.

I can't use my leg. So I'll use what I have.

With gritted teeth, Seth pulled himself up to stand on his good leg. Using his hands to drag himself upright, he felt like a wolverine was gnawing its way out of his chest. He'd had cracked ribs before and he had them again, or worse. His vision blurred as he pressed against the rugged stone to keep from falling the rest of the way off the mountain. As the world went black he felt again the voices in his head. The explosions and death and fire.

Wiping his wrist across his eyes to clear them, he saw blood on his shirt sleeve and dabbed at the cut on his forehead. Forcing back the visions of war, his world stopped spinning.

Ethan needs me.

He looked up. It was probably twenty or thirty feet to the top of the cliff.

I have to help Ethan and Audra and the babies.

It was more than Seth thought he could do with his leg beating at him, his head throbbing and his chest burning.

But a man didn't grow up on the frontier without learning hard lessons. While there was breath in his lungs he'd do what needed doing. He reached up, tested his grip, and pulled his good leg up to the first toehold. Breathing hard, he smelled smoke and saw a plantation house burning. There were voices in the fire, calling to him.

He rested his forehead on the rocky cliff, and the scratch of stone drew him back from waking nightmares.

Ethan!

He had to get to Ethan. He found that the pain reminded him of what was real. He'd survived the war by living one minute at a time. Sometimes one heartbeat at a time. And he'd do it the same now.

Inch by inch, ignoring how far he had to climb, ignoring the terror that he'd find his brother dead, ignoring the pain, he clawed his way up.

At last he gained the top of the ledge.

Peeking over he saw Audra shoved along in front of two men. It was the new hired men from Ethan's ranch. They'd tried to get Audra before. This time they'd succeeded.

"Take us to the money, right now." One of them, a skeleton of a man, had a tight grip on her arm.

Seth went for his gun and nearly fell. He had to grab the edge of the cliff with both hands. Then, before he could change his grip and try again, the men and Audra were gone behind the cabin.

Audra's sweet voice rang out. "You have no need to hurt my husband or anyone else. I'll take you to the cavern. I'll show you where Wendell hid the money, and I'll give it to you right now."

Seth had no one to shoot at.

With his teeth gritted to keep from crying out in pain, Seth rolled onto the ground above the ledge and began to crawl. His leg made walking impossible, but it was just as well not to with his head aching and his belly threatening to cast up its last meal.

Scraping along on the ground, he finally made it into the cabin to find Ethan, unconscious.

"Ethan!" Seth crawled to Ethan's side and saw his chest rise and fall. He was alive!

"Ethan. Ethan, wake up!"

"Ethan, wake up. You've got to help Audra."

Ethan's eyes flickered open to see Seth leaning over him, shaking his shoulders. Seth's face scraped raw. His skin as pale as milk. His mouth tight as if he was in agony.

"Audra? What? She needs help?" Ethan didn't remember anything except that he'd been walking along that ledge.

He felt the sticky warmth on his head and tried to reach to the source of the pain.

He couldn't move.

Seth was busy with his knife, and he had ropes slashed and Ethan's hands free about the same time the full force of the pain hit. He touched his face, ashamed of how his hand shook, and drew away bloody fingers.

"What happened?" He forced his mind to clear, forced himself to move past the wicked, throbbing pain in his skull.

"I saw them take her." Seth slid an arm behind Ethan's shoulder and helped him sit up.

The world spun around, but Ethan fought off the dizziness.

"The men that attacked our ranch?"

"Yes, it's those two newest hired men. I climbed to the top of that ledge just when they were dragging her out of the cabin."

"Let's go." Ethan staggered as he got to his feet and headed for the door.

"Ethan!" Seth's sharp call turned Ethan back, even though everything in him was driving him forward. Seth was still sitting on the floor.

"What are you waiting for?" Then Ethan really looked at his brother. Still on the floor. His face drawn in lines of suffering.

"I can't walk, Eth. I think I've got a broken leg. Maybe some ribs, too. They hit me and I fell off the ledge by the corral."

He remembered. Ethan had seen Seth going over.

"I . . . I have to go after Audra." But could he leave Seth? He had to.

"I heard them. I know where they're going."

"Where?"

"They went into the cavern."

Ethan staggered back and almost fell. Hitting the cabin wall was the only thing that held him up. "No."

Seth's eyes said it all. He knew exactly how Ethan felt.

A black hole yawned at Ethan's feet. Worse than feeling it, Ethan knew he had to jump into it. He had to go after Audra. He had to go down into that cavern.

He forced the words past his lips. "Did they go across the creek into that entrance?"

"Yes. I heard Audra begging for your life, Eth. I'd just about dragged myself up that ledge. If I'd've been faster, I might have been able to get my gun into action."

"You did fine, Seth. You found me and got me untied so I can go." Ethan's head throbbed with equal parts fear and pain. He stood straight, squared his shoulders. He did it all for show, to behave as a man ought to. But he hated that cavern. He felt as if he were walking straight for his own death, Audra's too.

"I'll use the torches down there. I've got matches." Ethan

had one clearheaded moment to look again at Seth. Lines cut deeply into his face from the pain. "How long was I out?"

"They haven't been gone long. I crawled here as fast as I could."

"I should help you."

"Go. I'm inside. I'll keep the girls safe. They may not be happy, but they won't be left alone."

"The girls." Ethan had forgotten his daughters. He had to pull himself together and start thinking. "They're sleeping."

"I know."

Ethan jerked on his pistol and quickly checked the load. He reached in his pocket and produced a small tin of matches. "I'll be back as soon as I can."

"I'll say a prayer for you, Eth."

That was the sanest thing his little brother had ever said. "I'd appreciate it."

He turned and ran out of the cabin. He was across the creek in minutes and saw the ladder hanging over the edge of the cavern entrance. Ethan dropped to his knees by the opening and looked down, listened for any sound.

Nothing.

He turned and forced himself down the ladder. Ethan felt the blackness press on him as if he were in the belly of a beast. Each step down the ladder was a horror.

When he reached the ledge it was there, just as he remembered. He only had to think of Audra to control the fear, or at least endure sliding down the throat of Satan, and being swallowed up by hell.

CHAPTER
22

"Turn here," Audra said.

Mitch, in the lead, looked back at Audra, who was pointing for him to go down the tunnel on the right.

Mitch was ahead of her, Grove behind. Both carried a torch, which they'd found at the bottom of the ladder they'd climbed down. Mitch kept his lifted above his head, the tunnel was high enough to allow it. If she'd had any hope of slipping away in the dark, those hopes were dashed by the torches. She had to douse them somehow.

She was sure this tunnel led to the place Seth had fallen so many years ago. If she hadn't been sure, based on the directions she'd been given, she would still know by Julia's charcoal arrows and the dramatic X above the arrow. A warning of danger.

They were black lines on dark gray stone in dim light. She

didn't think her captors had noticed them. But so what if they did? Someone had marked the walls? Audra would simply claim Wendell had done it, and she knew that it marked their way.

She kept up a good pace, which kept Mitch moving in front of her. All she could think was that she needed to get them as far from Ethan as she could. She hoped her assured step led these men to believe she was going in a direction she'd learned well, aiming straight for the treasure.

Planning each step, she wondered where that hole was ahead and what it would take to best two ruthless men. Fear shook her hard, but she fought against it. She kept going. And she braced herself to do what she could, knowing she was upheld by God's righteous right hand.

The image of Audra in the hands of his two hired men, maybe suffering a terrible fate, kept Ethan moving. He found a torch on the wall, then hesitated before he struck the match to light it. There had always been torches down here closer to the entrance. They could have been taken out years ago for all he knew, but if the two men with Audra had light, then they'd be easy to find.

God, give me the strength to face my fear of this dark place.

With the lit torch in hand, he went on. He knew this section of the cavern well. Despite never coming back, it had haunted his dreams for years.

He walked straight for the tunnel he and his brothers had always taken. He walked as quietly as possible, listening for any sound.

He reached the opening that led to the pit Seth had fallen

into, and paused. Audra knew little about this cavern. The men who had her most likely knew less than she did. They'd talked about this place, though, with Audra listening in. They'd talked more about this tunnel than any other. If she was pretending to lead them somewhere, she'd go this way. Sick about returning to where his brother had almost died, Ethan turned and started forward. Each step was harder to take. He felt the darkness thicken until it was a solid wall that his meager torch couldn't penetrate.

Trying to listen for Audra ahead, instead he heard a child screaming, the ground cracking, the fire roaring like a beast.

Hanging by his belt for long soul-shredding seconds. He forced himself to take a step and he stopped, terrified the ground would break off, become a mouth full of jagged teeth, biting at him, devouring his whole family, devouring his soul.

Numb with the effort to go on, he dropped his torch just as he'd dropped the lantern.

Flames shot up like a lake of fire that burned but never consumed.

Seth, on fire. The screams.

The slam to the back of his head.

Ethan had to not care. He had to find a way to shut off the fear.

The only way that worked was to not feel anything too deeply. Not care. Not love. But he couldn't separate himself from his heart. Not with Audra. Terror had him in its jaws and seemed to be shaking him to death, like a cat shook a rat. The fear drove him to his knees.

Ethan couldn't move. He knelt there, too much of a coward to throw off the fear and save his wife, the woman he loved. He reached out for God, for miraculous strength, but he only heard the echo of his own fears and the laughter of Satan. His head lowered to the cavern floor as if evil were a hand pressing him down.

The cavern was too strong.

No.

Ethan knew the truth. He was too weak.

The cavern had won.

Audra saw another heavily drawn X on the tunnel wall. A warning.

She moved closer to Mitch and felt Grove close the space behind her. She pictured what she'd do. She needed darkness and speed. The torch would be her first goal. Strength sufficient to the task. She asked for it, begged for it, and prepared to fight as if God himself were fighting through her.

She was watching the tunnel floor intently and saw what she knew had to be that hole. It was only a darker shadow in a tunnel filled with shadows. Only knowing it was there warned her. She launched herself at Mitch, slammed him forward, clawed at the torch, and jerked it from his hand. Mitch screamed as he fell. Audra whirled and hit Grove in the face with the fire. He staggered back, shouted furiously while raising his gun.

She brought the torch down hard on his gun hand with a loud scream. He dropped the weapon and clawed at his face, his hair on fire.

She stomped on his torch when it hit the ground, to extinguish it.

"You can't get away from me!" Grove's rage was murderous. Audra took one second to jam the torch she held into the tunnel wall, and as Grove slapped out the flames on his own body, all light was gone. Then, again aware of what she'd been told about this place, she rushed to the left side of the tunnel and ran out on the ledge Julia and Rafe had told her was there. Running in the pitch-dark.

A gun roared behind her, but with no light, Grove couldn't aim. She moved more carefully, quietly, to give him nothing to aim at. The bullet whizzed past her in the dark. It caromed off the tunnel wall with a high whine. Praying with every step, Audra knew Grove could get a lucky shot. She kept on moving until she thought she was past the gaping hole in the collapsed floor and then stopped. Now silence was the weapon she'd use. She crouched down and felt along the floor to be sure she was past the pit and on solid ground. Now to go forward, find the entrance into Rafe's valley, and run for home. It was a long way, but she was healthy and strong, with God on her side. She could do it.

"I'll find you, woman!" Grove roared. "You're not going to get away from me."

Then she heard footsteps coming fast.

The scream brought Ethan to his feet. He was running before he made a conscious thought to do it. He'd left his torch behind without realizing it. Even after he thought of it, he still didn't hesitate. Where he'd had nothing but the blackest of terrors before, now it was as if God had wiped it all away. He remembered his mother saying, "God's strength is made perfect in weakness."

That had never made sense before. But right now, God certainly had His chance for perfection in Ethan Kincaid. His mind cleared further and he realized exactly where he was. He had relived this awful place so many times that even in the pitch-dark, he knew how far he had to run to reach that hole. And the scream was such a powerful reminder of Seth that he knew the noise was coming from that exact place.

As he neared it he moved all the way to the left, remembering what Rafe and Seth had talked about, how there was a way across. He found it. The darkness wasn't even touching him now. As he crossed he heard running steps ahead of him and then an awful, ugly grunt, followed by a scream.

For one heartbreaking moment he thought he was too late. Then he heard screaming. A man screaming, only a few feet ahead. Screaming and falling.

There was a dull thud from about twenty feet below. The scream cut off and there was only silence. Ethan hurried forward.

"And don't you ever touch me again!" Audra's voice echoed in the darkness.

"Audra, honey, it's me! Ethan." He decided he'd better warn her if she was busy shoving men into the hole.

"Ethan? Ethan, you're all right! You came."

Ethan stepped across the slender ledge. "Seth said there were two men. Where's the other one?" He still couldn't see her, but she was talking and he followed her voice.

"There were two. Both of them fell."

"Two men? You won a fight against two men?"

"Of course. I had to save you and my children. Did you say Seth talked to you? They said they'd killed him."

"He found me and untied me. But we've got to get back. He has a broken leg. I left him with the girls, and he can keep them safe, but he's in a lot of pain. He needs help." Finally, Ethan found her, reaching, going by feel, following her voice in the echoing tunnel.

"I'm so glad you're both all right," she said.

Ethan pulled her into his arms. The most courageous woman he'd ever known. "You're not hurt, either? You were able to throw two men into that hole in the ground? What a woman!"

"Well, they hurt you and th-that made me really, really mad." Then she threw her arms around his neck and broke down in tears.

CHAPTER
23

Audra had trouble doing anything but clinging to Ethan for what seemed like far too long. Finally her tears subsided. "We've got to get back," she said.

Ethan turned, caught her hand, and took two steps toward the ledge just as the sharp crack of a gun being cocked sounded in the cavern. He pulled Audra to the floor as the gun roared. Bullets ricocheted around them. Ethan covered Audra with his body and whispered, "Shh . . . he's firing blind."

The gunfire went on and on. From this angle, Ethan could tell that Mitch had somehow climbed out of the pit. The bullets shattered rocks, which pelted Ethan's back, but none of the bullets came close, at least not that he could tell. Ethan heard the click of a trigger on an empty gun.

"I'm going to get you, woman!" Mitch shouted. "No one attacks me and lives."

Ethan judged where Mitch stood and launched himself in that direction. He landed hard on Mitch and brought him to the cavern floor. He heard the gun clatter across rock.

In utter darkness, Ethan grappled with a madman, crazy with rage. Mitch slammed a fist into Ethan's shoulder. The blow was so hard it would have knocked Ethan cold if it had landed on his chin. Ethan swung a fist and Mitch grunted. They rolled on the ground. Ethan could feel the pit only inches away.

Mitch knocked Ethan sideways. Ethan clung to whatever he could grab, dragging Mitch down, slugging at him, taking blows. Hanging on to keep the man away from Audra.

Mitch's hands found Ethan's neck and began to squeeze the life out of him. Ethan pounded blow after blow to Mitch's face, but nothing broke that crushing hold. Ethan grabbed Mitch's arms, desperate to take the pressure off his neck.

Then a sickening thud sounded. Mitch arched upward, releasing Ethan's throat. Another thud sent Mitch tumbling sideways.

When no renewed attack came, Ethan fumbled in his pocket for his tin of matches. He was desperate to see what had happened.

"Are you all right, Ethan?" Audra was there, on her knees, running her hands up his arm, finding him by touch. "Ethan, speak to me. Ethan!"

"Yes . . ." His throat nearly failed him, so Ethan coughed and tried again. "I'm okay. Audra, you . . . you saved me."

With a sudden laugh she did a fair job of launching herself into his arms. "I did, didn't I?" She laughed and he hugged her tight.

A groan from right near them had Ethan setting his dangerous little wife aside to again get his matches. He struck one just as Mitch reared up from the floor. The light stopped him, but then he looked around and dove for his gun, which lay on the edge of the pit. As Mitch bent down for the gun, Audra, sitting on the floor beside Ethan, spun and kicked out, landing a solid foot on Mitch's backside. He went tumbling through the broken-off floor. Roaring as he fell, he clawed at the gun and took it over the edge with him. Ethan heard Mitch land, along with the metallic clatter of the gun.

"I'll get you!"

The revolver clicked on an empty chamber. Ethan heard the crack of the revolver being opened and pictured Mitch's loaded gun belt. Grove had one, too. He heard the slide of a bullet being loaded. They had only seconds before he reloaded his gun and began firing.

Ethan jumped to his feet, grabbed Audra, and together they moved up the slope leading to Rafe's valley. He was amazed at how unafraid he was of the dark tunnel.

They heard another shout from Mitch and the sound of him falling again. His luck at climbing out in the dark so swiftly the first time hadn't held the second.

Mitch was still roaring from the depths.

Ethan tightened his hand on Audra's. "I figured something out here today, Audie, honey."

"Stop calling me that awful name." She didn't sound that upset. "What did you figure out?"

"I've spent years being afraid of things that only lived in my imagination. I'd turned a bunch of dark tunnels into something evil, like the tunnel was alive and intended to harm me. Facing down bad men in this tunnel helped me to realize I've wasted a lot of time worrying over something that doesn't exist when there are plenty of real things to worry over."

"And you think that's a good thing?" She sounded doubtful.

"Don't know if it's good. I only know it's true. And I'm not so scared of this stupid cavern anymore."

Ethan paused, and in the darkness he listened to Mitch shouting out threats. "Do you think he'll be able to find his way out of there?"

Audra was silent as they listened to the ugliness. It seemed to still be from the depths, as if Mitch couldn't find his way out of the pit a second time. "I wouldn't underestimate the man."

"I hate the idea of leaving anyone in here. It was my own personal nightmare for too much of my life."

The gunfire started again. Six shots.

"They have a lot of bullets between them," Audra said. "I'm not going back for him."

"Let's leave him to calm down for a few hours," Ethan said.

They would come up in Rafe's valley. Grab horses there and ride for the cabin. They'd make sure Seth and the girls were all right, then with some backup he'd come back for Mitch and Grove.

Plenty of backup.

Again Mitch's gun clicked on an empty chamber. Ethan caught Audra close and held her. "We'll wait until he starts shooting again. We don't want him to get his bearings at all. I'm hoping in the dark he won't know what direction to take."

Guilt gnawed at Ethan to abandon these men. He knew how the place could drive a man mad.

Mitch began spewing such profane evil it hardened Ethan's heart. As Mitch's voice rose and bounced off the wall, Ethan decided they could move again, but quietly. They'd gone about twenty paces when the gun began firing, with Mitch working his way through his ammunition supply. If he knew Grove was down there, Mitch could empty his belt of bullets, too.

Ethan and Audra traveled at a near run until even the sound of gunfire faded away—or maybe stopped. Ethan wasn't sure. They hurried up a steep tunnel, still in the pitch-dark but with only one possible direction to go. There were smaller tunnels off this main one, the place Maggie had nearly fallen. The side tunnel where Seth had come out. But Ethan couldn't stumble into such small places by accident. He hoped.

They ran into a stone wall. It then occurred to Ethan that he still had matches and could have lit them once they were out of Mitch's sight. But now there was no need. He'd been in this part of the tunnel. It led straight out to Rafe's caldera. It didn't have branches off it to get a man lost. Or holes in the floor to let a man fall to his death.

"I know where we are." Ethan pulled Audra to the right, and within a few steps they saw a dim glow that grew and grew. They rounded a curve and saw a circle of sunshine. Ethan emerged into the light and turned to Audra to make sure she was unhurt.

"I can't believe you outsmarted them, Audra." He grabbed her around the waist and hugged until her toes left the ground.

"And you got there in time to save me from Mitch." Her arms went around his neck so tightly that Ethan probably should've been afraid of being strangled again. But he couldn't work up one speck of fear.

She laughed, her face buried against his neck. "We've got to go," she said. As Audra pulled back from him, her smile faded. "You're bleeding." Her face turned into a scowl. "I'm going with you when you go back in there. And I'm going to teach those men a lesson they'll—"

Ethan kissed his bloodthirsty little wife. "I'd forgotten I even got a conk on the head until now. I'm fine. The blood will wash off. Now let's go—we need to get back to Seth and the girls."

They ran for the horses.

As they rode hard toward Audra's cabin, she explained just what the men had done, and Ethan told her about Seth's broken leg.

"We've got to get to that tunnel opening and get the ladder pulled up before Mitch and Grove get out," Ethan said. "They probably don't know there's another way out. But maybe they're turned around in the dark enough they can't find anything."

Audra nodded. "Mitch had matches. I threw the torch he was carrying. But he could find it, or light his way with the matches until he finds another one."

They urged the horses faster.

Soon they rode up to the cabin, and Ethan heard Lily crying to beat all.

Audra jumped off her horse. Ethan caught its reins and said, "I'll corral the horses, then go draw up that ladder and come back to help you. We'll need to bind up Seth's leg and get him home somehow."

"Rafe and Julia were going to meet us where the trail split toward Rawhide. If we don't show up, they'll come to meet us."

Ethan glanced at the sky. "That's right. It's well past noon. They'll've had time to search in town and be headed home. They could come riding up here any minute, unless something delayed them."

Audra rushed for the house as Ethan made short work of

crossing the gorge and getting the ladder up and out of reach. He saw no footprints that indicated the men had beaten him to the ladder.

Now they were trapped.

In the dark.

Would they go mad? Maybe. That place had done so much damage to the Kincaid boys, though back then they were more children than men. Two tough brutish outlaws might stay calm. Find a torch. Remember their way. And if not, maybe they could handle the dark.

Whatever happened, they wouldn't be coming out this way.

Ethan rushed back to the cabin and found Audra shut in the back bedroom.

"She's feeding Lily." Seth looked up from where he sat on the floor. Very still, with Maggie straddling his leg.

Ethan flinched when Maggie twisted around to grin up at her uncle. "Let me get her."

"It's not so bad. She's not bouncing on the broken leg." Seth leaned down so Maggie had to look at him. "Hey, look who's here."

He lifted her and turned her to face Ethan. Maggie squealed and her little legs churned in midair as if she were running to him.

"I think she likes you, Eth." Seth set her down, and Maggie toddled to Ethan so fast that she fell over. Ethan snagged her before she hit the floor. He hoisted her and she gabbled at him.

Ethan was pretty sure she called him Papa. He rested her on one hip. "How's the leg?"

"Broken for sure. But I'm getting by." Seth sounded pretty good, but his face had a grayish tinge that told the truth about how much pain he was in.

"Audra." Ethan raised his voice a bit, yet he didn't have to yell; the walls were thin.

"What, Ethan?"

"I'm taking Maggie with me to find a couple of boards or something to use to splint Seth's leg. We're not going to get any more treasure hunting done for now."

"Did you get the ladder pulled up? Are you sure those awful men didn't get there first and climb out?"

"I've left them down there for a fact, honey. They could get out into Rafe's valley if they figure out how to find that exit. But even if they do get out, we'll know who to be watching for now. We'll get them."

Ethan started to leave when he noticed a pile of something that looked like trash or maybe a rat's nest behind the small pile of kindling by the unlit fireplace.

With a frown he went and shoved the logs aside, wishing he'd find treasure. Instead he found . . . "Audra, why do you have cigars?"

Audra laughed. "They aren't mine. Wendell was a cigar smoker. You must've found the last of his cigar stash. After he died, I started throwing them on the fire. They burn pretty well, though they stink."

Ethan looked at the cigars, mostly crushed and dried out. He extended the pile of rubbish toward Seth. "Want a cigar, little brother?"

Seth grimaced. "Of all the crazy stuff I've done, I've never picked up the habit of tobacco. I don't think I'll be starting on a cigar as ugly as those."

Audra came out of the bedroom with Lily against her shoulder, gently patting the little one's back.

308

Ethan recapped the adventure with Audra while he bound up Seth's leg.

"How'd you like being down in that cavern again, Eth?" Seth asked as he went about ripping up his shirt to help tie the splint in place.

"I managed." Ethan really thought about it for the first time. Up until now he'd just gone forward, doing what he had to do. "God's strength is made perfect in weakness." He turned to Audra and smiled.

She smiled back.

"Well, that sounds good." Seth worked on his shirt without even looking up. "You oughta be about perfect then."

Ethan would have slugged him if Seth didn't have a broken leg.

"What happened down there went about as perfectly as we dared hope, didn't it?" he asked Audra.

"Me getting the best of those two men. You coming for me right when I needed you most."

"After you'd done everything yourself is more like it."

Audra laid a finger on his lips. "I like knowing I fought back. I think I finally believe I'm a strong woman."

"I've believed it for a long time."

"And you faced that cavern. I know you hate it down there, but you faced it despite that."

"I did."

"God took our weakness and made things come out perfectly."

"I don't think I'd have a broken leg if things were completely perfect," Seth added.

Ethan looked at Seth and smiled. He knew, even if Seth didn't, that he never would have gone into the cavern if Seth had been able to. Yes, a broken leg seemed like a hard result for poor old Seth, but he'd heal. And now Ethan's fear was broken while Audra had a new confidence. Their lives together would be better now.

Ethan knew it was still a hard land, but without outlaws on their trail, things were going to calm down.

Finally, life would be good.

"This town suits you then, Jasper?" Trixie sounded exhausted.

Jasper didn't blame her. She'd wanted to stop now for hundreds of miles. Jasper had dragged her along until they'd reached Colorado City. This was close enough.

"Yes, and the man at the station said he knows of a house or two for sale. The bank is the place to ask."

"Let's go to the hotel and worry about a house tomorrow." Trixie moved slowly down the board sidewalks. Jasper knew his joints were creaky; it looked like hers were, too. "I can't face making a decision this important without a good night's sleep."

"If you'll trust me with this, you can go lie down for a while and I'll scout out the houses. It's a good-sized town. I'll make sure there's a yard for chickens and a garden and a barn for a milk cow or two." It sounded like Jasper's very own vision of death.

The drudgery of the life she wanted to live made him want to growl like a mangy wolf.

"There's the bank, and the hotel isn't in sight." Trixie pointed to a sign, swinging over the bank's front door just ahead of them. "I'll go with you. I want to hear about the houses and help pick out the one we buy."

Biting back his impatience, Jasper smiled. He'd hoped to get to the post office and see if there was a letter for him. Maybe Mitch would have left word with details about Jasper's money.

He didn't want to even ask for that letter with Trixie watching.

The bank had exactly two houses for sale. Trixie picked the bigger one, which ended up being real little.

"We can be happy here." Trixie leaned against Jasper as they stopped and looked at the house.

"It's a nice house, all right." Jasper lost the impatient feeling that rode him most of the time. It was a nice house. Two stories. Board instead of log. Glass windows and a solid-looking porch with a row of spindles along the front. The house was on the edge of town with a wooded lot behind it that came with the place, and mountains and forest stretching away forever beyond their property line.

Jasper's hunger to get his money faded as he gazed at the house. "It's almost familiar," he said under his breath.

"What?"

Jasper tore his eyes away from the house and turned to Trixie, smiling. "It feels like home already."

"Let's go inside." She handed him the key the banker had given them once the papers were signed and the money handed over.

They reached the front door, and Jasper used considerable flourish to unlock it. He swung the door open and turned to look at Trixie. Jasper's house in Houston was a mansion. Of course he'd borrowed heavily against it when he'd converted his holdings to something far easier to carry. This whole house would fit in one corner of his Houston place.

"We're home." How strange that it almost sounded good. Jasper was nearly fifty, but he suddenly felt as awkward as a teenager.

With a smile he swept Trixie into his arms. With a little squeak of surprise, she grabbed his shoulders. Their eyes met and she laughed and hugged him tight. Jasper carried her in. He kicked the door shut and set her on her feet, then leaned down to kiss her.

She pressed her palms flat on his chest to stop him. "Jasper, I want to say something now that we're really in our own home."

A twist of frustration tightened his jaw, but he straightened away from her and said with an easy smile, "Say it, wife."

Her expression grew somber as she studied him. Finally, when Jasper began to think maybe she wasn't going to speak at all, she said, "I know you, Jasper Duff, better I think than you know yourself."

Jasper sincerely hoped not.

"I know you came along with me, even married me, mainly because I had money and bullets were flying."

Jasper did his best to control a flinch. She did know him. "Now, Trixie, that's not—"

"Let me finish."

With a mocking sweep of his hand, Jasper said, "Fine, go on."

"I know you're still crazy to get back what was stolen from you. And I know that your mind is twisted with ideas of revenge, of regaining power, of continuing on with the dishonesty that's been part and parcel of who you've been your whole life."

Not his whole life. Just the last forty years.

"So here's the thing." Trixie crossed her arms.

Jasper braced himself.

"I'm going to hide the money I have left. I'll hide it just as carefully as I hid it before."

"Do you think I'd steal your money?"

"I think you've got a rare knack of justifying anything you want to do."

Which was no more than the plain truth. "It's your money— do with it whatever you want."

"I will." Trixie's expression was firm, but there was real kindness behind it. She really did love him. "I want you to give up on all the madness of finding your money. We've got enough. We need to live quietly. If suddenly we're rich, if we live in a big house in a big city, we'll be found out. You know the Hardeseys have arms that reach a long, long way, especially in a city. They'll find us and they'll kill you. And I'll probably take a bullet because I'm standing next to you."

Jasper felt a pang of regret for the truth in that statement.

"So I'm home now. I'm staying here." She looked around the modest entry area of the little house and seemed to plant herself solidly and deeply right there in the front entrance.

It reminded Jasper a bit of the house he'd grown up in. It reminded him that he'd loved his mother. His father, too. He wondered for the first time if his father had ever regretted turning all his fury on Jasper. Had his father, possibly, in the depths of his grief, gone a bit mad? Had he struck out at his son only to regret it later, when it was too late?

Jasper had been too hurt, too twisted up with his own grief and anger and guilt to ever go back to see.

"I'm not stupid, Jasper. I know you picked this place for a reason. So I'm guessing you're thinking to search for your money from here. If you go, if you set out on this madness to find money that will almost certainly destroy you, then don't come back. Don't come in here with the wealth you're so hungry for and expect me to be excited and leave with you to some mansion that will get us killed."

"I'm not going to lie to you, Trix. I have one place I want to check. I want to see if my men left a letter for me in this town."

"You can read your letter, but when you leave to chase after whatever that letter tells you, don't bother coming back."

Jasper wondered if he could do it. He had to read the letter, if it was even there. What if there was enough information to send him off on the hunt? What would he do? Trixie was right about that money being as good as a noose. He'd want to spend it. He'd want a big house and silk shirts. He'd live high. And he'd be found out. And he'd die.

Jasper was struck by the strange business of being honest with someone. And was impressed with just how smart Trixie was. He wondered for the first time if maybe he really could find happiness in a small house with a chicken coop in the backyard.

CHAPTER
24

Ethan flinched with sympathy as he lifted Seth astride his horse. Seth's jaw was tight with pain, but no words of complaint escaped his lips.

"I'll ride ahead, Seth. Audra, you bring up the rear and keep an eye out for any sign of those outlaws." Ethan was pretty sure there weren't any bad guys, so he took some pleasure in leaving his feisty little wife as the rear guard.

She smiled so sweetly it was all Ethan could do to not laugh at her wish to be tough. But he didn't laugh because handling two dangerous hombres was all the proof anyone needed that she was a lot stronger than she looked.

They rode slowly toward the Kincaid Ranch. Ethan planned to mark the trail when he got to the place Rafe and Julia should intersect with on their way home from Rawhide. When they finally reached the red rock wall, Ethan glanced back and knew they had to take a break before Seth fell off his horse.

He reined in his mount and swung down. "Let's rest."

"I don't need rest, Eth." Seth spoke through clenched teeth. "Don't stop for me."

"There's a spring near here. We can have a drink of cold water and the jerky and biscuits."

"Ethan, stop acting like—"

Ethan came to his side and dragged him off his horse. Seth tried to stand on his good leg and his knee gave out.

Catching him before he could fall, Ethan as good as carried him to the wall. When they got close, Seth sank to the ground and twisted to look at a tree that seemed to grow right out of the rock. "Look at that."

"What?" Ethan turned to see what Seth was so interested in.

"Is that a . . . cave?" The sun was getting low in the sky, and although they were in a nice clearing, it was heavily shaded.

With a sinking stomach, Ethan looked closer. Then closer still. "Yep. It's a cave."

Ethan had made his peace with that cavern, but he didn't think he was ever going to really love caves like Seth. He tried to distract Seth from this one. "This looks like the best place for you to build your cabin." Except for that cave. He nodded at a little spring. "Fresh water, year-round."

"I remember this spring from when we were kids." Seth licked his lips, and it reminded Ethan that they hadn't eaten or had more than a sip of water yet today. "Can you get my canteen, Eth?"

While Ethan fetched the canteen, he said, "That spring never runs dry. And we're about halfway between my place and

Rafe's. So it's within easy riding distance. You could come and eat with us most of the time."

With the canteen filled, he handed it to Seth, who took a long drink. Once his thirst was quenched, he gave the canteen back and began dragging himself along on the ground toward that blasted cave.

"Seth, leave it for now. I don't want you bumping that leg around."

"I just want to look inside." Seth poked his head in the cave, and his voice echoed. "I want to see if it's big or not." Seth went the rest of the way in.

Ethan looked at Audra, who rolled her eyes. "Your brother is a very nice man, but he's a little strange, Ethan."

"I think I might just live in here." Seth's voice echoed a bit, but he hadn't gone in too far. Ethan hoped that meant the cave wasn't a big one. "What are the rules about homesteading? Do you have to build an actual house?"

The sound of hoofbeats turned Ethan and Audra around. Ethan's hand went to his gun just as Rafe rounded a bend in the wooded trail.

Looking away for a second, Ethan said, "Maybe they found the treasure. I've only thought that we didn't get to do any hunting, but if they found it, then it doesn't matter."

They rode up. Rafe dismounted and wrapped his reins around a tree branch. Julia was at his side before Ethan and Audra could walk the few paces over to them.

"Where's Seth?" Rafe asked.

"I'm in here, Rafe." Seth's voice sounded hollow from inside the cave. "I'm thinking of living in here."

Rafe jammed his gloved fists on his hips. "Seth!" Rafe's voice could've shaken the cave, it was so loud. "Get out here."

There was a scratching sound.

"Seth, right now."

"I'm coming, Rafe."

"How deep did he go into that dumb cave?" Ethan bent down to stare in the dark hole.

"What's taking him so long?" Rafe demanded. "I've got some questions for him."

Ethan could see that something was bothering Rafe. It wasn't about Seth liking to explore caves. Rafe's usual icy temper looked fiery hot right now.

"He broke his leg." Audra's announcement drew Rafe and Julia's attention.

"How?" Julia pulled her riding gloves off, her brow furrowed with concern.

"Those men, the ones who shot at you yesterday, attacked us."

Julia gasped and looked from Audra to the children. "Are you all right?"

"We've got them."

"Got them where? How?" Rafe's eyes narrowed on Ethan, and he realized he still had dried blood on his face.

"We trapped them in the cavern." Audra patted Maggie on the back while Lily slept in her little pack.

"Audra single-handedly captured both of them, shoved them into that hole Seth got burned in, and by the time I got there, she was ready to just walk right out on her own."

"That is not how it happened. You saved me." Audra threw her free arm around Ethan's waist. He smiled down at her and tucked her under one arm, loving the feel of her.

"Audra got the best of two men?" Julia looked at Audra, impressed.

"You went into the cavern?" Rafe looked at Ethan, doubtful.

Audra and Ethan took turns telling about the day, but they made it quick.

"We need to get Seth home. He got knocked over a cliff."

"Hi, Rafe." Seth stuck his head out of the cave.

"You've got a broken leg?" Rafe stalked toward his brother.

"Yep. My ankle. Hurts like crazy, too." Seth didn't sound all that upset about it as he came the rest of the way out, crawling on his hands and knees. His heavily splinted leg appeared last.

Rafe pulled a paper out of his shirt pocket. "Seth, I got a letter while I was in town."

With his usual wild smile, Seth said, "That's nice. I don't reckon I've ever gotten a letter before."

Rafe pulled a second piece of paper out and extended it toward Seth. "You have now. There were two of them—one to me, one to you. From. Your. Wife."

Ethan felt his jaw drop open. He sputtered for a while before he could say, "Wife? Seth? You've got a wife?"

"Didn't you want to marry me a few weeks ago?" Audra stepped away from Ethan. Who braced himself to tackle her if Seth was in danger. His brother had a broken leg, after all.

"And I'm quite sure you expressed an interest in being married to me, too," Julia said.

"But that was after you were already married to Rafe." Seth took the letter slowly, staring at it as if it might bite. "There wasn't much chance of you actually saying yes."

Seth opened the letter and read silently for a while. "Callie. Uh . . . she says we got . . . got . . . got . . ."

Rafe shook his head. "I think married is the word you're looking for, little brother."

"You said her name once," Ethan said, remembering.

Seth looked up from the letter. "I did? When?"

"Yesterday, when we got shot at. You said you didn't like the idea of building a cabin and living in it alone. Then you said you missed Callie."

"It sounds kinda familiar."

"Well, it oughta be if you married the woman." Ethan swatted Seth on the head with his hat.

Seth ducked and kept reading.

Rafe looked down at his own letter. "It says she's worried about you and has been looking for you ever since you ran off from her. She says you had nightmares from your time in the war and she doesn't know if you're thinking right."

"She's got the right man," Julia muttered.

"It also says she's coming here," Rafe went on. "Apparently you talked about your family and she wants my help in finding you. In fact, she demands my help."

Seth went on reading his letter, and his eyes got so wide that Ethan was afraid his eyeballs would fall right out of his head.

"If she knew your name, Rafe, why'd she take a year to come hunting for Seth? Don't seem like she cared much about him."

"She doesn't say, but Seth told her he had family in Rawhide, and that's why she wrote to me here." Rafe's eyes lifted from Seth to Ethan.

Seth squirmed from where he sat on the ground and stuck his nose even deeper in his letter. "Callie's really upset."

"I think killing mad is a better description." Rafe held his letter up. "Some of the time she sounds worried, then she kinda

320

switches over to 'he'd better be dead.' She's not happy with you, little brother."

Seth's attention was riveted on the letter. Audra's fingers itched to see what the woman had written to so completely trap Seth in the words.

"Seth, for heaven's sake, you ran off and left the woman?" Julia looked tempted to start pounding on Seth. Ethan wondered if he'd have to protect his brother from both women.

"We've got to find her and help her. Get her out here." Audra chewed on her bottom lip to keep it from trembling.

Ethan edged closer to her. She was strong. She'd beaten up two men today. She hadn't oughta ruin it now by crying.

"No Kincaid is going to abandon his wife. Not while I'm alive." Rafe looked torn between pounding on Seth and mounting up to find Callie.

"Does she say how she's living?" Ethan asked. "How she's coming out? Can we go meet her? I hate to think of a woman alone, just like Audra and Julia. No one to protect her. Helpless."

Julia swatted Ethan on the arm. "We weren't helpless."

"My letter says she's headed for Rawhide." Rafe handed the letter to Ethan. "She wrote the letter right before she started out on the train for Denver, planning to take a stagecoach the rest of the way."

Julia frowned. "There aren't any stagecoaches to Rawhide."

"I reckon she's finding that out about now."

Seth looked up from his letter, his confusion giving way to determination. "We've got to go meet her. How will we find her? I wonder what she looks like."

Julia slapped herself in the face with the palm of her hand and shook her head. Ethan heard a little groan of pain.

"This letter is at least a month old," Rafe said. "You know how poor mail delivery is out here." He looked back in the direction of Rawhide. "She could be here any minute."

Seth tried to stand, and his gasp of pain reminded Ethan that the boy had a broken ankle. "Not sure how far I can ride."

"I'll ride out in the morning." Rafe looked at Julia. "We'll ride out in the morning. We'll head for Denver and hunt until we find her."

"There's hardly a decent trail between here and Denver." Ethan frowned. Then he remembered when he'd done nothing but smile. Ethan kind of wanted those old days back.

"And what trails there are wind from town to town," Ethan went on. "She could be coming down a dozen different directions, probably on a freight wagon. You can't hope to find her, Rafe."

"We've got to get those men out of the cave first," Audra reminded them. "We really can't leave them in that hole. Worse yet, if they get out, they could attack us again."

Ethan looked from Julia to Rafe. "You didn't find that money, did you?"

Rafe shook his head. "Had quite a while to look, too. I didn't even think of a letter."

"I get mail from time to time. I thought of it," Julia added.

"When she asked," Rafe said, "they handed those to me. Eth, Callie's letter was to you and me both. Reckon Seth had nightmares about both of us."

"That cave isn't deep enough to live in and there are no tunnels at all," Seth said, pointing at the cave he'd just come out of, smiling. He'd been surprised for a few seconds about having a wife. But now he was his old loco self. "Where's the fun in that? I guess I'll need to build a cabin."

"Big enough for a wife." Ethan felt very sorry for poor, abandoned, forgotten Callie Kincaid.

Seth perked up and smiled wide at Audra. "Are you going to live here with me? And bring the babies? That'll be fun."

"Maybe Callie shouldn't be in that big a hurry to get here," Julia said. She sounded exhausted.

CHAPTER
25

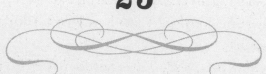

"We've got 'em." Rafe emerged from the cave entrance in his mountain valley, dragging Mitch along.

Audra looked at Mitch and clenched her fist. "You are an awful man!"

She didn't slug him because he had his hands tied behind his back. It wouldn't be one bit fair, though the scoundrel deserved it.

The man's head drooped low, and Audra saw an ugly bleeding cut on the back of his head. "Did I do that to him?"

Ethan came next with Grove in tow. The man had a make-shift sling on his arm, and his head was covered with dried blood.

"Did I do that to him, too?" Audra swallowed hard as she looked at the battered men. She felt tears well in her eyes, but she fought them down. She didn't regret what she'd done in fighting for her life, but it was a shocking day all around.

"The cut on Mitch's head looks like a bullet wound." Ethan sat Grove on the ground with no care at all. "I'd say he shot himself. Probably ricocheted one of his own bullets. But it's a scratch. Unless it turns septic, he'll be fine."

Audra exchanged a look with Julia. They'd been forced to stay behind with the children while the big strong men went in to capture the bad guys.

As if Audra hadn't already done all the hard work. "We know that can happen, don't we? That's how Wendell died. From an infected scratch."

"But Grove here, yep"—Ethan nodded toward the man with the sling—"I'd say you did that."

The tears threatened again, yet Audra was determined to be a ruthless, courageous warrior. She didn't even let tears thicken her voice. "Where did you find them? You weren't gone for long."

"They were still in that pit," Rafe said.

Led by Steele, five more of the Kincaid hands came out of the cavern. Every one of them had a lantern. Rafe and Ethan hadn't tackled these men in that dark hole alone. The day was wearing down and it had been a long one.

"Mitch climbed out before with no trouble at all," Audra said. She thought of the way he'd come out of the hole in the pitch-dark, fast, unharmed, killing mad.

"The way rock was shattered," Ethan said, "I'd say Mitch's wild shooting busted off any footholds he found at first. He probably knocked himself out cold with a ricocheted bullet, though he was awake when we got there. Both of them were conscious."

Audra cleared her throat and squared her shoulders. "I'm surprised he didn't have a few b-bullets left."

She was strong. She was fearless. She was dangerous.

Ethan looked at her. "Nope. Their guns were empty."

She was going to cry.

"Mitch must've shot 'em all off at us—his and Grove's," Ethan added. "Which left them in the dark for a long time, and when we got there they were hurting enough and scared enough to be glad to see us."

"Not sure glad's the right word," Steele muttered.

"They let us drag 'em up without any real escape attempt," Rafe said. "At least no attempt until we had them trussed up tight." Rafe jerked his head at the secure knots holding Mitch's hands behind his back and a sturdy rope tying Grove's good arm to the one in the sling.

Mitch looked back at the entrance as if it were a monster's mouth, complete with jagged teeth. "I hate that cavern. I'd rather be in a jail."

"You're gonna get your wish." Ethan sat Grove down beside his partner.

Audra and Julia had stayed behind with Seth and the children. They'd done their best to rewrap the bandage on Seth's leg and tried to get him to remember more about his wife. By the time the bandaging was done, Seth was ashen with pain.

Julia had made enough supper for all of them and gotten a meal in Seth and Maggie both. Seth had finally settled into bed and fallen asleep as peacefully as Maggie. Then Audra had fed Lily and she'd gone to sleep in the fading light.

Audra and Julia had paced in front of the cave, occasionally going back to the cabin to check on their charges, awaiting their men's return.

Now they were back and her eyes went to Ethan. She saw none of the terrible stress he usually bore with a smile when he'd had anything to do with that cavern. Its hold on him was finally broken. That made her so happy she almost cried again.

It was going to be a wonder if she got out of this day without crying her eyes out, and she'd been doing really well at being a strong woman.

Not counting right now.

"I'm going to ride to town with these men." Rafe looked at Julia. "You come with me, Jules. And you men ride along, too. I don't want even a chance of these men escaping and endangering any more of us."

Rafe turned to Ethan and continued issuing orders. "It'll be late into the night before we get back. Can you get Seth home?"

"Yep. We'll manage."

"My boss won't quit," Mitch snarled from where he sat. "He wants what you stole from him, and he won't quit until he gets it. If you were smart, you'd give us that money and let us go."

"We don't know where it is." Audra wanted to cry. Which seemed to be her theme for the last hour or so.

"I think if a man pushed you hard enough, you might come up with some ideas. The boss might just come himself. He's not a patient man."

"You want a gag to go with those ropes?" Rafe asked.

Mitch subsided into a sullen silence. He'd made his point.

Audra wondered where in the name of heaven Wendell had hidden so much money that a man could afford to send these men after it.

"You don't need all of us riding with you, Rafe." Steele returned his hat to his head. He'd left it behind when he entered the cavern. "I'll take one man and head for the ranch with Ethan, help him get Seth home. We need to be watching for more two-legged varmints."

The sleep had given Seth renewed energy and he made the trip well enough.

Audra didn't have much chance to talk the day over with Ethan because of the men riding with them. Instead, she concentrated on making good time in the heavy woods. And fighting tears. For a woman who'd beaten up two armed gunmen today, she was feeling like a terrible weakling.

Once they got home they were busy getting the girls tucked in and Seth settled in bed, his leg carefully propped on a pillow.

It was late when Audra finally pulled the covers over her in the cool mountain evening and sank into her feather ticking.

As Ethan joined her in their bed, Audra opened her mouth to say good-night and burst into tears.

Ethan pulled her into his arms and held her close. Her face rested on his strong shoulders as he caressed her, murmuring soft words. Audra couldn't hear them for a long time, but when her tears finally ebbed, she heard him say, "I'm so sorry, sweetheart."

He sounded as if his heart were breaking.

"Why am I crying? We survived this h-horrible day."

Ethan hugged her closer and she felt his soft kisses on her hair. "That's why you're crying, because you had a horrible day."

She cried harder and nestled against his sturdy chest, loving his strong arms. "I was so afraid, Ethan. I'm such a coward."

"No, you're not. You're about the bravest little thing I've ever seen."

Audra raised her head and Ethan handed her a handkerchief. She wiped at her soggy face and noticed she'd soaked the poor man's nightshirt.

Dabbing at it, she said, "I've been trying to be brave, but

today all I've done is be afraid. Afraid they'd hurt me. Afraid for my children. Afraid for you." Her voice broke again. When she could talk again, she added, "You're the one who was brave. You hate that cavern but you faced it. You went down in there to save me. That's the bravest thing I've ever seen."

Just the thought of what it cost him to come for her sent her into another fit of tears. "I have to quit crying. What is wrong with me?"

There was silence while he held her, rubbing his hands on her back and her shoulders, caressing and soothing. Finally, into her hair, he whispered, "I love you, Audra."

The words hit her with the power of a lightning bolt, and she wrenched out of his arms to sit up. With her back to the window, she cast his face in a shadow and couldn't read his expression. But why read an expression when she had the words?

"You do? Really?"

He dragged her back down and rolled her onto her back, leaning over her. "I really do. When I faced that cavern today, it was because loving you was stronger than my fear. I don't think I'm ever going to like it down there, but the thought of losing you helped me realize the cavern . . . well, I've given it too much power over me. I've let that fear control my life. I let it send me away from a home I missed and brothers I loved. And the things you did today, leading those men away from me. Fighting them in that cavern, thinking and planning and remembering all you knew about the caves and tunnels—and doing it all when you were in so much danger, a lot of people wouldn't have been able to make their heads work. It's the bravest thing I've ever seen."

"No, I wasn't brave. I was terrified."

"Only a locoweed wouldn't be afraid of armed men spewing

threats. Fear is the only possible sane reaction. But being afraid of something really frightening isn't the same as being a coward."

"Yes it is."

Ethan leaned down and kissed her until she started feeling really brave. Her arms wrapped around his neck just as he pulled away, but not so far she couldn't hang on.

"If a rattlesnake struck at you, you'd be afraid, right?"

"Well, yes."

"That would be natural. And you'd either run or you'd shoot the rattlesnake. Neither of those things is cowardly."

"It's just good sense." Audra felt all the tensions of the day ease away, washed away by the tears and now by Ethan's kindness . . . and his confession of love.

"That's right. And those men today attacked with just as deadly of intentions as a rattlesnake. Worse because a rattlesnake is only trying to protect itself. You kept your head. You picked your moment."

"I did. I knew about that hole and I fully intended to try and knock them into it." Audra felt her cheeks heat up. "What a terrible thing to admit."

"You were thinking. You were defending yourself and your children and your worthless napping husband."

"Hush." She pressed her fingers to his lips. "Getting knocked over the head isn't the same as taking a nap."

She saw him smile behind her fingers and knew he was teasing her. She dared to say, "So maybe I'm not a complete coward."

"Not even close."

"And maybe you're not a complete coward, because you faced down your worst fear and triumphed over it."

Ethan shrugged one of his broad shoulders. "Okay." He kissed her. "Maybe neither of us did so bad today."

He kissed her again and this time she held on tight. When he paused to take a breath, Audra asked, "So where in the world do you think Wendell hid all that money?"

"I don't want to hear another word about your first husband while you're in bed with me, is that understood?"

"I'm happy right where I am. And thinking about nothing except how much I love the man I married."

"I was wondering when you were going to say it back."

The world spun away as Ethan pulled her too close for her to have a single thought in her head except for loving him completely, passionately, deeply.

ABOUT THE AUTHOR

Mary Connealy is a Carol Award winner and a RITA Award finalist. An author, journalist, and teacher, she lives on a ranch in eastern Nebraska with her husband, Ivan, and has four grown daughters—Josie, married to Matt; Wendy; Shelly, married to Aaron; and Katy—and two spectacular grandchildren, Elle and Isaac. Readers can learn more about Mary and her upcoming books at:

maryconnealy.com
mconnealy.blogspot.com
seekerville.blogspot.com
petticoatsandpistols.com